Improper Relations

Janet Mullany

First published in 2010
by LITTLE BLACK DRESS
An imprint of HEADLINE PUBLISHING GROUP

A LITTLE BLACK DRESS paperback

1

Cataloguing in Publication Data is available from the British Library

ISBN 978 0 7553 4780 3

Typeset in Transit511BT by Avon DataSet Ltd,
Bidford-on-Avon, Warwickshire

Printed and bound in Great Britain by
Clays Ltd, St Ives plc

Headline's policy is to use papers that are natural, renewable and recyclable products and made from wood grown in sustainable forests. The logging and manufacturing processes are expected to conform to the environmental regulations of the country of origin.

HEADLINE PUBLISHING GROUP
An Hachette UK Company
338 Euston Road
London NW1 3BH

www.littleblackdressbooks.com
www.headline.co.uk
www.hachette.co.uk

To Steve, because it's about time
(people were beginning to talk), but you don't
have to read this one either.

Acknowledgements

All the usual suspects, and if you think you should be here and aren't, my apologies. Big thanks to: the design and editorial teams at Little Black Dress, in particular Catherine Cobain, Sara Porter, and Leah Woodburn; my agent, Lucienne Diver; the ladies of the Risky Regencies and History Hoydens blogs; the Beau Monde; Maryland Romance Writers; the Wet Noodle Posse; the Bad Girls Critique Group; the staff and volunteers at Riversdale House Museum; writing friends Anna Campbell, Julie Cohen, Kate Dolan, Colleen Gleason, Delle Jacobs, Christie Kelly, Kathy Love, Miranda Neville, Pam Rosenthal, Robin L. Rotham, and Leanne Shawler; non-writing friends Gail, Lucy, and Maureen, and my daughter Alison.

Miss Charlotte Hayden

My story begins with a wedding.

Not, I hasten to add, mine. I have been assured from allegedly reliable sources that certain farmyard creatures would sprout wings and fly were I to receive a proposal. My brother George, a year older than me, has declared me a filly no one wishes to mount, and although he was in his cups at the time, and I deplore his vulgarity, it is true I look to gallop in last to the finishing line of matrimony. Or, as my father thunderously pronounced, while I braced myself for the rigours of polite society, 'If you can't catch one this time, Charlotte, it's off to the country and good works for you.'

I felt rather as an elderly horse must when the glue factory is pointed out.

Besides, the family needs a social triumph following the recent unpleasantness (or as my mama phrases it, the *Recent Unpleasantness* – you can hear the italics when she utters the phrase, usually with a flutter of hankerchief, a sigh, and the consumption of another glass of cordial) regarding my eldest brother Henry. Shortly before Ann came to live with us, Henry was hastily fitted out for a commission in a regiment, his debts paid off, and more parents of naïve heiresses (who anticipated marriage whereas Henry clearly did not) placated. Henry barely had time to shake his golden frogging at a few more fresh victims and run up a few hundred guineas more in gaming debts before the regiment left for Liverpool.

I was relieved. Mama was *Prostrated with Grief, the Likes of Which One Who is Not a Mother Cannot Conceive*.

But the wedding. Yes, Ann's wedding. My best friend Ann, from whom I have been inseparable ever since she came to our family a few months ago. I had not seen her for years. She was someone who visited occasionally when we were both little girls, and with whom I swore vows of eternal friendship before she went home and we forgot about each other until the next visit. She was a vicar's daughter in a family infinitely more shabby and far less money-grubbing than mine, who had spent the last three years as house-keeper to some obscure, dreadful old cousin, so as not to be a burden to her parents. And then suddenly Ann, dear Ann, orphaned and with all that money inherited from her cousin and employer, and with no one to look after her . . . of course she should live with us, for was not my papa her godfather and now her guardian? So it was off to London and high society as Papa managed Ann's inheritance.

Fortunately she inherited so much money that Papa's expenditures – or, *giving the dear girl what she needs to triumph in society and Charlotte with her*, as he puts it – have barely made a dent.

She is a beauty, the gentle and sweet-natured one who always knows the right thing to say, whereas I am the clever one, or so they tell me. I'm not too sure of this, for it sounds remarkably like a sop of kindness tossed in my direction. Not that I break mirrors – certainly by knocking one from the wall, but not merely with the impact of my reflection. I am moderately pretty. But compared to Ann – well, there is no comparison.

I don't believe I'm more or less clever than any of the hopeful young ladies paraded in the marriage mart. I speak some dreadful French, embroider with a minimum of bloodshed, produce lifelessly correct watercolours, have several easy pianoforte pieces at my disposal for the drawing room and occasionally I read something other than fashion papers. In truth, I am quite accomplished.

But Ann. This is her day at this elegant gathering in the Earl of Beresford's drawing room – nothing so vulgar as a church. Dear me, no. This ceremony is performed by special licence, with a fashionably languid clergyman brought in for the occasion, while the cream of the *ton*, London's most fashionable and well-born – of whom today I am one, acting as Ann's bridesmaid – speculate upon the bride's innocence (I shall not say a word) and dowry (larger than you might think).

Gentlemen had flocked round Ann (and her fortune), and incidentally round me, to my father's gratification. I have enjoyed some popularity as a conduit to Miss Ann Welling, until she met the man who is at this very moment becoming her husband.

'Charlotte, I met a gentleman,' she murmured as we travelled home from the stultifying boredom of a soirée a few weeks ago.

'I met several. Dreadful, weren't they.'

'Oh, no.' She turned the full force of her sapphire blue eyes upon me (and if you think that's an exaggeration, you should see some of the poetry her admirers have written). 'Oh, not this one.'

I felt a pang although I couldn't exactly describe what it was – jealousy, anticipation? I must be glad for Ann, I told myself. For of course every woman wants to fall in love and have her own establishment and babies and all the rest (but what is all the rest?) for so we were raised. And so I became the onlooker as Ann fell in love with the Earl of Beresford, a handsome gentleman possessed of a large fortune, a large family (of which I am now a very small part) and, as of a few minutes ago, a wife. While he wooed her I became her confidante, privy to what the Earl said and did, and speculated with her for hours on what his lordship really meant. Each of his words was picked apart as though his conversation was an old stocking we intended to knit into something better. Were his intentions really honourable? What did he try to say when he sent a fan, ivory with seed pearls, fashionable to the point of plainness? The Greek vase? The books of poetry? Or the saucy garters, red ribbons, paste jewels, gold embroidery? They made Ann blush and we debated for hours whether she should allow his lordship a glimpse of them or whether merely telling him that she wore them was enough.

I'm not quite sure what the result of the garters was.

I was the one who sat with her, our hands tightly clasped, when Beresford called on my papa and they shut themselves in his study for what seemed like hours. Ann and I worked our way through a decanter of brandy while the settlement was thrashed out – or something, for the two gentlemen emerged talking of dogs – and Ann burst into drunken tears in her lover's embrace and then fell asleep on the sofa. Beresford gazed at the trail of drool falling from her mouth and sighed.

Oh yes, he was in love too.

Between then and the wedding, I became the one who declared with great innocence that I had no idea where Beresford or Ann had gone (into dark corners and walks of gardens, into clumps of bushes, unused rooms, and so on). I would help her rearrange her hair and straighten her gown when she emerged, giggling and dishevelled.

She smiled sweetly at me and thanked me, but there was an end to confidences and giggled secrets. No word on the garters, the assignations. She received letters that she would tuck away into her bodice, and spring to her feet crying that we must try my hair in a new style, or make some adjustment to a gown, for she was convinced that now I must marry before the season was out.

And I realised that I was losing her, although I did not understand why. All I knew was that our short-lived intimacy was fading away, leaving me to the tender mercies of my family. She was Beresford's now, becoming Lady Ann Jane Trelaise, Countess of Beresford, preparing to cross the divide between maidenhood and marriage and leaving me behind.

Now the new Countess, on her husband's arm, turns to face the elegant congregation with a smile that somehow combines maidenly modesty with triumph. The Earl gazes at her, her hand in his. My mother is weeping like a sieve and my father blowing his nose. And I—

'Pardon me, ma'am.'

I look up. Oh, my prayer book, which I must have dropped at some point, and a large, linen, masculine handkerchief.

I blow my nose and mumble, 'Thank you sir, I must see to Lady Beresford.'

I gather Ann's fan and bouquet of silk flowers, and take them to her, dropping a curtsy to the Earl, who beams at me in an alarmingly toothy way. He is a large, loud man, whom I would dislike if he were not Ann's choice; whom in fact I do resent to a certain extent as he is the one who has taken her from me.

And I suspect he is not terribly clever.

'Well, cousin Charlotte,' he booms, taking my hands in his, 'I may address you so since you are one of us, now. And we'll marry her off soon, eh, Ann?'

Had I not returned the silk flowers to their owner I might have been tempted to slap him with them at this public declaration of my marital failure. 'Thank you, sir, please do not go to any trouble on my account. I shall—'

'Any help would be much appreciated, Beresford,' my father interjects. And it is true that becoming a minor planet of the rich, powerful (and in my opinion, pompous) family of the Earl and Countess – they swarm over the drawing room, loud, voluble, handsome – should increase my chances of an offer.

I look at Ann to see if she shares my mingled embarrassment and annoyance, but she gazes at her new husband as though there is no one else in the room; and for her there is not. A swarm of Trelaises, declaring their happiness complete and what a charming bride, etc. etc., descends upon them, and I step aside. I still clasp the linen handkerchief and look about me for the gentleman to whom it belongs. Since

I did not actually look him in the face – and there was no chance of an introduction since he arrived late, and I barely noticed him, other than realising someone had slipped into place beside me – I'm not quite sure how I shall recognise him.

While the others cluster around the bride and groom, there is one who remains sprawled on a chair. He wears plain black, very fashionable for a gentleman, of course, but on this man it looks as though he intends to fight a duel and possibly conduct the funeral service over his unlucky opponent all in the same day. His dark hair is unruly, also eminently fashionable, but in a way that, along with his unshaven chin, suggests he has but recently risen from his bed.

Goodness.

He is lean, dramatic, handsome as the devil, and I suspect the bed was not his.

A rake!

Will my reputation fall around me in tatters if I approach him?

I regard the soggy handkerchief in my hand and regret that the bosom of my gown, fashionably brief, does not allow for extra cargo.

While I have been staring at him I have in fact been moving towards him, like a mouse fascinated by a snake, so I arrive in front of him as he looks up – his eyes are shadowed, naturally, his eyelashes dark and lush, his face lean and bony – and gazes straight at my bosom.

He yawns.

'Sir, I thank you for the loan of your handkerchief.' I should really have waited for an introduction. I hold out the soggy item to him.

Then, as though his manners return, he lurches to his feet, blinks, and bows. 'My pleasure, madam.'

His pleasure. I blink at that. But we cannot stand here blinking like a couple of owls. I dip a small curtsy, and watch as his hand – long, beautiful fingers – takes the handkerchief, folds it, and tucks it into his waistcoat pocket. I should of course turn away at this point, but I cannot.

'I regret we have not been introduced,' I say.

'Ah. You must be Miss Hayden. Beresford told me all about you.'

This is nonsense as Beresford knows nothing whatsoever about me, except that I serve a useful purpose in allowing him to steal away with his affianced.

'Indeed. And you, sir, are . . . ?'

He smiles and his eyes dance with amusement or something more sinful. 'I, Miss Hayden, am Jonathan Trelaise, Viscount Shadderly. I hold the distinction of being the wicked cousin – *your* wicked cousin, now.'

'Perhaps I already have one. Besides, Ann is not a blood relative; my father is her godfather.'

'Oh, I'm far more wicked. And doubtless far better bred. Look at us all.' He gestures at his family. 'Although soon I shall mend my ways.'

'Why is that, sir?'

'I intend to marry.'

Dreadfully, I feel a pang of disappointment. 'And is the lucky woman here?'

'I don't even know who the lucky woman is, Miss Hayden. It's a theory only. The family thinks I should marry.'

'Oh, then of course you should.'

He gives me a quick glance as though he is trying to work out whether I'm making fun of him. I suspect this is a man who takes himself, particularly in the role of wicked cousin, rather seriously.

I assume my best innocent expression.

'And as to you, Miss Hayden? Any luck recently?'

'I beg your pardon?'

'Beresford told me your family was exceedingly put out that your cousin married before you.'

'That's none of your business!' How dare he criticise my family – although what he says is absolutely true. I unfurl my fan in a businesslike way. 'Possibly we should kill two birds with one stone by becoming engaged, my lord.'

For one wonderful, brief moment, he looks shocked. Then he laughs. '*Touché*, Miss Hayden, although generally I believe it is the gentleman who does the asking.'

Viscount Shadderly

My cousin Beresford looks as red and gleaming as a side of beef as he beams upon his tender little bride. She is as lovely as even he, with his limited capacity, could describe – *remember how snowdrops look when you see them first in the spring, so pure and white, Shad, before your horse treads on them or your dog pisses on them? She's a capital girl!* He'd paused then, and refilled our glasses. *Should I tell her about my mistress?*

I'd advised him to be discreet. At least it was only one mistress. I wonder how Beresford's snowdrop will fare with our family, who are all agog with curiosity that he should marry this unknown. I believe she was raised in a vicarage, orphaned, and taken in by the Haydens, a shabby, genteel, grasping sort of family. Had she not been the sole heir of a rich, miserly relative, she would have stayed with them as an unpaid companion indefinitely, darning stockings and reading novels aloud for her bread. Under the caring and tender wings of the Haydens she had her London debut and staged a comeuppance by becoming engaged within months, unlike the troublesome and troubled Miss Charlotte.

Now, of course I've only heard Beresford's side of the story, and a drunken side at that. 'I think Charlotte's in love with me, Shad. Looks at me all the time. Poor girl.' He gazed into his glass, sighing. 'I feel sorry for her. No one's going to marry her. D'you think I should, you know, just to—'

'Absolutely not.' Just to . . . what? Cheer her up? I saw his disappointment and added, 'What if Miss Ann found out?'

'Of course, of course. You're absolutely right. Where would I be without you? Thank God you've come up from the country to help me.' A hiccup. 'How long until I get married?'

I squinted at the clock. 'About ten hours.'

'Maybe we should . . .' His words became incoherent and his wineglass tipped and spilled as Beresford slumped on to the table with a snore.

One of the ladies of the house – regrettably, we were in low company – offered to help his lordship into his carriage, and thus it was that the Earl of Beresford spent his last bachelor hours.

I guess, correctly, that the lady to whom I lend my handkerchief – I arrive late and crapulous, after our carousing the night before – must be the lovelorn Miss Charlotte Hayden. She does not appear to cry more than any other woman at the wedding, and if her cousin Miss Ann Weller, now becoming the Countess of Beresford, is daylight and sunshine, she is an indeterminate sort of dusk. She lacks the poreelain complexion, blue eyes and curling fair hair of her cousin; her hair is brown with a reluctant wave, her eyes an uninteresting grey, her face narrow and sharp-featured, and somewhat red around the eyes, and she is of middling height. To be blunt, her best feature is her bosom.

A certain sharpness of tongue has doubtless frightened off most suitors, although I find it the second most attractive thing about her. I do however feel no compulsion whatsoever to take the lady up on her offer of marriage; no, I need a nice docile sort of girl, a pretty thing who will adore me and pop out babies regularly so the estate will pass directly to my line.

I know the price is a terrible boredom, but it is my duty.

After an hour or so spent at the wedding breakfast, the weight of so many relatives lies heavy upon me. Yes, I am come to town to take a wife. Yes, I am settling the lamentable state of affairs left by my dreadful old father (every day, it seems, a new creditor or other problematic visitor arrives). Yes, I should be most grateful for a good word to the patronesses of Almack's, for my bloodlines are perfectly respectable, even if my bank balance is not.

Pleading fatigue I leave early, as I have business with a Mrs Jenny Perkins – or rather, Beresford's business. She is the mistress in his (mostly) untarnished past, and I offered to end the liaison. Beresford himself has been far too busy waxing poetic about spring flowers to deal with this matter, or so he tells me. I've met Mrs Perkins before and wonder at how a sensible man could entangle himself with this grasping tart, although when her maidservant admits me to the lady's presence, I am reminded of exactly why.

'Why, my lord, what a surprise!' She rises from her dressing table and offers her hand. 'Pray be careful of my headdress, it has taken me an hour to arrange. Is not Berry with you?'

Ostrich feathers bob on her head, but she is wearing very little else; so little, in fact, that I am immediately suspicious that another lover is on the premises. If this is so, it will save Beresford a great deal of money.

'I regret not,' I reply. 'The marriage was today.'

She sniffs, not in sorrow, but in disdain, while I examine the room for discarded breeches etc.

'Is that a mouse?' I cry.

Mrs Perkins shrieks and climbs on a chair, clutching her shift to herself.

I fling open the door of the linen press, expecting to find Beresford's rival quivering in fear. No, only gowns and sheets.

'I suppose you are come to pay me off,' Mrs Perkins says, still atop the chair.

I offer my hand and she steps down, rather too close to me, moving very slowly.

I clear my throat. After all, I have been busy in the country and not in an amorous sort of way. I am beginning to find Mrs Perkins' generous charms overwhelming.

'Outstanding bills, ma'am,' I manage.

She sits at her dressing table again. 'Well, sir, there are these garters—' hoisting her shift so I may view them and assess their worth, 'blue silk, embroidered with forget-me-nots. I believe I paid five shillings for them. The stockings are clocked silk – handsome, are they not? I paid—'

'Your bills, ma'am. I do not need to see the goods themselves.'

'Oh, sir. You are so hard upon me.' She glances at me to assess the effect she is having and dabs at her eyes with a lace handkerchief that probably is not paid for. 'I am most put out that Berry should cast me off so.'

'Of course. Would those be bills by your left elbow?'

She hands them to me. 'You should know also that I have ordered another new gown—'

'Indeed.'

'Oh, but you must hear, for I had a longing for a blue muslin, but Sally Pratchett, who used to keep company with Captain Allbright, although he has left her since – well, when I took her to see it, Sally said it would not wash, and persuaded me to try a madras, although I thought the colour not at all becoming, but then I realised I could dye the flowers for the bonnet to match. I have also a new cloak to be made for which I have chosen a most beautiful blue velvet – I shall show you a cutting—'

'Unnecessary, Mrs Perkins.'

Mrs Perkins' idiot babble of milliners and dress-makers does not distract me from her alluring person;

it serves much as the landscape in an erotic piece of art.

'A moment while I review the contract.' Ostrich feathers and bosom wobbling, she fiddles with the lock of a writing desk.

I've had enough. 'Put on some clothes, Mrs Perkins, and stop bending over in front of me.'

'Oh, sir!' She swipes at me in a friendly way and produces the contract, dripping with seals and red ribbon. Beresford assured me there was no mention of an annuity to be paid to her, only that he was to settle her bills to date (considerable) and continue payment on her rooms for another quarter, something I must see to soon.

To my relief, she drapes herself in a silk dressing gown (which does not hide her charms but is more a gesture of good faith) and we then embark upon a discussion of how much Mrs Perkins can expect to receive at the conclusion of her services – a 'present', as she calls it. She calls me a blackhearted villain and I call her a greedy trollop until we settle on an appropriate amount, although there is little animosity when all is said and done. She professes to all sorts of sentimental feelings towards Beresford (of which I am sure a good nine-tenths are professional embellishments), and sighs gustily when I describe the wedding, although I prove sadly inadequate in describing the ladies' gowns.

'And are you alone in London, sir?' she asks in a

businesslike way when we have struck our deal.

'I am, ma'am, but I have a great deal with which to occupy myself.'

The silk dressing gown slides from one comely shoulder. 'Then you will need some company where you can rest from your affairs.'

I grin at her. 'Cast your net wider, Mrs Perkins.'

She grins back and we part on reasonable terms.

I have no doubt she will find another protector, possibly sooner than I will a wife.

Miss Charlotte Hayden

Five days after Ann's wedding I plead a headache and stay home while Mama pays afternoon calls. Papa is in the House and George is out doing whatever it is he does in the afternoons (I suspect it is not the sort of activity about which he would chat over the family dining table). I have had enough of the veiled looks of pity directed at Mama, and occasionally at me, whenever Ann's marriage is mentioned.

I am not even sure where Lord and Lady Beresford are on their wedding journey – the arrangement was that Ann should write to me giving an address – but I decide I shall start a letter so that I can amend it when she writes and she will receive my reply all the sooner.

'Beg pardon, miss.' Our youngest footman, Jeremiah, who seems to grow all the time, lurks at the doorway of the drawing room. I swear another inch of wrist has emerged from his livery since the morning.

'I'm not receiving anyone.' I've heard the ring of the doorbell but am confident that no callers shall interrupt my solitude.

'Yes, miss, but Mrs Hayden said . . .' He shifts from one foot to another and grimaces. 'You have a caller, Miss Hayden.'

'Send them away. What's wrong with you?'

'My shoes, Miss Hayden. They're pinching me.'

'Ask another footman if he has a spare pair.'

'My feet are the biggest, miss,' he mutters. I fear that Jeremiah will wake one morning too big to emerge from his bedchamber and we shall be obliged to saw off the roof to free him.

'I'll tell Mr Finn. Please send this caller away.'

'Mrs. Hayden told Mr Finn, miss, that if a gentleman were to call, we should let him in.'

So Finn, our butler, is part of a nefarious plan to marry me to any stray caller to the house!

'But—'

And at that moment Viscount Shadderly pushes past Jeremiah, handing him his gloves and hat.

'Your servant, ma'am.'

I gaze at him in astonishment, and, as I grope to cover my letter, the inkwell rolls from the desk and leaves a trail all the way down my gown and on to the carpet, where I tread on it as I curtsy.

'Thank you, Jeremiah, we'll take tea,' the Viscount says.

'Jeremiah, we'll need the carpet cleaned,' I say in a

panic. I don't want to be left alone with this rake, and I'm sure he was not what Mama had in mind when she conspired with Finn to make me receive gentlemen alone.

'Yes, sir.' Jeremiah limps away and I suspect he has ignored my order about the carpet.

I'm longing to stand on one foot and see if there is ink all over the sole of my slipper – I do not see how it could possibly be avoided – and already plan a hopscotch on the darker shades of the carpet to the sofa. I hope if I sit on the sofa Shadderly will take a chair. I wonder if I should excuse myself to change my gown, but God knows I do not want to put any ideas about removal of clothing into this man's mind. Do I?

He, however, looks merely amused.

'How do you know our footman's name?'

'I find it useful to know servants' names.'

That reply raises all sorts of indecent possibilities in my mind – I suddenly remember all the novels where conniving liasions and illicit letters and secret elopements take place – but I don't want to look too interested.

'I regret I am not receiving visitors today, my lord,' I say, in as dignified a voice as an ink-covered woman can muster.

'Such a pity, but here I am, Miss Hayden, so we'd best make the most of it.' He smiles and it's . . . dazzling. It's like the sun coming out from behind dark clouds and I feel weak at the knees. I almost grab on to the desk for support. 'Shall we sit?'

'Oh. Oh, yes, certainly.' I wave towards the sofa. 'Please do sit down.'

He waits for me to sit first.

'Why not kick off that shoe?' he murmurs, as intimately as though he'd suggested I strip down to my petticoat. 'You don't want to spread ink all over the carpet, after all.'

Praying that no toes poke out from my stocking, I discard the shoe and rush over to the sofa, tugging down my skirts.

He sits next to me.

'What are you doing here?' It's not the most polite beginning to a conversation, but I do have the habit of blurting out exactly what is on my mind.

My unwelcome visitor is spared, temporarily, having to make an appropriate comment as at that moment Jeremiah limps in with a tea tray. I avoid looking at the Viscount while pouring tea rather messily and handing him a cup.

'Well, Miss Hayden.' He pours a quantity of spilled tea from his saucer back into the cup. 'What am I doing here? I wonder myself. Perhaps I have been thinking about you.'

'I doubt it.' I put my teacup and saucer down with a thud and a splash. 'My lord, you don't need to flirt with me. I am most honoured that you should call, but—'

'Beresford suggested I pay a call on you, and that I should become acquainted with your family now you are part of mine.'

'What? You have heard from them?'

'I have, by this morning's post.'

'Oh. I expected that . . . I mean, was there a message for me? From Ann, that is, Lady Beresford?'

'I'm afraid not.'

I stand and walk away from him, so that he will not see how upset I have become. She promised to write as soon as she could. I know that she cannot possibly miss me as much as I miss her – after all, she has a husband to occupy her – but to not even include a message when she knew the bearer of the letter was to call upon my family! Oh, it is a dreadful disappointment.

I hear the creak of his boots and the rustle of his coat as Shadderly stands. 'The letter was very brief, and mostly about some rather boring business matters that needed to be cleared up, and which I had promised to take care of.'

His sympathy makes me even angrier; humiliated, too, that he recognises my feelings for what they are.

I turn back to him. 'Of course. It has been charming to see you, my lord.'

He glances at the teacup in his hand and then at me. 'My friends and my family call me Shad.'

'I don't believe you can presume so far, my lord. Our acquaintance is by marriage only.'

'Very well. Your servant, ma'am.' He drains the cup, places it on the table, and bows. 'I expect I'll see you at Marianne's soirée tonight. I'll claim the first dance, if I may.'

'Who is Marianne?' What soirée? Now I vaguely remember some talk at breakfast of gowns and so on. What a bother. I want to stay home and sulk.

'My sister, Mrs Shillington. She's very fashionable. The first dance, ma'am?'

I shrug. 'I suppose so.'

'Your feminine charms overwhelm me. I'll bid you good day.'

I say a bad word after he leaves.

The door opens. 'I'm quite shocked, Miss Hayden. I'll have my manservant, who has quite enormous feet, send over an old pair of shoes for your footman. Until tonight, ma'am.'

Viscount Shadderly

I'm not sure why I called on Miss Hayden. Possibly it was an excess of dimpling, giggling misses paraded in drawing rooms for my benefit that made me long for something astringent, as one might after a surfeit of sweetmeats.

I'd expected the family to be home but decided that collaring Miss Hayden in her lair might be entertaining. I didn't expect to feel sorry for her or almost admire her for her lack of manners and grace. In fact, she rather reminded me of some of my more elderly relatives who are past caring about social niceties; or of a captive animal, trapped in that hideously over-furnished room of gilt and velvet where nothing quite matched and everything shouted of newness and expense, as though money had fought good taste and won. The Haydens' house is in the most expensive and new part of town, where the newly rich outdo each other in ostentatious vulgarity. (Old families such as ours outdo each other in boasting of our older London houses' inefficiencies and unhealthy locations.)

It was also obvious that Beresford was probably right about her feelings for him. She was so flustered to be caught writing a letter that she spilled ink all down herself, and then became mightily distressed that I had heard from him. She tried to cover it up with an enquiry about Lady Ann. I was afraid she might burst into tears. But not Miss Charlotte. She became even surlier and had the audacity to refuse my friendship – although why I offered it in the first place I'm not sure. After all, I came to town for a few weeks of pleasure, a reward for dealing with the problems at home, at the end of which I should acquire a suitable bride. And what has happened? I find myself embroiled in Beresford's loose ends, for my pains, and attempt to befriend an unsuitable and foul-mouthed woman; I am relieved that I can dispense with her after the first dance tonight.

*

'Who are you looking for, Shad?' my sister Marianne murmurs into my ear. Sets are forming for the first dance in the Shillingtons' ballroom. The room is an extravagant excess of gilding and naked deities above, the *ton* parading around below looking for suitable subjects for the next day's gossip.

'No matter. Are you engaged for the first dance?'

'Oh, you rogue!' She smacks me with her fan. 'Of course I am. I am to dance with Shilly. What would people say if I was to dance with anyone other than my dearest husband? Besides it is so very vulgar to dance with relatives.'

Shillington approaches and frowns. 'Have you not found Shad a partner, my dear?'

'Of course.' Marianne turns to a group of simpering misses nearby. 'Miss Bretton, may I introduce Viscount Shadderly, who would like to claim your hand for the first dance. He is excessively wicked and you must take no notice of anything he says.' To me, in a rapid whisper, 'Ten thousand, trade, Scottish, very innocent.'

Having presented me with vital information about my dancing partner, she furls her fan shut with a determined air and trips off on her husband's arm.

Miss Bretton regards me as a mouse might a cat as I offer my arm and make an innocuous yet insincere comment to her on the decoration of the ballroom. She reacts as though I offered to strip her naked, blushing and looking around wild-eyed for help.

We take our place in the set and the music starts, I looking to see if the errant Miss Hayden – who has had the audacity to refuse a viscount – has thrown me over for another partner.

There's no sign of her. I ask Miss Bretton how long she has been in London and receive her reply, in a terrified whisper, that she has been in town one month. We work our way down the set – an intolerable amount of time for me, and I suspect, for my partner – and then I glance at the doorway. I stop dead in the dance and there is some consternation as couples bump into me and I hear some fabric rip; probably a train from a gown.

'Sir!' A well-muscled elderly woman shoves me back into position and I hurry to catch up.

Yes, she's here, with her family in attendance. Mr Hayden, stout, red-faced, and with a halo of grey hair floating around his bald head; Mrs Hayden, her faded prettiness marred by a look of dissatisfaction (I suspect she is still mightily put out by the god-daughter from nowhere marrying before her own daughter); and a younger, less bald version of Hayden, whom I remember from the wedding as being their son George. Charlotte is, well, she is Charlotte; a cynical smile on her face and a gown that exhibits an interesting mix of excess decoration with drabness (I regret my first thought is that I should introduce her to Mrs Perkins).

Finally, thank God, the dance ends and I escort my

partner back to her party; I swear she fights to get behind her companions and away from me. I bow, turn away, and come face to face with Miss Hayden.

She stood me up, by God! Since I am determined not to dwell too long upon my injured feelings, I bow briefly to her, and pass by.

I see Marianne approaching, ready to foist me on to some other unwilling partner and I turn away to take a glass of wine from a footman.

Behind me an interesting conversation takes place. Mrs Hayden is the first I hear speak. 'Charlotte, why did you not say before? He is a viscount, after all. He does you great honour—'

An inaudible mutter from Charlotte.

'By God, daughter, you'll not insult a peer of the realm. George, go and strike up a conversation with Shadderly. Tell him our horse went lame or some such.'

'I must respectfully decline, sir. Let my sister explain—'

I drain my glass of wine and listen to the family bicker a little more. Now they seem to be going over familiar territory: how Charlotte, the ungrateful girl, does not repay their strenuous efforts to marry her off.

Someone taps me on the shoulder. I turn and, to my surprise, see Charlotte.

'They don't realise how loud they are,' she says.

He raises one eyebrow. He's in black of course, since it's evening, and he looks devastating, slender and powerful at the same time, and I chide myself for reading too many unsuitable novels.

'No matter,' he says.

'You don't have to ask me to dance again. Even if you were intending to, thank you very much, my lord,' I add, in case he had decided to disown me entirely.

'Ma'am.' He bows.

'I'm sorry. Mama wanted to arrive fashionably late, and I didn't want to tell her you had asked me for the first dance, because, well . . .' I don't want to give the reason, namely that they would fuss and make so much of it. I'd only told them when they commented on the Viscount's coolness as he greeted me.

'Oh, I think I have a pretty good idea of your family, Miss Hayden.'

My face grows hot. 'They are *my* family, Lord Shadderly, and you don't have the right to criticise them.'

He's silent and I wonder whether he will storm off like a black thundercloud (good riddance!), but then he bows and takes my hand. 'You are absolutely right, ma'am. My apologies.'

I nod in acknowledgement and feel quite awkward, particularly as my family is looking on with undisguised interest. But I quite like having my hand in his although I would rather die than admit it to him.

'Would you care to dance, Miss Hayden?'

'Not particularly. I'm not very good at dancing, and you always have to have such stupid conversations. I'd like something to drink, if you please.'

'Of course.' He looks around and a footman appears. Shadderly hands me a glass of wine before turning to my parents.

All of a sudden, he is quite charming, and apparently sincere, and, to my horror, asks their permission to take me for a turn around the ballroom, since the next dance is already well underway. I gulp down the glass of wine, take another, and drink that too.

Shadderly, social niceties dealt with, offers me his arm. 'Your glass is empty, Miss Hayden. Would you care for another? Or some lemonade?'

'Wine, please.' Reminding myself that I must sip this glass, I place my hand in the crook of his arm and we set off together. What the devil am I to talk to him about? At least if we danced I could pretend to be concentrating on the steps.

'So,' he says, 'you don't like dancing, you obviously don't care about fashion – what do you like, Miss Hayden?'

'Of course I care about fashion!'

'I beg your pardon.'

He must have deduced that I prefer to slop around the house in a day dress than put on finery for the evening, and I'm aware that my gown is unbecoming.

'You should go to the modiste with Marianne,' he says carelessly, as though going shopping with one of the wealthiest and best-dressed women in London is the most natural thing in the world to do. 'I'll have her call upon you.'

'But—'

He stops to chat with an ancient raddled lady, who sports patches and a wig and an exceedingly old-fashioned gown, whom he introduces as Lady Hortense Renbourn.

From her painted face she regards me with sharp eyes.

'Heh, you're too plain to keep Shad's interest,' she says. 'He'll get under your skirts and leave you, mark my words. He'll have no use for you after, and you're too low for him to marry.'

I open my mouth to remonstrate, although impressed against my will by her old-fashioned forthrightness, but Shadderly smiles and kisses her hand. 'You're the only woman in the room for me, Aunt Hortense.'

'Rogue!' She whacks him with her fan and addresses me again. 'So you're the one who brought the pretty interloper into the family.'

'Yes, milady.'

'She married better than she deserved.'

'On the contrary, she deserves happiness as much as any woman, milady.'

'Happiness!' She snorts. 'That's not the point of marriage, miss. Take her away, Shad, and don't make any more scandal.'

We continue around the ballroom. 'My congratulations, Miss Hayden, on standing up to her. She has a reputation for making young women cry.'

'I don't see why.' Fortify yourself with enough glasses of wine and you can stand up to any old hag, I think. I am amused by Aunt Renbourn and I wonder how long it will be, if I prove to be unmarriageable, before I can transform into an outspoken eccentric.

Now, however, I'm intensely curious about the scandals in Shadderly's past, and wonder exactly what they have been. I really don't know much about him. My brother George, who claims to know everyone, told me Shadderly's naval career was interrupted when his older brother died and he had to return home to take over the title and family responsibilities. It all sounds tediously unscandalous, if sad.

Shadderly pauses to purloin a bottle of wine from a footman and escorts me through some doors to a terrace.

'Why are you doing this?' I ask. I'm not sure whether I'm asking why he is showing me such interest, or taking me outside, or both.

'Good lord,' he says, leaning against the stone balustrade. 'I've never met a more prickly girl. Don't you realise, Miss Hayden, that being seen in my company raises your stakes in the marriage mart?'

'I'm delighted to be the recipient of your lordship's charity.'

He takes a swig from the bottle and passes it to me. 'You're not the recipient of my charity, Miss Hayden, or of excessive politeness. Possibly I enjoy your company.'

'Indeed.'

'Yes, I know it's difficult to believe.'

I snort wine from my nose at this and he takes the bottle from me while I dab at the neckline of my gown. I hope it hasn't stained.

'Sometimes you're quite rude, Shad.' I take a swig from the bottle to cover my confusion at using the familiar version of his name. 'What was the scandal that Lady Renbourn said you'd caused?'

'Oh, let's see. The usual sort of thing: I ride around the countryside on a black stallion looking for women to seduce. I fight the occasional duel, as naturally I am a hot-headed sort of fellow who is eager to take offence, and now and again I gamble away part of my estate and have to win it back.'

'Poppycock.'

He laughs.

Somehow we have nearly finished the bottle between us. The air is soft and dark, and I step away from him, and find myself launched into thin air. I land on grass, somewhat surprised; apparently I missed three or possibly four stone steps that would have provided a more conventional descent.

'Good God, are you hurt, Charlotte?' He rushes to my side.

'Oh, no. It didn't hurt at all.'

'How much have you had to drink tonight?'

I consider. We shared the usual number of bottles at dinner, a couple of glasses before I encountered Shad in the ballroom, then the three, then my share of our bottle. 'Very little.'

'You're drunk.' He smiles.

'Will you take advantage of me?'

'Good God, no!' He looks quite horrified. 'What do you think I am?'

'But you're the wicked cousin. I don't think you're up to snuff.'

'We'll walk,' he says. 'I can't return you to your family in this sorry state.'

'I'm not sorry. May I finish the last of the bottle?'

'No.' He drains it himself and tosses it aside. 'On your feet, Miss Hayden.'

I take his hand and lurch upright, bumping into him. Or rather, I bump and stay there.

'Miss Hayden,' he says. His voice is slow and deliberate.

'Lord Shadderly.' It's like a dance, only this is one I seem to be quite good at.

I can't remember what colour his eyes are.

'I wish I had eyelashes like yours. Do you use lamp black on them?'

'Oh, for God's sake.' He bends his head and his

mouth takes and holds my upper lip. Good heavens, he is kissing me. I am so surprised I stop breathing, even though I was the one who made an indecent suggestion a minute or so before. If I have had doubts about his status as wicked cousin, they fly away now, for his kiss is full of wickedness and sin.

I compare what he is doing to other kisses I have received, and come to the conclusion that this is how a kiss should be. And, yes, if you were wondering, I have been kissed before, but not like this. I have never been kissed by someone who knows exactly what he does, and who, I suspect, has put in a goodly amount of practice.

And certainly not by someone who presses against me with such insistence and with one hand draws me closer.

His mouth moves very briefly against mine and I, out of curiosity (and inspired by something Ann told me), touch my tongue to his lips.

He lifts his head. 'Well, Miss Hayden.'

We are still close to each other; I run an inventory of the parts that press into me. His stick pin (at my neck), coat buttons, breeches' buttons—

He steps back but keeps my hand in his. 'I trust my reputation as wicked cousin is restored.'

'A little.' I find myself smiling hugely at him. 'Shad, you asked me a little time ago what I liked. I liked that.'

'So you did.'

The quiet of the garden is interrupted by a roar of anger. 'Shadderly, what the devil are you doing with my sister?'

Miss Charlotte Hayden

My brother George, for it is he, punches Shad in the face. I've never seen anyone hit before, not in this way – my brother makes a great deal of noise about his boxing prowess to anyone unfortunate enough to listen – and am surprised at the sound it makes, a fleshy, cracking thump, and how Shad falls without a sound, flat on to the ground.

George grabs my arm. 'You fool! You're ruined.' He begins to haul me towards the house. 'The devil, you must marry him.'

I try to shake myself loose. 'What if I don't want to? Let me go, George, you great lummox.'

'Don't you call me names, miss,' he bellows. 'Why, to let a notorious rake take liberties with you, a man you hardly know—'

'Enough.' Shad's voice is cool but quiet. He's on his feet again, brushing grass from his coat. 'I'll do what's honourable, Hayden, you need have no fear. Miss Hayden, if I may—'

'I'll send you my second, sir,' George blusters. 'This is my sister you have assaulted.'

'Oh, stop it, both of you!' I finally manage to free myself from George's grip. Men! If George has his way he will haul Shad out to some deserted spot where they will go through the strange male formalities of trying to blow each other's heads off, and all over one kiss! I know too, that anyone George chooses to be his second, that is someone whose task is ostensibly to heal the breach without bloodshed, will be as bloodthirsty as he is. 'No one knows. It was a kiss, George; don't tell me you have never done the same yourself. I'm going back inside now.'

I run away from them, and ascend the steps I fell down a few minutes before. As light from the ballroom spills out on to the terrace, I see, with a sinking heart, that my gown is covered from grass stains. They were caused, I know, by my fall down the steps, but I am sure many will think the worst. As I hesitate, Mr Harry Dunbury, the worst gossip in London, and author (all suspect) of a certain scandalmongering newspaper column, steps through one of the doorways, raises his quizzing glass to his eye, and smirks.

Behind me, Shad and George come to a stop. I turn to look at them; George is nursing a fist, injured from his pugilistic efforts, and Shad's face and the ruffles of his shirtfront are covered in blood.

It is all too obvious what has happened.

Mr Dunbury bows and disappears back into the ballroom.

'Damnation,' George says. 'My hand hurts.'

'Good,' I say.

'I suggest you apply ice, sir.' Shad bows. 'I shall call on you, Miss Hayden. Mr Hayden, your servant, sir.' He disappears into the darkness as I wonder if his excessive politeness is designed to infuriate my brother further.

Meanwhile a dozen or so people find it necessary to wander on to the terrace, and there is much whispering and curious stares.

'If Shadderly doesn't come up to snuff I'll kill him,' George says for their benefit, swaggering slightly.

'Hold your tongue,' I hiss. 'You are making a spectacle of us. Have you no shame?' Even as I say it, I realise that the question is meaningless to George; in fact to any member of our family.

'Stay here, miss. I must ask Tom Hale to be my second.'

'Not the best choice, George. He kissed me last New Year's Eve.'

'What!'

'Several times.'

'Where?' George thunders.

'Behind the stables.' I assume he means a geographical location, not which part of my person. 'George, please stop shouting. Everyone is staring at us!'

But George growls at me and threatens me with expulsion from the family if I so much as move a finger. He disappears into the ballroom to tell our parents I am ruined. The full enormity of what I have done dawns on me as I see the sidelong glances and the ostentatious turning of backs, and hear the sniggers and whispered comments.

'Unmarriageable apparently . . . Not Shad's usual conquest . . . a duel . . . dishonoured . . . money-grubbing . . . the cousin was much prettier . . . shocking . . .'

I wanted to get out of the marriage mart but not like this. I didn't particularly want to do so by marrying, given the choice of gentlemen, and I certainly don't want Shad to . . . he said he'd do the honourable thing, and I'm not sure what he meant. Kill my brother? Allow George to kill him? Or the honourable thing towards myself, meaning, not with any involvement of pistols or swords, but marriage between us?

So he'll marry me out of duty, or pity, or . . . by God, I'd rather kill him myself!

'*Sharper than a Serpent's Tooth!*' My mother's arrival interrupts my unladylike musings, her fashionable gown taking on the appearance of tragic drapery. She bursts into hysterical tears.

Oh, this is dreadful. Now we shall entertain the onlookers even more.

'Fetch your mother some brandy,' my father, bustling behind her, commands George.

'Fetch me some too, if you please,' I say.

'Enough of your intolerable pertness, miss! Never darken my door again!' shouts my father, to the appreciation of our audience, as Mama heaves and sobs.

'May I come home to change my shoes? These are really inappropriate for the pavements of the Strand,' I counter.

He growls at me and then I see the tears standing in his eyes. 'Tell me, miss, did he take advantage of you?' He's staring at the grass stains on my gown.

I think I took advantage of Shad, but it doesn't seem politic to say so. 'I'm quite well, Papa,' I say, hoping this will calm him.

George returns, a handful of ice in his injured hand, a glass of brandy in the other. I snatch a lump of ice and drop it down the back of Mama's gown. She stops in mid-wail and makes a choking gasp.

'Now may we go home and stop entertaining the *ton*?' I suggest.

I shall say only that neither the drive home nor the ensuing scene in our drawing room is pleasant.

A yawning servant, wig askew, serves tea and the brandy decanter is passed. My brother, still raging, sends another footman with a note to Mr Hale, so that the masculine proprieties may be observed.

We wait. My suggestion that we go to bed – well, what difference can it possibly make at this point? – is met with stony glares. How long must we wait before we may acknowledge Shad as the vile seducer he doubtless is and retire for the night?

And then the knocker on the front door is given a decisive thud. We hear a brief conversation between our night porter and a gentleman; it's not possible, at this distance, to determine whether it's Hale or Shad.

It is Shad. He enters our drawing room, the place where I entertained him only a few hours ago, and I am disappointed that he does not wear a swirling black cloak like the villain in a play.

He addresses my father, ignoring me altogether. 'Mr Hayden, I am come to ask for your daughter's hand.'

Oh, please don't ask me. I'm only a walk-on player in this drama, the wronged maiden – or rather, at this point, a put-upon, tired, and bad-tempered maiden.

I make sure my curtsy is as minimal as possible.

My father nods, and he and Shad leave to discuss this business undertaking in the privacy of the study.

George, yawning hugely, suggests our mother go to bed, and she, drooping and dabbing her eyes with her handkerchief, leaves the room.

'And you, miss,' he says, 'you stay here.'

'Why?'

'Shadderly will want to talk to you.'

'Why do you think so? He all but ignored me just now.'

'Have you no sense of decency?' my brother snarls,

and I sit, confused, for what seems a long time, trying to sort out the etiquette of the situation – it is indeed as though everyone else but me knows the role they should play.

So I am in the midst of a huge, unmaidenly yawn, the sort of yawn that could swallow an innocent bystander, when Shad and my father return. I shut my mouth, blinking, and struggle to stand, realising too late that one of my feet has gone to sleep, and I lurch in an odd way.

'The Viscount wishes to speak to you,' my father says.

'Oh, very well,' I grumble.

Shad and my father bow. I try to catch George's eye to get him to stay, but it's no use.

I'm left alone with a glowering viscount.

'We are affianced,' he says.

I'm at a loss how to respond to this. I finally come out with a feeble, 'Oh.'

'I have to set the town house in order. I'm staying with my sister at present, but I expect you know that. And then we'll marry by special licence, within the week.'

'But I don't want to marry you, sir. And you don't want to marry me. So—'

'Honour – my honour – demands it, ma'am.' He looks furious now. I regret that I find there is something quite exciting about his anger, and I can't help but wish again he wore some sort of Gothic costume for this pronouncement. It would be so much more effective.

'What about *my* honour?'

'You have none,' he says bluntly. 'It can only be restored by marriage to me – the man who took it from you.'

'It might be a matter of honour to me that I marry a man I esteem.'

He takes a step towards me. 'Very pretty, Miss Hayden, but a moot point.'

I feel absolute despair and wish fervently that Ann were here to give me advice or consolation; but she is gadding around the country on her honeymoon, something I may be forced to do very soon, and I don't like the idea at all. I had always assumed I would marry, since I know my family are most anxious for me to make a respectable match if I can't manage a brilliant one, but I'd hoped it might be to someone I liked, or at least knew a little. I really wish, too, that he had not kissed me, for that complicates things mightily. I should like him to kiss me again – not while he glares at me so, of course, but at another time when that teasing, flirtatious side of him is revealed. At the moment I doubt it ever will. And don't men think there is one sort of woman who is available for kissing and flirtation, and another who is available only for marital intentions?

I'm not really sure I want to be categorised as either. Tears prick my eyes and I sniff, but I'm damned if I'll cry in front of him.

'Miss Hayden – Charlotte – here's the thing. I came to London to find a wife. Sentiment is all very well, but I must secure my line. I offer you my name, and therefore the restoration of your reputation. Once you've had our son, you're welcome to, ah, seek affection where you will.'

'How extraordinarily generous of your lordship.' I hope I sound sarcastic. How terrible if I sounded sincere.

'Actually, yes, it is. I'll be willing to turn a blind eye to your liaisons, as you'll do to mine.'

'I see.' How very fashionable; how cold. I wonder if Ann and her earl will come to a similar understanding if they tire of each other.

'There's no reason why we can't treat each other with civility,' he says. 'We could be . . . allies, if not friends.'

'What a delightful prospect.' I'm tired, I'm feeling more bad-tempered by the moment, and somehow I feel . . . cheated. I don't want to be the brood mare for Shad's line, and I'm sure Shad won't wait until a son is born to hop into another woman's bed. 'I trust my dowry was sufficient for your needs.'

'Perfectly adequate, ma'am. I'll bid you good night.'

'Good morning, sir.'

'Why, so it is. Good morning, Miss Hayden.'

He bows and leaves.

The room is cold, the fire having burned down some time ago, and I can hear sounds coming from downstairs, where our scullerymaid bangs around with a mop and bucket. At least I have a warm bed to go to and my family can maybe forgive me.

But oh, how I wish Ann was here.

Viscount Shadderly

For all his honest natural stupidity, Beresford would be a useful person to have around at such a time. I have found he serves as an excellent sounding board, on which I may bounce ideas and fancies, and come to a sensible conclusion. Occasionally, to the surprise of all, he'll produce an idea so brilliantly simple that it has not occurred to anyone else.

Somehow, I have suffered a fit of temporary (I hope) insanity.

It began, innocently enough, with lending a plain and ill-tempered woman my handkerchief and ended with my engagement to her. Worse, there is no way out, unless the unlovely Miss Hayden has another fellow lurking elsewhere (and not Beresford), for whom she will throw me over. I am not over-optimistic.

In practical terms this marriage is better than I anticipated from the general appearance of the Hayden family. They may convey an air of grubby gentility and penny-pinching, but certain hints – the brash new furniture, the extravagant gowns of the Hayden ladies, and rumours of the sons' high style of living – indicate that the family is spending money with a vengeance, investing in their awkward daughter's future.

It has paid off.

'Charlotte Hayden!' my sister exclaims. 'Oh, Shad, why?'

'Twelve thousand.'

'But . . . but you hardly know the girl.'

'Marianne . . .' I glance at my niece and nephew next to me on the sofa, 'I *have* to marry her.'

'You mean after last night.'

'Yes.'

'Uncle Shad, I want to put a ribbon in your hair.' Elizabeth, my three-year-old niece, has her mind on more important things than the near disgrace and marriage of her uncle.

Charles, my nephew, gnaws on a fist and kicks his legs. He seems to approve of his elder sister's attempts to make me an object of beauty, but Charles, a fat, smiling infant, approves of most things.

'Say please, Elizabeth,' my sister interjects. She leans forward to place a hand on her daughter's forehead. 'She feels a trifle warm to me. What do you think, Shad?'

'Please, Uncle Shad.' My niece climbs on to my lap and ties a ribbon in my hair, humming softly to herself. 'Pretty, Uncle.'

'Well,' says my sister, 'now you are properly

beribboned and adorned, what shall you do today, Shad?'

'I'd best take a look at the house.'

She nods. Neither of us has happy memories of the family's town house, that has stood, silent and empty, shuttered close and the furniture shrouded with holland cloth, for the previous two years. I have not set foot in it since my last departure from England to take command of the *Arcturus* five years ago.

'And then I'll take George Hayden to Jackson's.'

She makes a face. 'Why?'

'I thought it might foster family feeling. Will you come with me to the house? And as a further favour, will you take Charlotte to your modiste to see if you can persuade her to dress more . . .' I hesitate for an appropriate word.

'I believe you mean less grotesquely.'

'Precisely.'

'Oh, Shad.' She shakes her head. 'Well, your reputation as the wicked cousin is confirmed. But if the *ton* could see you now, with my children on your lap and ribbons in your hair – you'd be ruined, my dear. Absolutely ruined.'

I had hoped that Marianne would be cheered by a visit to the family house in London, but as we walk through gloomy old-fashioned rooms, curtains drawn to protect the carpets, she sighs deeply. It is not a cheery place; even when inhabited, it was not so.

My manservant Roberts follows a few deferential paces behind, dutifully taking notes, and murmurs quietly to the housekeeper who has managed the place during the family's absence.

My sister stops in front of a portrait of our mother that hangs beside the fireplace in the dining room. 'I miss her, Shad.'

'I too.' We pass by a matching portrait of our father on the other side without comment. Few miss our father.

'I remember him beating you,' she says.

'I was a wilful child.'

She looks at me steadily. 'I trust you will not treat your own children so, however wilful they prove to be.'

'I will not, I promise.'

My sister snaps into her usual brisk self. 'Roberts, there is a great deal of work to be done. Fresh paint here – a yellow, I think, to bring cheer to the room, for painting is about all we can do in this short time. Shad, your wife should choose wallpapers and such, and window hangings. I shall be pleased to assist. And you'll need at least half a dozen footmen and their liveries to be made . . . do you wish to be fashionable and hire a French man cook, Shad?'

'No, a female cook will suffice. I doubt we'll stay in London more than a month.'

'You don't plan on a wedding journey, then?'

I shake my head. 'No, we'll stay in town and brazen it out. Once we're seen at the play and the park, tongues will cease to wag and the gossipmongers will find someone else to prey on.'

'Very wise,' Marianne says. 'Shad, I wish you did not have to marry her. Not like this. I'm sure she's a nice enough girl, but . . .'

'Nonsense. It's high time I married.' I agree with my sister but I'm damned if I'll say so.

'And did you tell her about the Bastards?'

My sister is becoming meddlesome. 'Not yet. I shall.'

I instruct Roberts and Mrs Williams the housekeeper to hire footmen and female servants as necessary. I don't even know if Charlotte will bring her own maid. Already I feel I am drowning in domesticity and I can't wait to leave this house. The next time I enter it will be on the day I am to be married.

Miss Charlotte Hayden

'*Most Condescending*,' my mother pronounces. 'We are *Most Deeply Honoured*, Mrs Shillington.'

Mrs Shillington, dressed in the height of fashion and supremely elegant, allows a smile. I suspect she is here under duress. Her gaze travels around the room and her eyebrows arch a little, making her look ludicrously like her brother. I do not think her expression conveys admiration of our taste in furnishings.

'I have always thought my Charlotte a *Most Lovely Girl*,' Mama continues. 'Such *Regularity of Features*! And her complexion – why, at home, she is accounted the *Most Handsome Girl in the County*.'

What a pack of lies. I don't think Mrs Shillington believes them, but she maintains her composure. 'I shall have Charlotte back safe and sound in a couple of hours,' she says. 'Pray do not concern yourself, ma'am.'

My mother, who I knew wanted to accompany us and entertain us with a succession of pronouncements, looks taken aback for a moment. But I'm full of admiration at Mrs Shillington's adroitness and – or do I imagine it? – one eyelid flutters in a tiny intimation of a wink.

Thus I find myself, feeling dowdy and uncomfortable, in Mrs Shillington's elegant carriage, headed for her modiste's establishment. She is silent, elegant, aloof and I feel a fool for thinking she might be an ally. But I feel that one of us should make an effort to break the silence.

'Mrs Shillington, this was not my intention.'

'To go shopping?' She raises admirable, arched eyebrows.

'To marry Lord Shadderley.'

'Oh, that.' She frowns a little. 'Think nothing of it, Charlotte. It is time he married.'

While I ponder the possibilities of this – that she has deigned to address me by my first name, but does not invite me to use hers, and the implication that I am merely some sort of marital conduit for Shad's obligations – we draw up at a small house with a sign announcing that it is the establishment of Madame Bellevoir, Modiste. We are not in Bond Street or one of the other fashionable shopping streets; this is an entirely more modest neighbourhood, with a chandler's opposite, and a couple of children playing with a dog at the side of the street.

We alight and a young woman runs out of the shop to greet us with a deferential curtsy, while another opens the door from inside, the shop bell jangling. A woman, some years older than Mrs Shillington and very plainly dressed, meets us at the doorway and ushers us inside.

'So this is she,' she says to Mrs Shillington.

I am becoming exceedingly tired of people talking of me as though I am elsewhere.

'I am she who what?' I dare say I sound bad-tempered as well as ungrammatical. I am not in the best of moods.

They both ignore me and Madame Bellevoir, for I guess it is she, walks around me as though I were some sort of item on display.

'Not bad,' she says to Mrs Shillington. 'Not bad. The gown – *mon Dieu*.'

I want to blurt out that the gown cost a lot of money and at least I am not dressed like a . . . I do not know how she is dressed, only that you notice the woman, her height and carriage. Similarly, Mrs Shillington is a picture of refinement and elegance although I should be hard put to describe exactly what she is wearing.

'And you, *mademoiselle*,' at last she addresses me directly, 'you are to be married? And you are how old?'

'Three and twenty.' What does that have to do with my gown?

Madame and Mrs Shillington begin an earnest conversation in French about horses and I wonder whether they are both insane, or whether it is my knowledge of French that is at fault. When Madame takes the pins from my hair and lifts the locks in her hand, I realise that they are talking about my hair – *cheveux*, not *chevaux* – and I gather they plan to cut it.

'Absolutely not! *Non!*'

'*Mais oui, mademoiselle.*' Madame beckons to one of her assistants, beside whom I now feel horribly overdressed, who comes forward with a sheet and a pair of scissors. 'You will be *très élégante*. It is the highest of fashion. When your hair is cut, then we talk of the new gown for the wedding. Your husband, the milord, will like the hair short, for you will look like a boy and all Englishmen, they—'

'Not my brother,' Mrs Shillington says.

A stool is shoved beneath me, the sheet tied round my neck, and as the scissors snap, locks of hair tumble down my front and on to the floor. There's so much of it I'm quite horrified.

'A true elegance of bone, that is what creates *la mode*,' Madame says and both she and Mrs Shillington nod with satisfaction. The assistant darts around me, tipping my head this way and that, snipping, tugging, a frown on her face. Meanwhile Mrs Shillington, seated with a glass of wine (how I envy her), leafs through fashion illustrations and scraps of fabric. I have the feeling that I am to have as much say in the cut and colour of my gown as the style of my hair.

Madame tips a bolt of fabric, dusky pale green, on

to the counter, and tosses a gold ribbon that loops and unspools on top of it. She and Mrs Shillington look at the fabric and trim, then at me, and they both shake their heads. Madame removes the gold ribbon, and substitutes a narrow silver one in its place. They both nod, as two men who have dug a hole might toss their spades aside and express satisfaction at a job well done.

'I hate green,' I offer, and have to spit out a mouthful of hair.

They ignore me.

The snip and clatter of blades around my head slows and halts. The young woman moves to stand in front of me, peers earnestly at my head, and lifts and pats my hair.

'So!' Madame says. She flings a length of fabric over my shoulder and the pale silk slithers over my bodice and cascades about my feet.

Her assistant produces a mirror and I stare at my reflection.

I gasp.

Marianne – for she invited me to use her Christian name – declines to come into our house when I return home. One of her children, it appears, was slightly unwell earlier in the day and she is anxious to return. We have had very little conversation but I feel she is an ally, possibly a friend. I feel, in fact, warmer towards her than I do towards my future husband, whom I now realise I may not see until the day of our marriage.

As I enter the house I refuse to let the footman take my bonnet and, my shorn head covered, I enter the drawing room.

Much to my relief, I am not to be the principal in a family drama. My brother George has appropriated that role, stretched upon the couch (his muddy boots still on his feet, something only he and Henry would be allowed to do), while my mama laments and groans, a basin in her hand.

'Why, George, what's the matter?' I ask.

He sits up. 'Capital fellow, Shad!' I see now he has a dreadful black eye, and his appearance is not improved by a beefsteak dribbling blood on to his neckcloth. 'Did a few rounds with me at Jackson's, and you should see his right hook! Tremendous fellow, excellent sportsman, damned fast on his feet—'

My mother makes a tremulous whimpering sound at his strong language.

'Beg your pardon, ma'am,' he continues. 'I wasn't too keen on the idea of you marrying him, Char – he's a trifle high in the instep I thought, for a fellow who's got an estate in a pretty bad way, won't enclose, you see, so he's squandering money on his tenants, bad money after good. Or do I mean good after bad? So—'

'You mean Shad did that to you?' I'm horrified.

'Yes, and he got a few blows in on my ribs. Thought he'd broken one, but it's not so bad now.'

'Pray, lie down, *Dearest Boy*,' my mother intones.

She places her basin on a small table to reach for her decanter of cordial.

'Are you completely mad, George?'

He shrugs, the same stupid proud grin on his face. 'Damned gentlemanly of him to invite me to a round, that's all I can say. I'll be proud to shake his hand and call him brother.'

'But you wanted to kill him last night.'

'Oh, that . . .' He waves a hand. 'We're the best of friends, now.'

'How charming.' I remove my bonnet and am gratified by the sudden silence that falls. George stops his idiotic babble and there's a loud clink as my mother's cordial glass lands on the table.

'Good God!' my brother said. 'You look like a boy.'

'No, I don't.'

'Your *Crowning Glory*,' my mother moans and reaches for the decanter again. '*Gone, Forever Gone*.'

'And this is my dress.' I thrust Madame's sketch at her.

George peers over her shoulder and a drop of blood falls on the paper.

'Looks like a damned – beg your pardon, ma'am – shift to me. Needs a few bunches of flowers around the . . . somewhere . . . frilly things.'

'Thank you, brother. I'll be sure to consult you next time I visit the modiste. Or maybe you'd like to come with me and she could punch your face?'

'Very funny,' my brother says, swinging his muddy

feet from the sofa to the floor. 'Why, it's time for me to go to the club. Can't wait to tell the fellows there about Shad. Wonder if he'll put me up for White's?'

He leaves the room, whistling unmusically.

My mother moans. 'This gown. This gown has no . . . *No Bosom*.'

'You are mistaken, ma'am.'

'You will be an *Indecent Spectacle* at your own wedding. Oh, the shame.'

'Well, ma'am, you surely understand why the bosom is so low cut?'

She refills her cordial glass by way of a reply.

'As I understand it, ma'am, it is so my husband does not mistake me for a boy, for both Madame Bellevoir and Mrs Shillington were kind enough to explain that if he did, then there would be no chance of an heir.'

'*Impertinent, Ungrateful Child!*' My mother reaches for the bellpull as a drowning man might reach for a rope. 'Send for my maid,' she tells Jeremiah who stares at my head with undisguised curiosity. 'Charlotte, you may leave to reflect upon your *Most Miserable Lack of Filial Affection*.'

I am only too happy to retire to my bedchamber, where I light a dozen candles so I may admire my daringly cropped hair.

I cannot wait to see my father's reaction at dinner.

And I wonder what Ann will think of it?

And Shad. I have been persuaded, by Marianne and the dressmaker that, as in every novel I have read,

Shad will see my new hair and elegant gown and be overcome with admiration at the vision of loveliness he sees before him. He will fling himself to his knees before me and kiss the tips of my gloved fingers, while muttering incoherent expressions of adoration. Like a horse in blinkers, all he will see is me.

I do wish I could believe this sentimental nonsense.

Shad's List of Necessary Tasks Before Wedding

1. Retrieve family jewels from bank.
2. Send for coachman and family and coach from the country.
3. Inspect house.
4. Meet servants.
5. Acquire special licence.
6. Buy wedding ring.
7. Pay Mrs Perkins' next quarter rent.
8. Ask Marianne to find a lady's maid for Miss Hayden.
9. Find mistress.

Shad

On the day of my wedding I arrive early at my house – for so I must think of it now – and inspect the drawing room which has been scrubbed and scoured and looks almost presentable. The bedchamber is in fine fettle, with the bedhangings washed, the dead flies cleaned from the windows, and the bird's nest from the grate – Roberts assures me all the chimneys have been swept. To my surprise, my new household includes the gangling Jeremiah from the Haydens, who has decided to leave his position to stay close to the only man in London whose feet match his in the hopes of cast-off boots. Roberts follows behind me with a clothes brush, taking unnecessary swipes at my coat in the way of an inept fencer chasing a reluctant opponent.

'You'll do, sir, you'll do,' he says finally.

Below, activity around the front door indicates the

arrival of guests. For a moment the floor tilts as though I am on a quarterdeck and I feel that particular thrill of electricity in my wrists that indicates we are about to engage the French. I look up almost expecting to see the swell of a mainsail.

'Get a ladder, Roberts, and clean the cobwebs from the plasterwork.'

'Yes, milord, I'll see to it directly.'

I descend the stairs to meet my guests. I'd hoped Beresford might have returned to town – I'd written to him that I and Miss Hayden were to marry, but had received no reply – so could only assume he and his bride were billing and cooing still in some deserted place. I have chosen in his place an old friend from the Navy, Captain Carstairs, a gentle soul possessed of a wooden leg and paralytic shyness.

And in only a few hours I and my new Viscountess will have to perform some form of billing and cooing when we are alone, our guests dispersed, and the wedding breakfast over.

My sister has been extremely reticent on the topic of her visit to the modiste's with my affianced. The most I can elicit from her is that I shall have no cause for embarrassment, other than the presence of the Hayden family at the ceremony, a necessary but unavoidable nuisance. I regret it is not possible to marry by post.

But, as is my wont, I shall do my duty.

Below a shuffling, tapping sound indicates that my

best man is on the lookout for me. Sure enough, he appears below and his mouth begins to work in the familiar way that indicates he wishes to speak. Oddly enough he's perfectly vocal on a ship during engagement, where he curses and bellows with great clarity and fluency, but in polite society he is tongue-tied.

'Coming down directly, my dear fellow!' I descend the stairs and clap his shoulder.

He indicates the coat of his uniform. I don't believe he's trying to tell me his heart is broken or that he has developed a hopeless passion for my bride. I know, in fact, that he is reassuring us both that he carries the ring.

Now that would be an excellent solution; if only Miss Hayden would be obliging enough to fall in love with my best man and the two of them to elope while I go through the motions of jealousy and betrayal and remain an embittered bachelor. But I'm not sure I would wish the woman on to any friend of mine.

I am reminded that unfortunately, if Beresford's speculation is correct and not just male vanity, Miss Hayden may well be in love with Beresford himself – not something that bodes well for the future of our marriage. I am not sure there are any good omens at all.

'You have the ring? Excellent.' I sound revoltingly cheerful to myself. I'm glad Carstairs doesn't speak, or at least only spares his best efforts for matters of true importance, for if he were to utter any sort of jolly platitude at the moment I should be tempted to throw him out of the window.

He grips my hand and shakes it, much in the same way as he would do before a battle, when we were lieutenants together.

'Capital,' I say.

A clock nearby starts the humming sound that indicates it is about to strike the hour. Eleven of the morning.

Carstairs and I straighten our shoulders and shake hands again for no particular reason. Roberts, faced with a pair of unmoving targets, wields the clothes brush on us both with great energy.

At least the house is now in fighting trim, so to speak – the stink of fresh paint (and the occasional smear on footmen's livery) indicate our hasty attempts to make it habitable. It is still old and dark, with a ponderous oak staircase and much ancient, unfashionable furniture of the sort that will never wear out or be in fashion. There are very few guests: my sister and her husband, and a few other members of my family whom Marianne prevailed upon to attend. Those who have not met my bride are, according to Marianne, half mad with curiosity. Aunt Renbourn declined to be present, saying that there were altogether too many weddings taking place in the family, and she preferred to stay at home with her cats and particular friends.

Side by side Carstairs and I march into the drawing

room where our guests are assembled, and Miss Hayden turns to give me a welcoming scowl.

There's something different about her but I can't quite work out what it is. The bosom is still as magnificent and there seems to be more of it on display but before I can examine her more closely I am shoved forward to take my vows, Miss Hayden's hand in mine – slightly damp, with somewhat of a quiver.

Charlotte

Even my father noticed! Even if he did say I looked like a boy, he had the grace to say that the new gown was 'quite nice', a phrase he produced after much hemming and hawing, and wondering if I should have a shawl so I would not catch cold.

But this dolt I am marrying barely looked at me! He has not noticed the grace of my suddenly swanlike neck, the swell and curve and all the rest of it of my bosom – or maybe he has, for I do not recall that he has looked me in the eye once. Meanwhile the clergyman, who sports more feminine frippery of lace and embroidery than all the women in the room put together, binds me and Shad together until death do us part, while I wonder if lack of observation is grounds for an annulment.

I mumble my vows, Shad mutters his, and I wonder what would happen if I lunged for the door like a wild animal seeking its freedom. I could probably outrun his one-legged friend, but Shad has something of the greyhound about him.

As we are pronounced man and wife there is a scuffle behind us and a child's voice rings out. 'Uncle Shad! Uncle Shad, we have come to see you marry!'

We both turn round – I notice our hands are still joined and withdraw mine from his – to see a woman, who from her cap and apron looks like a nursemaid, with two children at the doorway to the drawing room.

Uncle Shad, indeed. One is a girl of about ten – what a busy youth Shad had, before he went off to expend his energies on the French – and the one who spoke is a little boy of about six. Both of them sport Shad's black hair and features.

The clergyman makes a low whimpering sound and clutches his prayerbook to his lacy bosom.

The boy runs to Shad, who hesitates and then scoops him into his arms. 'John, you must stand quietly and then you may have some cake.'

'Will the lady be our mama now?'

Married for less than a minute and the mother of two!

My mother gives a low moan and collapses into my brother's arms.

The girl comes forward and curtsies shyly to me and I cannot help but smile at her, charmed by her good manners and her resemblance to her father.

'We'll talk about this later,' Shad says to his children.

'Why does the lady have hair like a boy?' John continues.

'She doesn't—' Shad stares at me, confirming what I suspected, that he has barely looked at me until this moment. 'By God, she does. You do, that is. My sister's doing, I suppose? It suits you, ma'am. And the gown. Most, ah, elegant.'

'Will you not introduce your children to me, sir?' Oh, we are so polite to each other.

'Indeed, yes. This is John and this Amelia. Susan,' he addresses the nurse. 'You may take them downstairs for some cake, and . . .' They have a brief conversation before the nurse and children leave the room, presumably for the kitchen.

Shad's family does not seem particularly put out at the arrival of his illegitimate children. His sister gives them a friendly smile, and I suppose that such a high-born family (or at least, a family that has an earl at its head) will be worldly enough to accept a few such offspring into their midst.

My mother meanwhile, after my brother and father have fanned her and waved a vinaigrette beneath her nose, has come to her senses. 'Oh, the *Shame*, the *Shame for My Dearest Girl*,' she announces, which makes little sense to me, for it is not as though I was the one to produce my bastards at my own wedding.

'Would you rather he let his natural children rot in a ditch, ma'am?' I hiss at her, thoroughly annoyed, although I do agree that flaunting them at his wedding is a little vulgar.

'But the *Indelicacy*. My dear, can you not *Do Something*?' This to my father, who mops his brow with a handkerchief. He and I share a rare sympathetic glance.

'Well, ma'am, it's best he should sow his wild oats before the wedding rather than after, eh, Charlotte?'

My mother does not seem cheered by his observation and sinks into a chair again.

I, who know Shad intends to continue his habitual pursuits despite the acquisition of a wife, manage a smile. The sowing of wild oats has always seemed a particularly inappropriate metaphor to me – why should anyone sow something that grows wild? I envision a rake (and not an agricultural implement) striding across a field surrounded by lightskirts in flimsy petticoats. This may be quite an accurate portrait of Shad's country activities and I'm not sure exactly how Shad's wife fits into this charming rural scene.

My mother's flustered instructions to me regarding the wedding, and particularly the wedding night, did not include the correct etiquette for meeting one's husband's crop of bastards. I wonder where they live and whether they will be a prominent part of our lives.

The ceremony over, the company make its way downstairs to the dining room for the wedding breakfast. What a gloomy room. Portraits of Shad's late parents, his mother with a defeated expression, his father looking bad-tempered, preside over the gathering.

'Your mama was very pretty,' I lie to Marianne, who is sitting near me.

She gives a brief smile. 'Thank you.'

The silver shows signs of hurried cleaning – I wipe mine on my napkin – and all around me Shad's family laugh and talk of people I don't know and repeat stories that are not particularly funny but make them howl with laughter. I attempt a conversation with Carstairs, who has a particularly dreadful shyness.

Shad, I notice, is busy being charming to his relatives while I sit at his side, keeping a smile on my face.

And so it will go on, days and weeks and months. I'm terrified – not of the *Intimacies of Marriage*, to borrow my mother's term, but of the lack of intimacy inherent in the marriage.

How I wish Ann was here.

After the wedding breakfast I say farewell to my parents. At this point, thanks to copious champagne, even my brother is red-eyed and trumpeting into a handkerchief. To my surprise, he swears that if Shad does not prove a good husband, he'll horsewhip him, and then turns to Shad and embraces him like a brother. 'She's not a bad girl,' he says. 'She needs keeping in line, but she'll do well.'

'Oh, go away, George, you're drunk.' I wish I were.

I've hardly been able to eat or drink a thing.

George wraps an arm around my waist and breathes winey fumes at me while he whispers in my ear, 'He's after a mistress, Lottie. Just thought you should know. It's what they do, the *ton*. He was at the theatre with that wooden-legged fellow the other night, visiting bits of muslin in their boxes.'

'Thank you, brother. Now go home.' I wonder if I should instruct the large-footed Roberts to throw my brother out of the house, but to my relief my family leave.

At least, I feel relief for a very brief moment and then I'm terrified. I want to run after them and clutch at their arms, begging them not to leave me alone with this man who looks at me with . . . well, I can't quite decipher his expression. He stares at me with great intensity, but I'm not sure whether it's contempt or desire; whatever it is, it makes me exceedingly nervous. What if he wants to consummate our marriage on the dining-room table? I look around wildly for a biddable footman to remove some of the leaves of the table. My worst fears are realised when Shad sends his man Roberts out of the room and it is just the two of us, the table cleared.

I sidle to the fireplace and eye the poker. It's not that I'm averse to the idea of going to bed with Shad – part of me is extremely interested in the possibilities thereof, and has been ever since that memorable kiss in the garden.

Shad strides across the room towards me. It's like being approached by a wild animal and for one insane moment I contemplate jumping on the table and inviting him to have his wicked way with me.

But at the last moment his gaze shifts beyond me and he continues to the tall clock that stands against the opposite wall. He opens the case, retrieves a key and winds it. Grateful that I did not cast myself seductively on the table, I try to maintain an appearance of calm.

Roberts comes back into the room. 'Oh, sir,' he says reproachfully.

'Mind your place,' Shad returns, and I wonder if he's as nervous as I am.

'You know that clock has a particular way to it, my lord.'

Shad closes the case. 'Ma'am, my sister and I took the liberty of choosing a lady's maid for you. This is Annabelle Withers.'

I see that an elegantly dressed woman has also entered the room. She looks down her nose, smooths her gown, and manages to curtsy while conveying the deepest contempt towards us.

'How d'you do, my lord, milady,' she says with a twist of her features that may be a smile but is more likely a sneer.

'You'll help dress Lady Shadderly for the park and the play,' Shad says. 'You may go.'

Withers and Roberts leave.

'You're telling me what to do!' I burst out in indignation.

He raises one eyebrow – how I wish I could do that – and props himself up against the table. 'We're not quite so fashionable that we'd spend the day of our wedding apart.'

'And what if I don't wish to go to the park and the theatre? What if I don't like Withers?'

'Don't be difficult, Charlotte. You might want to save your energy for more important battles. She is pretty hideous, I agree, but according to my sister she has a definite way with silk stockings.' He reaches inside his coat and tosses a slim case on to the table. 'These are yours now.'

'What?' The case is sharkskin, somewhat worn. 'Thank you, sir,' I add as graciously as I can. I open the case and see the lustre of pearls and the flash of fire in rubies: heavy old-fashioned jewels. I look again at the portrait of Shad's late mother, and recognise the necklace and earrings.

'Allow me.' He lifts the necklace from the faded cream satin bed and moves behind me. His warm breath on the nape of my neck makes me shiver. The gold of the necklace warms against my skin and rests heavily on my collarbones.

'Look.' He turns me towards the mirror above the fireplace and our reflected eyes meet. I can't decide whether the jewellery is the ugliest I've ever seen or the most beautiful. It makes me look like a stranger to myself, but so I am. I have a new name, a new home, and very little hair.

The dining-room door opens again and Shad steps away from me. 'What is it now?' he says, sounding extremely annoyed, although I'm not sure why. This, plus the winding of the clock, makes me wonder if I have married a madman.

'Beg your pardon, milord,' says Withers, for it is she, and the phrase is less a commonplace than a command. 'Milady should change for the park now the hot water is ready.'

Shad says something under his breath about the park be damned, but bows, and I leave the room, Withers following. We go up the stairs and I realise I don't know where the bedchamber is. I hesitate outside the drawing room – actually two rooms with double doors that were opened for the wedding ceremony to allow for the crush of guests – and am aware, from her contemptuous silence, that this wretched woman is going to be of little help to me.

We proceed up the next flight of stairs and I see an open door and a fire burning in the grate. Relieved that I have not led her upstairs into the servants' quarters, thus revealing my ignorance of the house and everything in it, including my husband, I enter the bedchamber and allow Withers to change my clothes.

She is certainly an excellent lady's maid even if she behaves as though she is doing me the greatest of favours. She sniffs disapprovingly at my clothes, even the new ones I ordered under Marianne's guidance, and looks down her nose so much I fear she will become cross-eyed. I remove the necklace which she places in the case, saying Roberts will lock it up for me, and I prepare to make my public entrée as Lady Shadderly.

So, the park, Shad expert with reins and whip and a handsome pair of dapple greys pulling a suitably dashing phaeton. We attract stares, whispers – people must know we are married, and I am vain enough to hope they admire my new clothes.

A pretty woman driving her own equipage salutes Shad with her whip and a lusty wink. He raises his hat but does not stop to introduce me to her.

'Who is that?' I ask.

'Mrs Gundling.'

'Does not Mr Gundling care for the park?'

He looks at me, possibly for the first time that day, a long, thoughtful look. 'I believe Mr Gundling to be legendary.'

'Indeed? Legendary in the sense that he may not exist?'

'Precisely, ma'am.' He flicks his whip and the greys break into a canter.

'Is she your mistress?'

'That's a very indiscreet question to ask on our wedding day.'

I shrug. 'Very well. I'll ask you tomorrow.'

He laughs. 'By tomorrow you will have other matters on your mind.'

I ponder this statement which is definitely obtuse and possibly indecent.

Shad

I have been unsettled all day but I presume that is what marriage does to a man.

I show off my new wife, gilded with my respectability, to the *ton* in the park and at the theatre. The same gown, its long sleeves removed for the evening, reveals my wife's strong, slender arms – not a part of a woman that has interested me much before. I find myself gazing at her with indecent thoughts on my mind, the same sort of thoughts I entertained earlier that day in the dining room, of tipping her on to the table and consummating the marriage then and there.

I don't think Roberts would have approved, and now I've probably broken that damned clock, the only thing that tolerated my father and which has not worked properly since his death.

Charlotte seems remarkably self-possessed, engaging even Carstairs in some sort of conversation at the theatre, and being almost – no, not charming. I don't think that's a word I would associate with the new Viscountess, but she certainly engages the interest of the various people who wander in and out of my sister's box.

We return to the house and engage in some stilted conversation over supper, for which neither of us have much interest, and my bride retreats upstairs to the ministrations of Withers, who has proved quite unbearable in the two minutes or so that I spent in the same room as her. I try not to think she and Charlotte deserve each other.

I dismiss Roberts for the night after he fusses around with my clothes – he seems to have formed an unnatural attachment to the clothes brush – and enter the bedchamber, intent upon doing my manly duty.

Best to get things started and over with quickly. To my surprise I am more than ready, but consider it a condition of my enforced celibacy; my wedding arrangements have interfered damnably with my hunt for a mistress. I stride into the room, slamming the door behind me.

Charlotte, propped up in the bed, looks at me with astonishment.

I know she's about to say something wiltingly unpleasant. I fling my dressing gown off and toss it to the floor.

She laughs.

Oh God.

Charlotte

'I beg your pardon,' I say and do my best to squash down another giggle that wants to force its way out, like a sausage out of its skin – oh heavens, what a comparison. No, not that at all.

'Hmm.' He doesn't seem particularly bothered by his nakedness and I have a feeling I should be more bothered, but mostly I'm curious as to how he will feel. Will the hair on his chest be soft or coarse? And that other part of him, pointing resolutely at the far corner of the room – shall I be allowed to touch that? Or expected to? Or possibly I should ignore it, as I ignore the various bumps, twitches, deflations and inflations on view in any drawing room, with gentlemen's fashions as they are. Perhaps I have not been as immune to these phenomena as I thought. Why on earth do not etiquette books cover the marital obligations?

He plucks the dressing gown, a lovely garment of dark blue silk embroidered with dragons, from the floor and covers himself up. 'Well, I suppose it's better than making you cry.'

'I'm terribly sorry. Just as you came in, I was thinking of something someone said earlier and although it did not strike me as being funny then, I—'

'Liar,' he says without much interest. 'Do you intend to spend the entire night in the centre of the bed?'

'You sound just like my brothers,' I grumble, shifting over.

'I beg your pardon?' He looks confused.

'In the nursery, when my brothers shared a bed.'

'Of course.' He disrobes, very fast, and gets into bed next to me, giving me time to see that his Rampant Condition is no more. I wonder if my mother would refer to it that way, rather as she lectured me with great solemnity but little clarity on *Wifely Duty* and *Undignified Yet Necessary Obligations of the Marital Bed*. Since she did not go into specific details of how I should encourage the undignified yet necessary obligations to get underway, I am at a loss; and since she also warned me that I should anticipate *Excessive Discomfort* I'm not sure I want to.

'Remove your nightgown,' Shad says. He's close enough so that I can feel his warmth.

'I beg your pardon?' I clutch the bedclothes to my bosom.

He looks perplexed for a moment. Then, 'Remove your nightgown, *now*.'

'No.'

'Ma'am, a few hours ago you promised to obey me.'

'Well, I'm sure that wasn't what that vicar was referring to. It's indecent!'

He shifts further down the bed and props himself on one elbow. With the other hand, just his forefinger, he very lightly strokes my wrist. He whispers, 'With my body I thee worship.'

Heavens! It strikes me that the concept of Wifely Duty etc. may not be so bad.

We stare at each other and he clears his throat. 'The nightgown, ma'am.'

'Very well. But you must blow the candles out.'

'The candles stay alight.'

He strokes my wrist again with one finger. I like his hands. I like the way he touches me. I don't know why I am so intent on arguing myself into a corner.

'Look,' he says, 'this is exceedingly awkward. Please bear in mind that I haven't done this before.'

I'm astonished. 'What! Sir, I am not a complete idiot. I have seen the evidence with my very own eyes today that you know very well what you are about—'

'Stop.' His fingers curl over my wrist. 'I owe you an explanation, but now is not the time. I meant, this is new to me – marriage, and lying with a woman of no experience, and a woman I don't . . . don't know very well.'

'You mean you don't desire me.'

He grins. 'I didn't say that. Give me your hand.'

I regret that I let out an undignified shriek and giggle, as the answer to one of my earlier, silent questions is revealed beneath the bedcovers. Apparently regeneration has taken place. How extraordinary!

'That's better,' Shad says. 'Now, the nightgown, if you please, ma'am.'

'No.'

'Very well. I'll have to rip it from your body.' He grasps the neckline of the offending garment and tugs. 'Good God, is it sewn with steel?'

'Wait, don't tear it.'

'I don't think I can.'

'I'll have to explain it to Withers.'

'You don't have to explain anything to a servant. You're Viscountess Shadderly. I'll sack her if you like.'

'No, don't, Shad. She won't get another place if you sack her after a day.'

'As fascinating as this discussion of the household is, I fear you're distracting me.'

He isn't at all distracted, judging from what I hold.

'I'll allow one candle to remain alight,' he says. 'That's my final offer.'

'Done.' It is after all my Wifely Duty. The stoutly sewn garment drops to the floor as he blows out one candle.

'You do know what I'm going to do?' He says it softly, a breath, a whisper against my mouth.

'Yes.'

Or so I thought. I thought I knew.

Shad

'May we do it again?' She sounds remarkably bright and cheerful. 'And I didn't bleed. My mother said I would experience great agony.'

'Half an hour.'

'I beg your pardon? You are mumbling.'

Eyes closed, I attempt to enunciate a little more

clearly. 'In half an hour or so. Probably. And your mother is misinformed.'

'What am I supposed to do in the meantime?'

'Oh. Read a sermon. Embroider something.'

She snorts. The bed shifts as she reaches for the wretched cotton nightgown and drops it over her head, without revealing an unnecessary inch of skin, to my great disappointment.

'You looked much better without your clothes. Maybe I should command you to be naked in the house.'

She sniffs. 'It would certainly enliven morning calls.'

'Where are you going?'

She comes round to my side of the bed, unfortunately beyond my reach, and dons my dressing gown. 'That's an indelicate question, sir. Where do you think? But – oh.' She pauses. 'You said it would take half an hour.'

'I miscalculated. There's a chamber pot behind the screen.'

'Certainly not.' She flounces towards the door, pausing to turn back and inspect me. 'What a peculiar thing it is.'

'Thank you.' I'm not sure she means to compliment my anatomy, which sturdily compliments her in the only way it knows how. I've never seen my dressing gown look more alluring.

And I thought I knew what I was about.

Charlotte

When I wake the next morning I am alone in the bed, but not in the room. Beyond the seclusion of the bed curtains Withers rattles around, nagging a footman to put more coals on the fire and not to make the carpet dirty. I hastily don my nightgown, which Shad thoughtfully stowed beneath my pillow, and wonder whether Withers will inspect the sheets and report to the rest of the household. Probably not; she's too high and mighty to exchange confidences with any of the lower servants.

I manage not to slap her while she laces my stays, looks at my morning dress as though it is a sack (and it is new, from Madame Bellevoir's – perhaps she thinks as I do, that it is rather too plain) and dabs at my hair with a comb. I style my hair by running my fingers through it, as I have seen my brothers do, and make my way downstairs to the morning room.

Shad is there, in boots and breeches, somewhat muddy around the legs, reading the newspaper. He must have gone for a ride before breakfast. Frankly I am amazed he had the energy.

He stands and bows.

I curtsy.

Oh curses, are we back to being polite after the indecencies of last night?

We both sit. 'Shall I pour you some tea, sir? Oh, what a pretty teapot. Is it—'

The newspaper in his hand creases. 'Charlotte, pray do not touch the spout that way. A footman might come in at any moment.'

'Which way? Oh. Oh, you mean . . .'

'Precisely.' He grins at me.

I help myself to some bread and butter, taking care not to fondle the handle of the knife overmuch, although I am strongly tempted to do so. It is quite refreshing to know that I can disturb him with the simplest of gestures.

He lays the newspaper on the table and smooths out its creases. Oh, I do like his hands.

'I owe you an explanation about John and Amelia,' he says and clears his throat.

I'm not sure I want to hear about his lurid past, but I nod.

'Susan Price, the woman who accompanied the children, is my coachman's wife,' he says.

'She's their *mother*?' I'm quite horrified. 'I thought she was their nursemaid.'

He shakes his head. 'Oh, good lord, no. Their mother – or rather, mothers – are gone. Amelia's mother left the village a few years ago. I don't know where she went to, probably one of the big mill towns. John's mother died in childbirth. Susan and my coachman, Matthew Price, have no children of their own so it's a good arrangement. I expected their arrival, but I assure you I did not intend them to invade our wedding in quite that way. They live above the coach house but the children will not bother you. I am afraid their presence must have shocked you, and I . . .'

Roberts enters the room with a letter for Shad. I expect Shad to lay it aside, but he breaks it open and smiles. 'Excellent news. Beresford will be back in town any day.' He passes the letter to me.

I read it, amazed at Beresford's dreadful spelling and the tedium of his comments on the places they have visited, but I am delighted to read a tiny, scribbled note in Ann's hand. 'Oh!' I exclaim. 'Ann sends me her love, and says she'll call on me when they return.'

'I see.'

'What do you mean?' Sometimes dealing with this man is like handling an animal or a small child, as prone as he is to illogical statements. Am I holding the note in a suggestive way?

'I think you know,' Shad says and regards me in a thoughtful way.

'Of course.' I decide to ignore that last cryptic remark. I fold the letter and hand it back to him, somewhat annoyed, despite my elation at Ann's note and the news of her return. He, after all, is the one with the crop of bastards and who, according to my brother, is searching for a mistress. 'You were explaining about your children. Pray continue.'

'As I was saying, they live with Susan and Matthew . . . yes, Roberts, what is it?'

'A lady, milord. Well, not a lady, sir, but . . .' he glances in the direction of the front door, where a loud female voice is raised against the placatory tone of one of the footmen. 'And all her trappings.'

'What? Oh, damnation.' Shad rises, pushing his chair away. 'I forgot . . . Charlotte, you'll stay here, if you please.'

He leaves the room with Roberts.

Naturally I follow.

In the hall a bosomy and good-looking woman is surrounded by a heap of boxes and bags. She weeps copiously into a large handkerchief.

'You promised, sir! You promised!' she says to Shad.

'I beg your pardon, Mrs Perkins. I—'

'And now I have no home, for that landlord said—'

'I'll see to it,' Shad says. 'Stop making such a noise.' He turns to me. 'And what are you doing here? Pray leave, ma'am.'

'No, I shan't. Who is she?'

The woman addresses me. 'Ask him, milady. He'll tell you.'

I'm really afraid of what he will tell me, or what she will reveal. But I don't need to be told that she is a discarded mistress and for a moment I am almost dizzy with shock. That she should come to his house and the day after our wedding and make a scene like this, and all because Shad did not have the decency to pay her off!

'Stay here,' he says to the woman. 'I'll write you a draft.'

He leaves, doubtless for his office, followed by

Roberts. The footman looks at me and then at Mrs Perkins, who continues to cry. She is muddy, her skirts bedraggled – she must have got dirty while unloading her goods from a hackney. Her nose and hands are pink and chilled and despite myself I feel sorry for her.

'Come into the breakfast room,' I say. 'There's a fire there. You can leave your things in the hall.'

She looks at me with deep suspicion, as does the footman. But what else can I do with her?

The footman springs into life and opens the door to the morning room.

'Thank you, ma'am,' she says and unties her bonnet with shaking hands. 'I am Jenny Perkins. Mrs Jenny Perkins.'

Of course. Doubtless she has a mythical husband. I offer her a chair and some tea, and she eats her way through the bread and butter and cake on the table.

Then she looks at me, or rather, not at me but at my gown. 'Madame Bellevoir?' she asks.

'Yes.'

'Most elegant!'

'Thank you.'

'Now, this gown looked most promising when I cut the picture from the paper last month but I do not think it turned out well. I should have used a narrower trim, I believe . . .' and she is off on a detailed description, telling me the price of the cloth and the trim like a living fashion paper, while I nod and inwardly rage at Shad for his involvement with such an idiot.

After a while Roberts comes into the room and hands Mrs Perkins a sealed letter, which she opens, nodding with great satisfaction. She curtsies to me and thanks me in a civil manner, retrieves her bonnet, and leaves. I sincerely hope that is the last I shall see of Mrs Perkins.

I regard the table scattered with crumbs and the cold tea in my cup. I'm afraid Shad will return to continue his explanation; I'm afraid he won't. I don't want to hear about his relationship with her. Frankly, I am insulted. I would have thought Shad might have sought out a woman with some wit and not a talking fashion magazine. I was shocked by the arrival of the Bastards yesterday, but they seemed nice enough children. Mrs Perkins, however, must have charms only a gentleman can appreciate, for I thought her quite dreadful.

I retire to the drawing room where yesterday I was married and ring the bell for a footman to light the fire.

Shad enters. He's changed from his muddy clothes and has a greatcoat slung over one arm. 'My apologies, ma'am, for what you witnessed.'

I don't trust myself to say anything.

'I have business to take care of. I'll return later.'

'More mistresses to pay off?' I find my voice, or rather I discover a particularly vicious hiss, as he is at the doorway.

He turns to face me and for one moment I have the sense that we are about to damage each other horribly.

'I'll trust you to mind your own affairs, ma'am. Your servant.'

He bows, and the door closes behind him without a sound which is even more unnerving. I would rather he slammed it. And his voice – like ice. For about ten seconds I consider returning home but envision such an onslaught of pronouncements from my mother, explosive huffing from my father, and stamping about from my brother that I cannot countenance it.

As I walk across the carpet my foot lands on something small and hard. I bend to pick it up. A toy soldier lies in the palm of my hand. I listen carefully and hear a small sound behind one of the sofas.

I am not alone.

Shad

It's a sorry state of affairs when a man cannot return to his own house.

Having fulfilled the business I set out to accomplish, I go to my club and meet Carstairs. I talk about nothing in particular, he listens and nods, and I wish I could tell him what is on my mind.

In short, my wife is on my mind. My astonishing, provoking, and deeply offended wife. I cannot blame her for the last. Neither can I think of a way to broach the subject again – that is, the two subjects, the Bastards and Mrs Perkins. For one, I do not think she will believe me; and I do not have to explain anything to anyone, least of all a woman, even if she is my wife and last night revealed such astonishing . . . I wish I had not promised Beresford to keep silent about his mistress, particularly to Ann's friend, but I never thought Mrs Perkins would come to my house and force me into that ridiculous and humiliating charade.

I wonder what I should tell Charlotte if she asked me about my amorous past. Now she will never believe a word I say. How could I tell her I took pains to leave no unwanted children or disappointed women in my wake, that my mistresses were as much friends and confidantes as bedfellows? (And a continent away, which might be the strongest point in my favour.)

Enough. What sort of fellow am I to even consider slaking my lust on my (annoying, unpleasant, extraordinarily alluring – stop!) wife? It's indecent. I'm quite sure the Church would not approve, not that I give a fig, but one has to set an example to the tenants and the servants and so on. A gentleman takes a mistress for that sort of thing.

I cannot guess what Charlotte will do next. What if she has left the house to return to her family? But I cannot believe she would prefer their company to mine.

I long for Beresford to come back to London so I may seek his counsel. I'm sure that he and his pretty sweet-tempered Ann get along famously. But at the same time I am afraid that my wife's not-particularly-secret hankering for Beresford will reveal itself to the detriment of all.

What a mess.

After I have bored Carstairs to death talking of horseflesh and we have progressed to a lively one-sided discussion of the latest events of the war, I stand to take my leave.

'My regards to Lady Shadderly,' Carstairs says quite clearly, his first complete sentence in what has passed for a conversation between us.

A horrible thought strikes me. Surely he is not in love with her? Or does he regard her as a similar challenge to a French frigate, cannons pounding away, bearing down on him with a strong wind in her sails?

This is so appalling I fairly dash out of the club into the rain, and return home before Carstairs takes it into his head to pay an afternoon call on my new bride. Like it or not I must return home and deal with a wife who is probably sulking, weeping, or doing both; moreover, she may take my peace-making gesture, the business of which occupied me for several hours earlier in the day, as a bribe to be quiet and complaisant.

Roberts opens the front door and takes my wet hat and coat. 'Milady's in the drawing room,' he says with disapproval.

'Indeed? Has she had any callers?'

'No, milord. She instructed me to say she was not at home.'

Worse and worse. I climb the stairs, bracing myself for what I will find.

What I do find astonishes me.

My drawing room has been converted to a nursery. John lines up his lead soldiers, the ones my brother and I played with when we were boys, in rows in front of the fire. Amelia hosts a tea party attended by a wooden doll and a collection of paper dolls cut from the newspaper. No wonder Roberts is annoyed; he considers the newspaper his property after I've read it.

In the middle of this domestic scene, Lady Shadderly toasts bread at the fireplace, sitting cross-legged on the carpet. She looks remarkably content, as though she is genuinely enjoying the children's pursuits, and somehow manages to participate in both a tea party and a war at the same time.

At my entrance, Amelia rises and curtsies and John runs over to me. 'Uncle Shad, we are having such a fine time! Look, I have a great battle here!'

'Will you take tea, sir?' Amelia tugs at my hand. 'Aunt Shad will toast you some bread if you like.'

'You must say please, Uncle.'

Aunt Shad, for so she is now, looks at me with a polite smile. 'Do take a seat, sir.'

She pours tea into a miniature cup and saucer, one of the set I gave Amelia for her last birthday, and I bow to the paper dolls and take my place on the floor next to them.

'I see it is raining again, sir.' Amelia hands me my tea. 'We were talking of the weather. Aunt Shad says it is most genteel to do so when paying calls.'

On the other side of the fireplace a walnut cannonball bowls down John's gallant troops. 'We have defeated the Frenchies, sir!' he shouts. 'Rule Britannia!'

'You may butter this toast for your uncle, Amelia.' Charlotte hands her a slice of toast on a normal-sized plate.

John, his enemies vanquished, wanders over to us. To my surprise, he plants himself in Charlotte's lap and I feel an absurd dart of jealousy that he has not come to me. She smooths down the lock of hair that sticks up endearingly at the back of his head. I wonder if mine grew that way too, and if my mother found it as touching as I do John's. I am fairly sure my father never noticed his children's hair.

I wonder when John's hair will tame itself and for how much longer he will be a child who wants to sit on someone's lap. He seems to grow by the minute.

'You look sad, Uncle Shad,' Amelia comments as she hands me my plate of toast.

'No, I am merely alarmed at what a polite young lady you are becoming.'

'Oh, the dolls. No, sir, that is only play. Aunt Shad made me the paper dolls, sir, are they not fine?'

'Indeed.'

'I have told Mrs Price the children may visit when I am not receiving callers,' Charlotte says. I am impressed by her good sense, both in consulting Susan and in making sure that the children do not disrupt our lives.

'It's very good of you.'

'On the contrary, they entertain me. We should like to go to the park when it is not raining if Mrs Price is agreeable.'

'And go to see the wild animals at the Tower,' John says. 'You should come, Uncle Shad.'

'Lady Shad and I will discuss it,' I tell them. I finish my toast and my thimble-sized cup of lukewarm tea. 'And now Lady Shad and I must go to the stables.'

'May we come, too?' John springs from Charlotte's lap. 'Oh, please, sir.'

'Another time. Now you should go back home.'

Charlotte spends a little time brushing crumbs from the children and telling them to pick up the toys and scraps of paper. Amelia takes the paper dolls and the rest of the newspaper, which Susan can use for some domestic activity, and nudges her brother into bowing. Then they both run off downstairs.

'Thank you for entertaining my children.'

'My pleasure.' She sounds polite, but not over-friendly. 'What will happen to them?'

'I'm planning to hire a tutor for them while I am in London. I wish them both to be educated. Amelia proves herself a voracious reader already.'

She nods.

Charlotte

The room seems very silent without the presence of the children. I wonder if now Shad will offer some sort of apology for their existence, which, considering the pleasure we have both taken in their company, seems rather absurd. He clears his throat.

I wait.

Finally, I break the silence. 'I don't think much

of your taste in mistresses. She doesn't even dress well.'

'I'm not interested in Mrs Perkins dressed or undressed.' He bends to pick up a toy soldier from the carpet and cradles it in the palm of his hand. 'These were mine when I was a boy, and my brother Frederick's before me.'

'Do you miss him? This was your brother from whom you inherited the title?'

'Almost every day I'm reminded of him,' he says, but does not elaborate. He does not need to, for it is clear on his face, that he loved his brother. 'And I should thank you, for entertaining the children. You're under no obligation to do so. It was most generous of you.'

'I wasn't doing it to be generous. I enjoyed their company.'

'I beg your pardon.' He bows. 'Come with me to the stables. It's raining, so we'll go through the servants' quarters.'

He sends Roberts ahead, to 'clear the decks' – I take this cryptic comment to mean that he does not want to cause mutual embarrassment by discovering the staff at abuse or dereliction of their duties. So we are greeted by the cook and maidservants wearing clean aprons and footmen in livery, their workaday leather aprons discarded, and everybody's face and hands very clean. Only a sliced loaf on the kitchen table, and a damp ring representing the recent presence of a jug of ale, suggests that we are disturbing a meal, and I am sorry for it.

Shad opens the back door of the house, revealing the stable yard in wet disarray – the deck-clearing has not extended to sweeping the yard. Straw floats in puddles among the cobblestones as the rain slants down. He looks at my feet. 'Those slippers will be ruined.'

'I can go upstairs and – oof!' I gasp in surprise as he scoops me into his arms.

'Good God, girl, do you eat stones?' He kicks the door shut and prepares to descend the brick steps into the yard. 'Pray put your arm round my neck. I'll certainly fall with your elbow in my chest.'

I quite enjoy being carried across the yard, all the while reminding myself that this is the man whose bastards invaded my wedding and whose mistress turned up the morning after. I regret I find it difficult to carry a single-minded grudge against him, and I attribute it to the charm of his children, not to mention his own charms on our wedding night. I wonder, with an indecent frisson, if he plans to seduce me in the hayloft or some such, and hope the grooms are not around.

As he sets me down outside the stable, rather fast, one of my feet goes straight into a puddle. He gives a sort of exasperated snort at my clumsiness and opens the door to the stables.

'You do like to ride, I hope,' he says, looking suddenly worried.

'Why, yes, I—'

'Because I thought maybe we should ride together. When the weather is improved, that is.'

To my surprise he looks shy and uncertain. He gestures to a loose box. 'I thought you might . . . when I went out today, it was to . . .'

'Oh.' I step forward to greet the bay mare that ambles to greet us, snuffing at my arm and hair with great friendliness. 'Oh, you beauty.'

I open the door and join the mare, stroking her gleaming neck and sides.

Shad follows me and slaps her rump. 'I ordered the grooms to give her a good brushing; her coat was a disgrace. I'm a bit too heavy for her – she's a lady's mount – but I put her through her paces and she's as sweet-tempered as—'

'Shad.' I drag my attention from the horse to him. 'Do stop fretting. She's beautiful. I love—'

'If she doesn't suit you the seller will take her back. I—'

He stands with his elbow resting on the mare's rump; she doesn't seem to be concerned, but turns her head, thus nudging me towards him.

'She has a most responsive mouth,' he continues.

So do you. I put my forefinger on that mouth (his, not the horse's). 'Thank you.'

He stills. He looks shocked and aroused (I can recognise it in him now, from the set of his mouth, the narrowing of his eyes). His lips move beneath my finger into a kiss – I am afraid I taste of horse, but he doesn't seem to mind.

'I love . . .' I say again and my mind goes entirely into a sort of spin as though it waltzes after downing a bottle of champagne. 'I love her.'

His tongue flicks against my finger and I lean against the mare as my legs begin to give way.

He turns the palm of my hand to his mouth. 'It is I who should thank you.' He continues, somewhat muffled. 'After all, it is your money that bought her. The money you brought to this marriage. It is only fair that you should have something beyond pin money. I wanted . . .'

I'm in a wonderful, terrifying state of desire and fear.

He lifts his head. 'Why in God's name . . .'

'What?'

He shakes his head. 'It's raining.'

'Yes.'

'So we can't ride.'

I nod. We both seem to have turned into idiots. To tell the truth, I am relieved that I am not the only one. Neither am I sure why he thanks me particularly, unless it is that I am compliant in the manner of his indiscretions – but then he gives me little choice. Besides, I like the children.

'So I thought . . .'

'Yes?' I say with what I hope is kindly encouragement.

'We should stay indoors.'

Well, that seems logical enough.

The mare, having gauged the level of stupidity between us, seems to have gone to sleep.

'Upstairs,' Shad says.

'I don't think the servants would want us to linger downstairs getting in their way.'

'No, *upstairs*.'

'You mean in the bedchamber?'

He lets go my hands and blushes. Shad blushes! I am thrilled.

He stirs the straw with one booted foot and mutters, 'I beg your pardon, ma'am, it was entirely a – a – an impractical suggestion – I am mortified. Indecent, even. Somehow, when I am with you, I am compelled to – that is, I don't know—'

'Shad.' I become bold and put my lips to his, stopping him in midstream.

It is much like urging a horse on, I find to my astonishment, as he responds with great energy and ardour, lifting me up against the side of the loose box. And he does not complain about my weight this time, nor about indecency, or indeed display any of the uncharacteristic uncertainty he has shown ever since entering the stable.

'Here?' he pants into my ear.

And indeed the bedchamber seems miles away. Some clumsy unbuttoning occurs, the loosening and shifting of garments and then—

'Beg pardon, milord. Oats.'

A groom, a wide grin on his face, stands outside, bucket in hand.

The mare, excited by his arrival and the prospect of food, lunges in the groom's direction. As he unbolts the door and pushes her away, for she wants to get her muzzle into the bucket, Shad and I attempt to make ourselves decent and I try not to laugh, even though my face, I am sure, flames as red as his.

'She's a greedy one for sure, milord,' the groom comments. 'But with a sweet gait, I'll be bound.'

I think he's talking about the horse. I find myself trying not to guffaw in an unladylike fashion.

Shad mumbles something to the groom about returning to the house, and we leave the stables – I linger to stroke the mare's sleek neck, but she ignores me, crunching up her oats with great energy. As soon as I am outside I tread in the same puddle, soaking the other slipper.

Shad removes his coat and places it over both of our heads, so it is much like a three-legged race across the cobblestones and back into the kitchen.

The servants stare at our dishevelled state. Shad's neckcloth is half off, his waistcoat buttoned unevenly; as for me, my hair stands on end (I see it reflected in a copper pot) and one stocking is collapsed around my ankle. Dirty water spreads from my feet over the flagstones.

'We'll take champagne and some cold meat in a

couple of hours,' Shad announces. 'Upstairs. Oysters if we have any.'

'Upstairs, milord?' How Roberts says this with a straight face is astonishing.

Fortunately at that moment something boils over on the range, preventing, indeed, unseemly laughter from the rest of the servants. There is a general rush to mop up, avoid burns, and to blame each other for the mishap.

'Some hot water for milady?' Withers, busy with an iron, looks at us both with contempt. 'I shall help milady change for dinner directly.'

'Absolutely not!' Shad barks. 'That is, there is no need, Withers. We will, ah, manage. I'll wish you all a good afternoon and evening. Roberts, there is to be an extra portion of ale for everyone.'

The servants thus disposed of, we make our way upstairs. It's a slow journey as we stop to kiss and make idiotic conversation.

'I love . . . your hair.' He ruffles through it with one hand. The other is – well, never mind where it is, but I fear I shall fall down the stairs with delight.

'I love yours too.' How daring, how unusual, to bury my hands in someone else's hair and feel it spring against my fingers. I have not touched anyone's hair since Ann and I experimented with headdresses and hairstyles, a pair of incompetent lady's maids.

'Is this usual in marriage? Is everyone like this?'

He kisses me as if to stop my mouth. I am learning

his kisses, their variety and hidden messages.

'I hope so,' he says as we come to the top of the stairs and he kicks the bedchamber door open.

Briefly, before I forget everything but Shad, I remember that soon Ann and I shall have the opportunity to compare husbands.

The next morning I am none too pleased to find that Shad has left early to breakfast with Beresford, for he and his lady came back to town late the night before. It's raining; it has rained most of the night. During one of Shad's half-hour regenerations (and that one was indeed half an hour for we had indulged ourselves mightily) we lay quietly and listened to the hiss of falling rain from the warm nest of the curtained bed. Beneath my cheek, my face pillowed on his chest, I heard the beat of his heart.

'Milady, the Countess of Beresford is downstairs,' the unpleasant Withers announces just as I'm wrapping myself up in the bedclothes to sleep some more.

'So early?'

She sniffs in reply and picks an oyster shell from the coverlet.

I jump out of bed, wash in a patchy sort of way, and don a wrapper. No one else will call at such an ungodly hour; besides, Ann and I have much to talk about.

I run down the stairs and into the morning room, where Ann sits, a cup of tea in front of her.

She looks absolutely delightful, wearing the blue gown in which she married, and a saucy bonnet decorated with silk flowers, a new one I haven't seen before. A pair of cream kid gloves lie on the table beside her. She sighs and strokes them flat.

Now if I were a true cynic I might think she poses for an artistic study – *Young Woman Contemplates Kid Gloves* (or our china, or the tablecloth) – because Ann has the gift of appearing in a state of perfection. You would not think that she has encountered the usual morning annoyances the rest of us mortals have suffered: dropping the soap on the floor and discovering the housemaids are sadly remiss in their duties, for instance. Even in stepping from her carriage to the front door of the house she has avoided getting mud on her dainty half-boots or the hem of her gown.

She truly is a miracle.

She looks up and sees me, grinning inelegantly I dare say, in the doorway.

She stands and runs to meet me.

I bound over and crush her bonnet against my face (I am somewhat taller than her). 'Oh, Ann, I am so very glad to see you. I have so much to tell you!'

'Oh, Charlotte!' she cries and bursts into tears.

Oh, lord.

I untie her bonnet, sit her down, and press more tea on her, managing to spill some on to the pristine kid gloves. 'I cried too, when first I saw it.' I pile a plate with bread and butter for her, feeling that I must encourage her to keep up her strength. Ann tends to have people fussing over her even when she doesn't burst into tears.

'No, it's not that. I like your hair.' A brief pause in the crying.

And then she starts off again. She cries for what I consider an extraordinary amount of time, while I wonder if I should use a napkin to improvise a cap, since my shorn head is such a shock.

'Ann,' I say, feeling a very slight annoyance at her extended weeping, 'Ann, I have so much to tell you. Please don't cry.'

She gazes at me with those lovely blue eyes, hardly reddened at all; she must be the only woman in London who can cry so elegantly. 'Charlotte, I am so happy you have married Shad, for he is Beresford's best friend as well as being his cousin.'

'But I don't think you're crying for happiness. What's the matter?'

'I have something for you.'

She has not answered my question, but naturally I am distracted by the parcel on the table and pounce upon it with a cry of delight. To open the box I have to cut through the string with the butter knife, which is a messy business. In it is a bonnet – a wonderful, flower-bedecked straw bonnet, which one day, when it stops raining, I shall wear, although it strikes me that it is the sort of hat that would make Ann look even more fragile and feminine, and me a caricature. But I am delighted that she should have brought me a gift, and besides, if I were to buy her something I should do exactly the same – purchase something I should like to have myself.

I try it on and find that my worst suspicions are proved correct. I look like a bald woman wearing a hat, since I have no fetching curls to peep from under the brim. 'Oh, it's splendid.' I almost convince myself. 'Ann, I have so much to tell you but I do wish you'd tell me what makes you cry so much, if it is not my hair.'

'I was quite astonished,' Ann says. 'By the hair, and by Shad's letter announcing your engagement and marriage. But so happy for you, Charlotte.'

'If I had known where you were, I would have written.' I don't want it to sound like a complaint – she was on her honeymoon, after all – but I do think she might show a little more enthusiasm for my introduction to the married state.

She nibbles daintily on a slice of bread and butter. 'Shad gave me a horse as a wedding gift.'

'Indeed? Beresford gave me my own equipage, a lovely barouche and a pair of matched chestnuts.'

My pleasure at Shad's gift diminishes a little. My mare, as lovely as she is, and without doubt of good spirit and breeding, does not match up to this extravagant bestowal.

'We should go to the park together, when it's not raining.'

'Oh my,' she murmurs. 'We shall be *so* fashionable.' This with a satiric sidelong glance at me reminds me in a rush of why I love Ann so much; that when you think she's nothing but sweet, womanly obedience, something, a glint in her eye, an inflexion in her voice, reveals her wicked sense of mischief.

I only hope Beresford appreciates her.

'Tell me about the honeymoon.' The words fly out of my mouth even as I realise the extraordinary impropriety of such a question. I really don't want to hear about that aspect of her married life. Well, I do, but only a little. Just for comparison's sake.

But Ann takes the question at face value and goes into a long (and to be honest rather boring) account of the beauties of the scenery and the sketches she made and which of the family's houses they stayed in. She tells me of witless comments Beresford uttered and which she seems to find endearing, like his observation that there's nothing like a pint of good English ale at breakfast. Every morning.

'Shad and I decided to stay in town,' I interject when she pauses for breath after a description of an aunt's pet donkey.

'Oh. And have you been enjoying the pleasures of the town?' Dear Ann. She blushes quite pink at the question.

So far the pleasure of the town, apart from the visit to the park and the play on our wedding day, have not extended much beyond the bedchamber door. So I deflect the question to the matter of Shad's bachelor pleasures. 'We do very well, but I was somewhat astonished to meet his natural children and his former mistress.'

'Oh. Yes.' She casts her eyes down in an excellent imitation of maidenly modesty, a talent I have often envied. 'Beresford told me about the children. I am glad you know of them, for I did not want there to be secrets between us.'

'They are quite lovely children and he seems most attached to them.' I'm not sure why I am defending Shad; should I not be expressing my shock and outrage?

'And the mistress? I didn't know Shad kept a mistress.'

'Apparently so.'

'But he hasn't had time to form an alliance in town, surely. He has been here less than a fortnight, and Beresford always complained he would not come up to town for anything before that.'

I hadn't even thought of this. I'm not sure how long it would take to set up a mistress. I shall have to ask my brother about it.

'Was she pretty?' Ann asks.

'I suppose so. I thought she was rather silly.'

She pats my hand. 'I am sure now he has you he will not stray.'

'Thank you.' I wish I were as convinced. I ring for more hot water and brew us some more tea.

Ann sighs and fiddles with a teaspoon.

'What's the matter?'

'Oh, you know me so well.' The tears gather and spill down her cheeks again.

'Please don't cry.' Now I'm really alarmed. Has Beresford been mistreating her or merely boring her to death? I try to phrase the question tactfully. 'He – he is a good husband to you, I hope.'

She dabs at her face with a dainty handkerchief. 'I never realised . . . he wants to do it *all the time*.'

'Do what?' And then I know. Of course. But why does this make her cry?

'All the time,' she repeats. 'I am sure Shad is not so selfish.'

'Well, it depends on what you mean by all the time . . .'

'Every other day!' she hisses.

Every other day?

'Except on Sundays. He says the Church would not like it.' She gives a small sob. 'And every morning, his— it prods against me as though we have a broomstick in bed with us and I try to ignore it, and—'

I, who have experienced this delightful male phenomenon only an hour or so ago, interject feebly, 'Well, he can't help it, and I'm sure he loves you dreadfully.'

'If he loved me he would not use me so!'

'He forces himself upon you?' Now I am alarmed. I did not think Beresford to be a violent man.

She shakes her head. 'He is always very polite and asks in a most gentlemanly way.'

I think fondly of some of the rather impolite things Shad has taught me, not to mention the impolite words he has used.

She continues, 'And last night – last night, he asked – I can barely . . .' Her face flames and her voice dies away into a mutter. I catch the word 'mouth'.

'Oh, that. Yes, well . . .' I flounder for words. 'It's not so very . . .' To give her credit, I was shocked too. At first.

'It is like being in a farmyard.'

'Well, not so muddy, surely.'

She ignores my slight witticism. 'He laughs when he breaks wind.'

'Oh. I think they're all like that. Gentlemen, I

mean. My brothers think it the greatest joke in the world.' I am becoming somewhat exasperated. 'Look, Ann, don't you think you're being a bit missish? He loves you. Everyone does it. The farting as well as the, ah, business in the bedchamber.'

'I hoped you would understand.' She smooths out the unwrinkled kid gloves again.

I make an inelegant huffing sound. Strange as it may seem, I'm jealous of her. She is not dealing with bastards and discarded mistresses, and a man who barely talks to her and did not want to marry her. Put simply, she has a husband who adores her, and mine teaches me indecencies. Yet she is unhappy and I – I am not. I would not claim to be in the throes of continual, unbridled happiness, but I do well enough; and I wonder that she loves a man yet cannot abide his company in the bedchamber, whereas Shad and I are mostly indifferent to each other except between the sheets.

I take her hand. 'Ann, maybe you should talk to Beresford. I know he is a good man and he wants to have an heir, so . . . Ann, you would like to have a baby, would you not?'

Her reaction astonishes me. She snatches her hand back and stands up. 'How did you know?'

I'm mystified. 'Know what?'

'Lock the door!' she says in a hysterical whisper.

'But what if we need more coals? Oh, very well.' My best friend has turned into a madwoman, driven out of her mind by Beresford's excessive sensual demands. (Every other day! Maybe there is something wrong with Shad. And me too, I suppose.)

The footman outside dismissed, and the door locked, I ask her to explain.

She doesn't sit. She roams, pacing up and down the room, fists clenched. I'm alarmed. I wish we were in the drawing room so I could offer her brandy.

'When – when I came to your house first, it was after my mama and papa died.'

I nod. I know this.

'But I hadn't been living with them.'

'I'm glad you weren't, for doubtless you would have caught the same putrid fever.' I'm not sure what she is trying to tell me, but I do my best to sound sympathetic. 'I remember how sad you were.'

'I had been housekeeper to my Uncle Padgett, the third cousin whose fortune I inherited.' That I knew. And then, 'While I was there, I . . . I gave birth to a child out of wedlock.'

I am dumbfounded. 'But Ann, why did you not tell me? Why—'

'I did not want you to think badly of me. Say you do not, please.'

'Of course not. I am – well, I am surprised. I . . .' She looks so fierce and desperate I don't know what to do. I am afraid to embrace her and I'm not even sure that's what she wants. And I hope my face does not show my feelings. I am shocked that a gentlewoman should have such an experience although possibly it happens more often than is talked about. I don't know what to say. I have a dozen questions on the tip of my tongue: what happened to the child (I do hope it is not dead although many would say this to be the best for all) and who is the father.

'Before you ask, the gentleman in question has washed his hands of me. He would not marry me. Promise me you will never ask about him.'

'But . . .' It sounds shockingly cold-hearted on his part. 'Very well, I promise.'

'Uncle Padgett left money to support the child also. He was the most generous and noble of men.'

I am afraid it crosses my mind that Uncle Padgett, whom I have always thought of as a doddering and elderly invalid, might well be the baby's father. 'And the child? What happened to your baby?'

She pauses in her frantic pacing. 'She lives. She is – oh, she is . . .' She sits down as abruptly as she has paced and seems to shrink in upon herself. 'I did not know what it would be like. The midwife who delivered her told me she might not live beyond a year, for many infants do not. She said I should put Emma – that is her name – from my mind.

'And I have tried!' She flares up with a burst of her former agitation. 'But I cannot. I think about her all the time. I cannot bear to see other women's infants for they remind me of her. She was too young to smile at me when I left her with the wet-nurse, but I swear she did. She is now almost a year old and I miss her so much.'

I am horrified that Ann has kept this secret to herself for so long. And, to my shame, angry that she did not trust me enough to tell me before. 'What shall you do?' I ask.

She shrugs. 'Go on as before. I have no choice. If Beresford knew . . . well, it would be the end. I do love him despite . . . the business in the bedchamber.' She hangs her head and whispers, 'Sometimes I think I shall die if I do not see my daughter again.'

'Do you know where she is?'

'She's in Camden Town with a nurse.'

'That's not so far away.' For the Countess of Beresford it might as well be the other side of the world, not a couple of hours' drive. She cannot order her husband's carriage to take her to see her bastard child, and certainly not drive there in her smart equipage.

But a friend could order *her* husband's carriage and whisk her discreetly out of London.

She seems to be thinking the same. 'Can you – if it does not rain tomorrow – no, I ask too much. You cannot.'

'I can. I shall.' I remember with a guilty pang that I promised to take Shad's children to the park when the weather is fine. I also promised to ride with him. But this is more pressing. I cannot bear to see Ann so unhappy. 'Shad will let me have the carriage, I am sure. I shall send you word.'

'Oh, thank you.' She throws her arms round my neck. 'You are the best of friends. But promise me, you must tell no one. Not even your husband.'

Why does she think I would tell Shad?

Shad

There's only one problem with Beresford being back in town and that is the extreme pleasure and interest my wife has shown at his return. The ostensible reason for her bright eyes and air of expectation is that she will once more be reunited with Lady Beresford and I am obliged to grit my teeth and agree. I am not such a jealous cur that I will accuse my wife of two days of adulterous intentions. Under the circumstances, following the arrival of the bastards and Mrs Perkins, I have very little moral ground on which to stand.

As is our wont, Beresford and I meet for an early morning bout at Gentleman Jackson's, to be followed by breakfast at a nearby tavern. We're the first customers of the day, as I discover when I enter the academy. A boy sweeps the floor and Jackson chats quietly with Beresford, who is already stripped and with his hands clad in padded gloves.

'Lord Shadderly.' Jackson's long, scarred face breaks into a gentle smile. 'A pleasure to see you here again, my lord. You missed quite a fight between milord and young Mr Hayden, Lord Beresford. An excitable young man, that Mr Hayden, but he stayed the course.'

'Your brother-in-law?' Beresford asks.

'Yes, young George. Fancies himself a blood.' I strip down to breeches and stockings and don a pair of slippers. I think I made my point with George Hayden that the only time he would be permitted to bruise me would be in defending the honour of his sister. He was exceedingly cheerful after I beat him bloody and bruised. You might have thought I did him a favour.

Jackson hands me a pair of soft gloves. 'Now, go more easily on Lord Beresford than you did on Mr Hayden, my lord, else you'll give the academy a bad name. We fight like gentlemen here, my lord.'

Beresford and I circle, eyeing each other. Our feet pad quietly on the wooden floor. The boy leans on his broom, watching us.

Generally we spar in a casual, friendly sort of way, apologising if one of us is careless enough to allow a blow to land, and making sporadic conversation. I suspect sometimes Jackson finds our nonchalance offensive, but neither does he approve of his clients trying to kill each other. This, after all, is a science and Jackson has a living to make.

'You're looking well,' I comment. 'You find the married state—'

I dodge a fearsome blow to the head and feint aside, jabbing under Beresford's lowered guard. He grunts as my fist lands on his ribs, then recovers, and rushes at me, his fists flying through the air. He has a greater reach than me and I retreat backwards, out of his way, swaying and ducking to avoid his blows, fists up, waiting for an opportunity to strike.

This isn't like Beresford, a cautious, friendly sort of fighter. What the devil has put him in this bellicose mood?

'Keep your guard up, my lord,' Jackson comments. 'Don't let Lord Shad tire you out, he's a cunning one.'

I take advantage of Beresford's momentary lapse in concentration to dodge in and land a fairly hard blow on his upper arm. I'm tempted to hit him in the head, to teach him a lesson and bring him to his senses, but consider a warning blow – showing that I could hurt him more badly but choose not to – more effective.

Beresford falters, regains his balance, and rushes at me, hands outstretched as though to grab my neck and throttle me, and we end up grappling and struggling to keep our balance in a savage and undignified way.

'Gentlemen, gentlemen,' Jackson reproves us. 'Not good form at all, sirs. Break it up, now, if you please.'

We separate, both of us sweating and breathing heavily, not from exertion, but from anger. Beresford looks as though he would like to kill me and I am afraid I shall have to hurt him in self defence. I wonder if he has gone mad. What has happened to my good-natured friend?

'Now, Lord Shad, you must remember to keep your left up; your elbow drops, sir. Lord Beresford, do not expend your energy chasing Lord Shad around the ring; you know he aims to tire you and turn on you. As you were, gentlemen.'

A few more early-morning boxing enthusiasts have wandered in by now and lounge around to watch us fight.

I wipe sweat from my face and neck with a towel and toss it aside. I notice bruises are beginning to appear on Beresford's arm and side where I hit him.

'Has he marked me?' I ask Jackson.

'A bruise on your collarbone, my lord, but . . .' He steps forward and allows himself a small smile. 'I do not believe we can blame that injury on Lord Beresford. It was inflicted by another, I believe.'

'Ah, yes.' To tell the truth, I'm embarrassed that Charlotte's enthusiasm is branded on my skin for all to see. Whatever her intentions are towards Beresford, he should know that at the moment her husband is the one who pleases her. I add, in a careless sort of way, 'I daresay Beresford carries similar trophies upon his person.'

With a roar of rage Beresford charges me like a wild bull before I have time to get my guard up and, his arms swinging in a careless and undisciplined manner, knocks me down and stands over me, breathing heavily. I do not doubt that if I try to rise, he will hit me again.

I roll and get to my feet in time for Beresford to charge me afresh but this time I advance to meet him and knock him sprawling, the shock of the blow travelling up my arm. He goes down and lies still. Our friendly bout seems to be turning into something quite different; now I want to kill him too.

I stand, out of breath, and wait for my friend, or my former friend, to recover. To my relief he does so after a few seconds. We eye each other warily.

'Why don't you shake hands, sirs. I think you have had enough for the day.' Jackson claps one hand on Beresford's shoulder, the other on mine. It may look like, and is indeed, a friendly gesture, but also serves the purpose of holding us apart from each other.

After shaking hands, this time a mere formality, Beresford and I retreat to our corners to dress again and another couple of fighters take our place.

Jackson gives us a curious stare as we leave, for generally we do so on good terms with each other, but this time we walk in silence an arm's length apart. Beresford has something of the stiff-legged gait of a dog about to attack and a frown on his face.

We emerge on to Bond Street where rain spits down from a ragged grey sky.

'What the devil's the matter with you?' I finally ask.

He turns to me, his face wretched, and mumbles, 'Ann.'

Shad

'I thought all was well.' Beresford, his face bright red with embarrassment, aims a savage cut with his walking stick at an innocent bush in the park. I have taken him there to try and calm him, and it seems he is now in the mood for confession.

'Damned embarrassing,' he adds.

'You may tell me anything you wish.'

'You're a good fellow, Shad. I'm sorry about – well, about trying to kill you.'

'At least you aren't French.'

He laughs at my attempt at a joke. I'm concerned. Beresford, my good-tempered, unimaginative friend, is desperately unhappy.

'Before we married,' he said, 'Ann was, well, amorous. For a gentlewoman, that is. Liked kissing and so on. Not that I ever – you know. I had Jenny Perkins for that.'

I make an encouraging noise.

'And then after we marry, she won't – well, she does, but she doesn't – oh, damn it, Shad, you know what I mean. In the bedchamber. A fellow likes the lady to show some – some . . .'

'Desire.' I think of Charlotte, my lovely wanton wife, and determine to kill Beresford and hide his corpse in the bushes if he has any hankering for her.

'Desire. Yes. In a proper sort of way, befitting her station.' More bushes are damaged. 'Yet she loves me, I swear it. So what's the matter with her?'

I'm intrigued by Beresford's insistence that gentlewomen should display some sort of genteel behaviour between the sheets, and question him tactfully about his previous experience with Jenny Perkins.

'Screamed her head off!' he announces proudly. 'And a milkmaid I had, my first, swore it was the best half-crown she'd ever earned.'

'Indeed.' I suggest, in a gentle way, that these ladies were merely giving his lordship what he paid for.

His face expresses outrage, disbelief, and sorrow in quick succession. 'No, no, I don't think so, Shad. They assured me I was the best lover they'd ever had. Jenny said . . .' He shakes his head. 'I feel like a great demanding clod with Ann. She's such a tender little thing. I try not to impose myself upon her too much, but I can't help it. I love her.'

Oh, the poor fool. 'Well, of course you need an heir.'

He nods, clears his throat, and examines the silver

top of his walking stick. 'You don't think – now this is ludicrous, my dear fellow – that I'm doing something wrong? You know, that maybe because Ann is a *lady*, there's something I should do differently?'

I consider my next words carefully. 'Possibly you should consider her pleasure.'

'Oh, I don't think . . . a gentlewoman, you know.'

Keeping a careful eye on the walking stick, I ask a few discreet questions and discover that Beresford is blissfully ignorant of the female anatomy. I take it upon myself to share what I know. He is startled and upset by my revelation, in much the same way, I imagine, that our forebears discovered that the earth revolved around the sun.

'Every woman?' he says with great suspicion. I wonder if he conducts a mental inventory of all the females he has ever known. 'Are you sure?'

'Yes, every woman.'

'And who told you this?'

'A woman in Italy. She was my first mistress. She married a sausage-maker after we sailed.'

'A sausage-maker!' Beresford echoes. His universe is in chaos. 'An Italian.'

'Yes.'

He turns to me in triumph. 'Well, of course, that explains it. She was a foreigner. So it can't possibly be something Englishwomen have.'

'They do. Every one of them.'

He looks troubled and pokes at the ground with his

walking stick. 'Even – even my mother? Aunt Renbourn?'

'My dear fellow, try to think of Lady Beresford.' I'm pretty sure that in her day, or perhaps even now, our aunt could have given any young man the education Beresford so sorely lacks.

'Very well.' He sighs. 'I'm still not sure I believe you, but . . . well, it's worth a try. Where did you say the, ah, item in question was?'

'I'll show you,' I say rashly. 'No, I mean . . . come with me. And don't tell Charlotte.'

I take his arm and lead him from the park in the direction of Mayfair.

'Surely we're not going to a house of ill repute?' he says.

'No, no.' We stroll along the streets full of elegant shoppers, our progress impeded by having to pause and raise our hats to acquaintances. I stop outside a print shop. 'I think we may find something here.'

The proprietor of the shop opens the door and bows us inside, rubbing his hands together, delighted to receive customers. He offers to show us engravings of classical antiquities, which sound promising, but turn out to be pictures of ruins. I lean an elbow on the counter, and engage him in frank, man-to-man conversation.

'Prints for gentlemen, sir! Why of course, sir.' He winks. 'For the very discerning gentleman.'

He opens a portfolio of prints of fox hunts.

I'm getting embarrassed now. 'You misunderstand me. We require prints like the one you have in the window of the, ah, unclothed nymphs.'

'Excellent, sir, excellent!' He dives beneath the counter and emerges with another portfolio. 'Most artistic! The beauties of the female form in exquisite and diverse detail.'

Beresford spends some time examining an exceptionally obscene print of a scene in a Turkish harem. '*Every* detail?'

I ask for a magnifying glass.

Beresford bends over the print. 'Extraordinary. Look what that fellow is doing. I wouldn't have thought it possible. But, Shad, I can't see, you know . . . it's all shaded out there.'

I take my turn with the magnifying glass and discover this to be true. Beresford, meanwhile, is leafing through the engravings, choosing which ones he is to buy, and discussing how they should be bound into a suitable volume for his lordship's library.

With the uneasy feeling that my attempts to educate Beresford may have backfired (there seems to be a strong possibility that he may prefer solitary amusement with his new collection of prints rather than the pleasures of the marital bed), I take him to my club, where we partake of beef and beer, and I call for paper and ink.

He watches me in astonishment as I draw. 'You're quite good, Shad.'

'I learned in the Navy.'

One of the club's dignified, sedate waiters approaches and I cover my paper. When he has left with our dirty plates, I hand my work to Beresford.

He frowns. 'I've never seen anything like this before.'

'I know. Wait, you have it upside down, although I suppose it depends where you are.'

'I'm not sure . . .' He shakes his head. 'I suppose I must commit it to memory.'

'Do you really think Ann would appreciate you coming to her bed with a map?'

He folds my drawing carefully and stows it in his pocket. 'She doesn't let me keep the candle lit.'

Charlotte

After Ann's revelation I feel at a loss. I would love to ride to clear my head, but although it is not raining so hard now, I know the ground will be damp and soggy; besides, I promised to ride first with Shad. She leaves, refreshed by her confession, and all smiles, excited by our proposed outing. I suspect, too, that since it is a Friday and she is expected to be on duty for marital obligations tonight, she has a two-day holiday to anticipate.

From upstairs I hear the sound of two young voices chanting lessons, a sound that takes me back to my own schooldays, and I find one of the spare bedchambers has been converted to an impromptu schoolroom. When I peer round the door, I see Amelia and John at a table, books open in front of them, and Susan Price sewing at the fireside.

Amelia, it seems, has taken it upon herself to be the teacher and currently gives this admirably terse summing-up of the reign of Henry VIII. 'He was a most wicked king,' she says. 'He had many wives, some of whom were quite wicked also and so he had to behead them, but he founded the Church of England so all was well.'

I don't want to interrupt their lessons so I wander back to my bedchamber and get dressed properly, ignoring Withers as much as I am able. I wonder how on earth I am to spend the rest of the day; then the notes and invitations begin to arrive.

First, a note from Mrs Shillington, inviting me to accompany her on afternoon calls; a note from Shad, announcing that he and Beresford will be spending the day together and that probably he will not return until late; and a note from Ann, who must have heard from her husband too, inviting me to dine with her.

Annoyed that I wear a morning gown, unsuitable for paying calls, I change into a walking dress. By the time I have come downstairs again, the silver tray in the hall overflows with invitations and Roberts is opening the door to Mrs Shillington.

'My dear!' She takes my hands. 'Marriage certainly agrees with you. You look quite ravishing.'

'I think it's probably the gown.'

'Nonsense! I am dying to go out and hear some good, juicy gossip; my daughter has been unwell and I have been at home these last couple of days, but now she rampages around the house like a young savage and so I conclude she is better, although she is still covered with dreadful spots. Now, whom shall we call on first?'

'I should visit my family.' I hope my voice sounds sufficiently enthusiastic.

'Of course!' She smiles as though I have made the most delightful suggestion in the world and somehow her pleasure spreads to me so I do not dread visiting my family as much as I have before, and even look forward to it. I hope only that my mother has not had too much recourse to the cordial bottle.

Marianne takes my arm with an affectionate squeeze and we board her carriage.

'We should shop next for hats,' she comments and I think again with an inward groan of the feminine monstrosity Ann gave me. Because it is a present from my best friend she will expect to see me wear it once but after that I shall give it to Withers, who will probably sell it, and good riddance.

As we enter my mother's drawing room I notice yet another piece of fashionable furniture has been purchased, a table with a marble top (I think it is painted wood) and gilded, clawed legs. I don't know which is worse, the hideous newness of the piece or the antiquated gloom of Shad's furniture, which I suppose is now mine.

'Charlotte, Mrs Shillington,' my mother intones from the sofa. 'You find me *Sadly Out of Sorts*. It is only that you are my *Dearest, Nay Only Daughter* and I have not seen you since your nuptials that I rise from my *Bed of Pain*.'

Tempted to say how well she looks, I murmur instead that I am sorry she is not well.

She waves a handkerchief in one hand and produces a letter from her person, rather like an incompetent magician. 'Read this *Dreadful Missive*.'

I give Marianne an apologetic glance. Since the letter is from Henry, I know it is not the sort of communication that one wants to share with a relative stranger, and I shall not read it aloud.

Marianne smiles and murmurs that since my mother is unwell, she will take it upon herself to pour tea, and busies herself with sending the footman for fresh boiling water.

I unfold Henry's letter and am assailed by a monstrosity of misspellings, crossings-out, muddled thought, and general vacuity. He has dreadful handwriting and it takes me some time to work my way through to the end. As usual, there is a long narrative of unfortunate events and unexpected expenses culminating in a request for an advance on the next quarter's allowance; since this is usually the reason for Henry's letters I am not surprised. However, there is more.

'Oh!' I exclaim. 'What excellent news.' I explain to Marianne, 'My brother Henry, who is with his regiment in Liverpool, is to marry.'

My mother moans. 'We do not even know the girl. She is from *Trade*.'

It's not so many years since our family emerged from their warehouses (my mother's side) and livery stables (my father's) into polite society, so I remain unimpressed.

'And at *So Great A Distance*,' my mother laments.

'I am sure Miss Claire Dithering is a lovely girl, as Henry says.' Besides, this way he may restrict his activities to making one woman, rather than many, unhappy.

'That a child of mine should *Sacrifice Himself Upon the Nuptial Altar for Gold*!' My mother empties her cordial glass and falls back prostrate upon the sofa.

And I think it's time Henry emptied someone else's pockets rather than those of my father, but it does not seem polite to say so. I am fairly sure Henry does not view his upcoming nuptials as any sort of sacrifice.

At this point my father and George enter the drawing room, somewhat muddy, talking loudly and drowning out the cadences of my mother's whimpers.

'Positively blooming!' My father plants a smacking kiss upon my cheek. 'Beg your pardon, Mrs Shillington, you're so quiet I hardly saw you there. Doesn't our girl look a diamond of the first water, eh, my dear?'

My mother fans herself but the effort is too much; the fan falls to the floor.

George retrieves the fan and applies it with great vigour. 'Come, now, ma'am, rouse yourself. We should have some punch to celebrate Henry's engagement. What do you say to a tipple, Charlotte?'

I am beginning to think that strong spirits may well improve the atmosphere of the drawing room, but murmur that Mrs Shillington and I have a great many calls to make. So we make our escape and I take a great refreshing breath of smoky London air when we are outside.

We go next to the house of Lady Hortense Renbourn, the raddled old witch whom I met the evening Shad and I became engaged – or rather, the evening on which I obliged him to become engaged to me. Her drawing room is infested with cats and a handful of decorative young men, all dewy eyes and careful curls. She is apparently fashionable in a strange sort of way – the young men hang upon her every word and seem grateful when picked out for any particular insult.

A cat climbs into my lap and proceeds to shed, purring with delight.

'I see Cleopatra likes you,' Aunt Renbourn says. 'Tom, show the lady what Cleopatra did to you.'

Obligingly the young man turns back his velvet cuff to display a collection of livid scratches.

'Love tokens!' screeches Aunt Renbourn. 'We'll

have claret, now. Johnny – damn the boy, where is he? – you'll pour. I won't have the footmen bothered; they're cleaning the silver. So, miss, give us the news. I hear you and Shad spurn the town to bill and coo at home. Most unfashionable, you'll regret it.'

'I trust your ladyship is in good health,' Marianne comments. She wipes cat hair from her glass.

'I'm at death's door, you hussy.' Aunt Renbourn, immune to polite conversation, takes a swallow of claret and belches. 'Those onions will be the death of me. Francis will play the spinet for us now. None of this newfangled stuff by foreigners, Francis – give us some Playford tunes.'

One of the young men shoos a couple of cats from the instruments and wipes the keys with a handkerchief. The spinet is ancient, like its owner, and sadly out of tune and missing a few notes. Aunt Renbourn listens with avid delight, thumping her ebony cane in time (mostly) to the music and occasionally humming along.

'Has Shad found himself a mistress yet?' she shouts across the room, apropos of nothing.

'I believe not, ma'am,' I bellow back.

'He will. And what think you of the Bastards?'

'They are charming children,' I respond.

She stands, scattering a cat or two from her lap, and hobbles behind a screen set in a corner of the room, where I suspect a chamber pot resides.

One of the decorative young men rouses himself to

make a comment on the weather. Johnny pours everyone more claret, Francis and the spinet continue to abuse Playford, and Tom extricates himself from fashionable lethargy to tell me he admires my hairstyle.

Aunt Renbourn emerges from behind the screen. She proceeds to entertain us for a good half-hour with an extraordinary narration of vice, dissipation, and depravity involving virtually every well-born family in England. Even Marianne looks taken aback at the revelation of young Lord L—'s indiscretion with his valet, the valet's sister, two military officers and a luckless goat.

'And they had to completely replace the wallpaper!' Aunt Renbourn concludes.

'Good heavens, look at the time!' Marianne rises. 'This has been delightful, Aunt. Regretfully we must leave you now.'

'Very well, miss. Tell your husband to call on me. Not yours, Marianne, he's a bore. Now you may leave so we may talk about you.'

'And we'll talk about you, ma'am.' I cannot resist this parting shot.

Aunt Renbourn cackles. 'Maybe you'll do for him. I'll bid you good day.'

'She likes you,' Marianne says as we enter her carriage. 'She becomes bored with sycophants and toadies. And she is quite right, Shad does like you.'

I wonder how anyone can tell and wonder what

Shad has said of me to her, but then we draw up at the house of a Mrs Garrand, who proves to be the complete opposite of Aunt Renbourn.

'She is my mother's cousin,' Marianne explains. 'She is quite unlike my dear mother, but they were the greatest of friends, so we must pay our call. I wish only that I liked her more.'

Their house is classically correct, everything in perfect symmetry, with Mrs Garrand lined up on the sofa flanked by two daughters on each side. The drawing room is as chilly as the hostess.

The daughters stare at me with thinly veiled hostility. Mrs Garrand holds forth on the weather with a challenging air, as though daring either of us to deny that it has rained much of late.

We agree that the weather has indeed been shocking.

Mrs Garrand tells us of her daughters' success at a recent ball where the family was received with great condescension. It is like being trapped in boring ice.

After a few more polite exchanges we escape.

'What a dreadful woman,' I comment when we are well out of the house.

'She fancied Shad for one of her daughters,' Marianne said. 'I am deeply grateful he chose you.'

'Thank you,' I mumble. To tell the truth I am beginning to feel like a travelling exhibit of some sort – step up, ladies and gentlemen, to see the bride of Viscount Shadderly, obtained in the deepest jungles of Essex and captured under the most dangerous of conditions for your edification. I am quite relieved to end our calls at Beresford's house, where I am to dine with Ann.

After Marianne has said farewell with a promise from me to go shopping soon, Ann seizes me and hauls me upstairs to view her new clothes. Her maid, in contrast to Withers, is a shy mouse of a woman who puts her mending aside, curtsies, and scuttles from the bedchamber as we enter.

A gown, a gorgeous concoction of palest pink satin with a silver net overlay, lies on the bed.

'I thought I should wear this tonight,' Ann says.

'Well, it is lovely, but if it is just you and I who dine, you do not need to change.'

'No, no, after!' she cries. 'We shall surprise our husbands at the play, for that is where they intend to go. Beresford was here just a little while ago to change for the evening.'

'I'd best go home, then and—'

'No need!' Ann rummages in her clothes press and brings out another gown. 'You shall borrow this. Your slippers will do well enough, and we shall make a headdress for you.'

'Well, I . . . I don't know. I have always understood that only certain sorts of women – loose women – go to the play without an escort. I'm not sure—'

'Don't be silly!' she cries. 'You are of the *ton* now, you know. It will be a great joke. But wait, here is something that will make it even better.' She delves into a drawer and plucks out a couple of masks.

'You think that will make us more respectable?' I take one of the masks, a plain dark blue with a few silver sequins. I can see that it will go wonderfully well with the gown she has picked out for me, a blue satin. I smooth the fabric of the gown with my hand and determine I shall get a gown made of this very same stuff. 'And, Ann, I'm taller than you. It's a lovely gown, but I'm afraid it may be too short, and certainly will be too small around the bosom.'

'No, it will do well enough. It's a trifle too long for me and I intended to have my maid hem it. We may have to lace you a little tighter.'

I still have severe misgivings about the outing. But I will be with Ann and she looks so happy and mischievous that I do not have the heart to turn her plan down.

Ann produces a gauzy silk scarf, white shot through with silver, that she knots around my head and embellishes with a paste brooch. She has to lace my stays tighter than normal and I can barely breathe and spill over the top of the gown in an indecent fashion. I shall have to be careful I do not turn too fast. I think Shad will like it, though.

We eat dinner – I eating less than usual, because of the lacing – and drink a lot of champagne, so that by the time we set out to the theatre in Ann's carriage we are both quite merry.

'Our husbands will be so surprised,' Ann says as we leave our cloaks with the footman who accompanied us and enter the theatre. 'This will teach them to abandon their wives for an entire day.'

'I hope they will be surprised in a good sort of way.' I adjust my mask, once again astonished that Ann, who is anticipating a whole two nights without her husband's attentions, should be so desirous of his company during the day.

The play has already started and we enter the area outside the boxes. A few women stroll there alone; they stop when they see us, giving us assessing glances. So do a pair of fashionably dressed young men, one of whom raises his quizzing glass. They confer and move towards us.

'Ann!' I tug at her arm. 'Do you not see those women?'

'What of them?'

I am amazed at her simplicity. Can she not see what I do? That these women, whose hemlines are a little high, their necklines far too low, and several of whom are masked, view us as competition in trade. 'Ann, they're whores.'

'Oh. Really? Do you think so?' She gazes at them as one might at an interesting painting. 'Surely you are mistaken.'

I pull her into Beresford's box before the pair of bucks can reach us. 'This was a very foolish idea!'

To my disappointment the box is empty. We both sit

down and look briefly at the stage – very little of interest to be seen there – and at the audience, which is far more entertaining.

'There's Beresford!' Ann waves at a box opposite. Her face falls as the inhabitants of the box, Mrs Garrand and her daughters and Beresford, look away.

'Take off your mask, you ninny.' Why on earth did I agree to this ridiculous escapade?

'Of course!' She removes her mask, and this time Beresford, who has already risen – doubtless he wants to see why two lightskirts have invaded his box – waves back, a smile of pure joy on his face. 'Stay here, Charlotte. I'll return in a minute.'

She runs out, leaving me alone.

Shad

At the theatre I have no desire to pay my respects to Mrs Garrand or her exceedingly tedious daughters and allow Beresford to attend them alone. I am glad to see that my friend's normally sunny disposition has been restored; he accompanied me backstage where he bantered with the actresses with far more enthusiasm than I.

'Splendid girls,' he says as we leave the backstage area. 'And anyone of them willing to be taken up by you, I'd say.'

I'm spared an answer as two sweating men carrying

a large Moorish arch shout at us to get out of the way, sirs. I'm heartily sick of women accidentally allowing their shifts to gape open or coquettishly allowing me a glimpse of garter. I'd far rather return home and find my wife in bed. I entertain thoughts of her asleep with a novel still in her hand and how she will half wake when I get into bed with her, and . . . I ask Beresford to repeat what he just said, wondering whether the visit to the print shop earlier in the day has inspired me more than I care to admit.

'Best make yourself scarce, my dear fellow, for Mrs Garrand will see you if you return to the box and I can't very well tell her you're an ill-mannered bore who declines to greet her.'

I linger, watching the lightskirts who parade their wares outside the boxes and glaring at any who look my way. Surely Beresford has exhausted the conversational possibilities of the Garrands by now.

When I open the door to the box it is not empty. A woman sits there, masked and mysterious.

She turns her head as I enter and the drapery she has tied round her head brushes against her bare shoulder. She wears no jewels but her eyes shine as she looks at me and her lips curve into a slight smile. There's something familiar about her and I wonder where we met before.

I close the door and lean against it, not wishing Beresford to barge in and make a nuisance of himself. 'Your servant, ma'am.'

She flutters her fan. Her bosom, mostly exposed, gleams white in the dim light.

I wait for her to speak. Her voice, I am sure, will be throaty and sensual.

She lowers the fan and closes it, her fingers running along the spokes in a gesture that is wholly arousing.

My breath catches.

Her smile deepens.

'I don't believe we've been introduced,' I say, 'but the pleasure is all mine, ma'am. May I know whom I have the honour of addressing?'

There's the rustle of silk as she shifts in her chair to offer me her gloved hand. Her skirts lift a little, revealing a shapely ankle. She still doesn't speak, but her teeth bite into her lower lip, deepening the natural red, as though she is amused by my presence.

I take her hand and kiss the palm. 'I'm Viscount Shadderly. I'd greatly like to become better acquainted. Tell me your name, divine creature.'

'You know my name, Shad,' says my wife.

She giggles.

Charlotte

'What the devil are you up to, ma'am?' Shad's flirtatious good humour has vanished. I've never seen him look so angry.

Before I can reply, he snarls, 'Take that damned mask off!'

I remove the mask. 'Shad, I—'

'How dare you dishonour me so? Whom were you to meet here?'

'Why, you,' I say, thoroughly confused.

He makes a sound perilously close to a growl. 'Do not attempt to jest with me, ma'am.'

'But I'm not. I—'

The door to the box opens and Ann and Beresford come in, his arm round her waist, and both of them wreathed in smiles.

'Lady Shadderly, may I congratulate you, ma'am,' Beresford says while Shad hovers like an infuriated black thundercloud. 'Two best friends married to two best friends – what could be better, eh? Why, Ann has sung your praises our entire honeymoon. Shad, you and your lady must dine with us on Monday.'

'We'll be honoured. We'll bid you goodnight, Beresford, Lady Beresford.' Shad grips my arm, his fingers like iron. 'Lady Shadderly is feeling unwell.'

'No, I'm not.' But he's dragging me toward the door.

What's wrong? Ann mouths at me.

I attempt to shrug with one arm immobilised.

Shad's fingers dig into my arm. He opens the door and fairly shoves me through.

'What is the matter with you?' I ask crossly.

And then I understand.

He wasn't being playful and flirtatious. He really thought I was one – one of those women (the sort who stroll around outside the boxes, bosoms exposed to the highest bidder among the ogling bucks). Not only that but he was pursuing me, or the woman he thought I was. I am outraged and hurt. Even though he told me he would seek his pleasures outside the marital bed I hadn't believed him.

How stupid I have been. I'd actually thought he liked me well enough that for a time he might stay faithful to me.

And he accused me of dishonouring him!

His anger is caused by embarrassment, that he has been caught red-handed in the pursuit of a mistress and that I have been the one to catch him.

'It serves you damned well right!' I respond with a snarl almost as fierce as his.

'We'll talk at home, not make a spectacle at the playhouse.' He hauls me down the stairs.

Ann's footman steps forward with my cloak; Shad snatches it from him and waves him away.

'Wait.' I attempt to fumble in my reticule.

'What?'

'A vail for the footman.'

'Why? You would reward him for being an accessory to adultery?' Shad hisses in my ear, but he fumbles in his breeches' pocket for coins and addresses the footman. 'Call us a hackney, if you will.'

His effrontery takes my breath away (and the stays do not help either). He has the audacity to accuse *me* of adultery! This man who has prowled round the theatre ogling loose women and is now hoist on his own petard!

We stand in angry silence until the hackney carriage arrives and Shad fairly pushes me inside, his face dark and grim. For some time neither of us speak.

'I ask you again, whom did you arrange to meet?' he barks at me from the darkness as the hackney jolts and rumbles through the streets.

'I didn't arrange to meet anyone.'

He gives a snort. 'And the mask?'

I don't want to betray Ann but I can think of no other way to explain it. 'Ann and I thought we should surprise you and Beresford at the theatre and since we had no escorts, that it was better to go masked.'

'I shall not allow my wife to appear at the play disguised as a common whore!'

'But I was masked. How would anyone have known who I was? *You* certainly didn't.'

'That's immaterial, ma'am!' he bellows with astonishing male logic. 'And I will not have you associate with Lady Beresford if this is the sort of indecency in which you are likely to become involved.'

The carriage stops at our house. Shad opens the door, steps down, and holds his hand out to me.

'She is my best friend.' I descend, ignoring his hand, and walk ahead of him.

The footman stationed to answer the front entrance for the night opens the door.

'Then you are a greater fool than I thought,' Shad says quite softly from behind me.

I ignore him.

I do not want supper. I am sick that within days of our marriage he plans to take another mistress. I do not think I could sit opposite him and make polite conversation over oysters and champagne. Not after he has insulted and shamed me.

I can scarcely bear to look at him, but I turn and curtsy before going upstairs alone. For the first time I am grateful for Withers' silence and indifference.

Shad does not come to my bed that night.

Shad

My sister once dragged me to some ridiculous opera by a German fellow where a woman disguises herself as a whore to attract her husband's attention. I suspect it's the basis of many a comic opera or play and now I play the role of the duped husband.

I honestly did not recognise her. First, of course, the light in the box was dim; second, she was masked; and third, I expected her to be spending the evening with her friend Ann in some sort of giggly schoolgirl way. If she'd not worn that scarf round her head I would have recognised her hair. You'd think the bosom might have jogged my memory, for I have spent some happy hours in contemplation of it in less undress than her gown tonight.

I am only human. Put an undressed woman in my bed, or even one wearing a stout, unbecoming nightgown, or a partially dressed woman in a box at the play and I shall rise to the occasion.

But none of my excuses hit the mark. The truth is, I have been caught with my breeches at my ankles (metaphorically). Had my wits been quicker than my loins I might possibly have laughed it off and pretended I knew it was she all along, but Charlotte, confound her, realised within seconds what I was about. She has every right to be insulted and angry.

Even more troubling, I was unmoved by the actresses backstage but the masked beauty heated my blood in an instant; and she is my wife.

So musing, I settle myself upon the sofa (hard, narrow, creaking) in my study where I have ordered Roberts to make my bed, and examine the mask that I stuffed into my coat pocket. Troubling thoughts arise in my mind. Does she plan to be unfaithful to me with Beresford, his wife an unwitting pawn in their game?

No, I can't believe it, not after seeing the obvious affection between Ann and Beresford tonight. Beresford's blushing confession earlier in the day, of his wife's indifference to him in the bedchamber, tells me that he is concerned with one woman only, and that is Ann. Why else should he be so distressed by her coldness?

I was of little help to him, I fear.

I turn the mask over in my hands. I think again of Charlotte at the theatre, the glint of silver from the scarf on her head, the seductive rustle of her gown, her bosom gleaming like a pearl in the dim light.

Two doors, from my study to my dressing room to the bedchamber, lie between us. Two pieces of mahogany, two agate handles and two brass locks. A few feet of wooden floor I could cross in seconds. Does she lie sleepless waiting for my arrival?

I think about how I could enter the room, and watch as she removes her hideous nightgown (the sartorial equivalent of a slab of solid mahogany). She will raise her arms to tie the mask round her head. Her skin glows lustrous and mysterious in the candlelight. She . . .

Enough!

I know it's more likely that my infuriating wife is wrapped in the bedclothes (she has the habit of dragging them over herself) fast asleep, now and again making a sound that is not quite a snore.

I settle myself on my narrow bed and prepare myself for a long and uncomfortable night alone.

The next day is Sunday. We meet at breakfast. We are icily polite to each other.

We put in an appearance at church so the *ton* may see us and we both give a creditable performance of married bliss à la mode – not over-affectionate, but very fashionable.

Charlotte

The weather has finally cleared by Monday and Ann and I exchange a series of notes early in the morning in which we agree that I should send the carriage first to her house. I fear that if she comes here first Shad may forbid the trip.

I crumple Ann's latest note in my hand as Shad comes into the morning room while I am at breakfast. I can scarcely bear to look at him without the deepest unhappiness but I notice he has dark circles beneath his eyes and looks tired. I should be glad he suffers from lack of sleep as I do, but I feel only sadness.

He regards me with deep suspicion. 'Who's that from?'

Mind your own business, sir, and a good morning to you, too. 'From Ann,' I say quite truthfully.

I throw the note on to the fire before he demands to read it.

'Indeed. You feel it necessary to destroy the evidence, I see.'

'Not at all. Oh, I'm sorry. Did you want the paper to curl your hair?'

'Most amusing. And what will you do today, ma'am?'

'I should like to visit an old servant who lives in Camden Town, sir.' I have practised saying this in front of the mirror. I blink innocently at him. I am a dreadful liar. 'May I take the carriage?'

'Camden Town, eh? A most salubrious spot. Maybe I should accompany you.' He looks pointedly at the teapot.

If I were going to visit an old servant I'd as soon take a dead dog. Or a mad one, and I ignore his unspoken suggestion that I should pour him tea. 'That is most kind of you, sir, but we shall talk only of female things. She is recently brought to bed.'

He pounces. 'I thought you said she was old.'

'Old in the sense of a former servant.'

'Quite,' he murmurs, and pours himself a cup of tea. A thin gush of liquid is followed by a great mass of tea leaves. He pushes the cup away. 'In that case, you should visit alone. I'll ask Roberts to see if the housekeeper has some nourishing jelly or some such you can take.'

'Oh, please do not trouble yourself, sir.'

'No trouble at all, I assure you.' He looks at his tea with distaste.

'I shall ring for more hot water,' I say in a long-suffering tone of voice, as though first I must scale a few mountains.

'No matter. I'll have Roberts bring me some ale. I shall be at my club. All day,' he adds with great emphasis.

'Very well, sir.'

'I'll bid you good day, ma'am.'

He bows, I curtsy, he leaves.

Thank God.

Shad

She's a terrible liar, and all my suspicions are confirmed.

She throws a note on to the fire as I enter the room, a clear sign of guilt. I see the relief on her face when I believe her preposterous tale of an old – or former – servant. If my head did not ache quite so badly I would pick a few more holes in her story, but I feel a great weariness.

I get a dose of willow for the headache from Roberts and spend some time in the butler's pantry with him, talking of this and that; how the crops do at home, which makes me desirous to return and see them for myself; how long we should stay in town.

Purely out of spite I ask Roberts to provide her ladyship with some invalid delicacy suitable for a new mother, and he goes to talk to the housekeeper.

I find that Withers has been instructed to give her ladyship's orders to the coachman, and my worst suspicions are confirmed. The coach is to go first to Beresford's house.

So it is true. I had hoped her lover was not Beresford – and even now, I cannot believe it of him. I wait in the alley opposite the house, astride my mare, my collar turned up and my hat pulled down against the fine drizzle. The whole world is grey and chilly and miserable.

Charlotte appears on the steps carrying a basket. She looks nervous and excited, and runs to the carriage as it pulls up. The blinds are drawn.

I wait until the carriage is a little way down the street, then I kick my mare forward. I shall find out the truth.

Charlotte

'What do you have in the basket?' Ann asks.

'Oh, some calves' foot jelly and some tea.'

'You didn't tell them?' She gasps and turns so pale I am afraid she will faint.

'No, of course not. I told them I was visiting an old servant who'd had a baby.'

'It's still too close to the truth.'

I want to tell her not to be ridiculous, but she is such a volatile mass of nerves that I pat her hand and tell her everything will be well, as of course it will be.

I'd looked forward to spending some time with Ann but she is highly agitated and I find it is up to me to calm her. I'd even hoped I might be able to ask her advice about how I should make peace with my angry, resentful husband. Instead I take her hand and chat to her about trivialities – I get her to talk of the play last night, and I tell her about my visit to Lady Renbourn. She smiles a little and asks if I am quite well after leaving the theatre so unexpectedly.

She blushes. 'I suppose – well, Shad may have become inflamed at your appearance. You looked quite lovely. I trust he did not make excessive demands upon you; it might have become quite unpleasant, and I am sorry if it were so.'

If only he had.

'Oh, Charlotte,' she breathes. 'Maybe you can tell him you are indisposed tonight.' Her face falls. 'I have been spared these two nights past, since yesterday was Sunday, yet I regret that tonight Beresford will become amorous. Tell me, Charlotte, what do you think of when . . . when, you know – to keep your mind off what he does?'

'I don't think of anything in particular,' I answer.

'I wish I were as stoic as you.'

I hesitate. 'I do not understand it. You and

Beresford love each other and you seem so fond of each other, yet . . . tell me, was it the same with the father of your child?'

'He was a perfect gentleman,' she replies, mystifying me.

'A perfect gentleman!' I cannot believe this. 'By all accounts he seduced and abandoned you. That is not gentlemanly. Oh Ann, Ann dearest, please do not cry. I am so sorry. I did not mean to hurt your feelings.'

'You don't understand,' she whimpers.

No, I don't. I don't understand any of it. I remember Beresford and Ann's courtship, when they were continually sneaking off to do . . . what? Whatever it was, Ann seemed perfectly happy to have Beresford disarrange her dress and hair and make her blush and giggle. Then, she did not confide in me. I am not sure that even now she tells me the whole truth, and certainly I do not tell her the truth of my sorry situation.

Ann indulges in a little more of her beautiful crying. As usual her tears improve her complexion and add to the brilliance of her eyes. She blows her nose into a dainty lawn handkerchief, pausing to show me the coronet embroidered thereon – I would not dare to show anyone a handkerchief after I had used it, and neither would anyone want to see it. Then she snuggles against me like a dormouse and falls asleep.

I put my arm round her shoulders, push her bonnet out of the way (the brim rubs against my face) and think bleak thoughts.

*

When the carriage draws up at the cottage in Camden Town Ann wakes and yawns like a kitten. She adjusts her bonnet and scampers out of the carriage, charming Price the coachman and James the postilion with a smile. I half expect her to burst into song and pick flowers like an actress in a play as she trips down the flagstone path to the cottage door.

I follow in a somewhat more subdued way after giving Price and James a half-crown so they may have the horses looked after at a local hostelry and buy some ale. I tell them to return after two hours.

When I enter the cottage, Ann is holding a beaming infant on her lap and is deep in conversation with the woman who cares for her, a Mrs Pyle. Mrs Pyle is a stout calm woman, apple-cheeked and missing her front teeth, clad in a brown gown and a sturdy apron.

'Look, Charlotte,' Ann says, holding the baby up. 'My little Emma. Is she not an angel?'

'As good as gold, she is,' Mrs Pyle says. 'Even with another tooth coming in, bless her, I had only to rub her gum with a little gin and the precious dear was all smiles.'

'A tooth!' Ann says. 'Oh, yes, look! Isn't she beautiful, with her tooth!'

The baby gives me a wide grin, revealing that she does indeed have four little white teeth, and belches the way George does after dinner.

I present Mrs Pyle with the calves' foot jelly and the tea.

'Thank you, ma'am, I'm most obliged.' She curtsies and busies herself at the hearth with the kettle.

I sit down next to Ann and tug at the baby's bare toes. She grins and coos.

Ann meanwhile engages Mrs Pyle in a conversation about how often the baby feeds, leading on to intimate details of the infant's digestion that really don't interest me. Emma is not the only baby under Mrs Pyle's care; a couple sleep entwined in a cradle; and a fat toddler staggers around the room. Mrs Pyle and a skinny girl of about twelve (I can't make out if she is a servant or a daughter) prevent this child from tripping over the hem of its dress, falling into the fire, pulling things off shelves, eating small objects it finds on the floor, or climbing on to furniture. It exhausts to me to see this creature in perpetual motion. It also impresses me that Mrs Pyle and the girl ward off disaster without undue concern and, in Mrs Pyle's case, while making tea and carrying on a conversation.

'Where is little Betsy?' Ann asks, looking round.

'God took Betsy to be his little angel last week, ma'am,' Mrs Pyle says. 'Oh, she was so pretty in her coffin, it was a treat to see.'

I am afraid Ann will faint. Her grip loosens on Emma and I take the baby from her.

Mrs Pyle hastens to reassure her. 'Don't you fret, ma'am, Betsy was never strong like your Emma. I knew she wasn't long for this world. She was too good for it, ma'am.'

Ann snatches Emma back and hugs her so fiercely the baby wails in fear.

'Now, don't you be making a fuss,' Mrs Pyle says, taking Emma with one arm, while somehow retrieving a spoon that the toddler gnaws upon, pouring hot water into a teapot, and taking a cheesecloth cover from a jug of milk. Emma stops crying and grabs hold of a descending lock of Mrs Pyle's hair.

The girl saws at a loaf of bread, removes the crusts, and dips them into the milk. Emma and the toddler each receive a crust and the conversation between Mrs Pyle and Ann turns to the subject of weaning. Emma is returned to her mother's lap.

'And may I ask when ma'am expects to be brought to bed?' Mrs Pyle addresses me suddenly.

'I – I'm not – no, I came with Lady—'

'With Mrs Longwood,' Ann whispers.

'Oh, yes. I came with Mrs Longwood to see her—'

'Her niece.' Ann anticipates me again.

'Yes, her niece. A lovely child. You take very good care of her, Mrs Pyle.'

'I offer the best of services to distressed gentlewomen,' Mrs Pyle says, as though she reads from an advertisement in the paper. 'There is no need for any unpleasantness in society when little accidents occur. Discretion is guaranteed, ma'am. If a lady has not yet quickened there are certain remedies to take care of the problem.'

Ann's little accident coos and chatters in baby talk.

The toddler grabs a fork from the table and attempts to ruin an eye. Mrs Pyle substitutes a pewter plate as a plaything. 'Or, ma'am, I assist at the lying-in, if you would care to see the bedchamber.'

'No, that's not necessary, Mrs Pyle—'

'And if you wish to take lodgings nearby when you begin to show, ma'am, I can recommend a most excellent hostelry. Many ladies find it best to—'

'Gentleman coming,' says Mrs Pyle's young helper, pausing by the window.

Ann gasps, shoves Emma into my arms, and runs through a doorway behind us, shutting the door.

The front door of the cottage crashes open. Emma, who has been gazing at me with some suspicion, takes this as the last straw, and opens her mouth in a deafening yell that wakes the two infants in the cradle. They begin to shriek in unison. The toddler sits down hard on the flagstone floor and raises its voice in a loud wail.

'Where is he? By God, I'll kill him!' says my husband, the blade of his rapier glinting in the sunlight.

He strides into the cottage of yelling infants.

'Put your sword away, Shad, you're frightening the babies.' I catch his sleeve and he turns on me with a look so fierce and desperate I am mortally afraid.

'Where is Beresford?' Now his voice is quiet and deadly. My knees give way and I sit down abruptly on a rush-bottomed chair.

'Sir—' Mrs Pyle advances towards him. I notice she has a poker in one hand and an infant under the other arm. I wish I had one, too – the poker, that is.

'Silence, you damned procuress!' He moves forward with a smooth motion, and wrenches a door open, revealing a cupboard. He stops before he stabs a large sack of flour to death.

He backs away to the centre of the room, and his gaze lights on a narrow staircase in one corner.

'Is he upstairs, ma'am?' he says to me.

'Beresford? Why should he be? He's in London, I expect. Put your sword up, please.'

I realise, to my dismay, that a warm dampness seeps

from Emma's skirts as she howls in my arms. The little girl is standing open-mouthed, holding the toddler by one hand, the other infant on her shoulder.

'Which one is yours?' he says, wheeling towards me. The tip of the rapier wavers somewhere at the level of my elbow.

'Stop it! Please, Shad.'

Emma reaches out to grasp the pretty shiny thing in front of us, and her action seems to bring Shad to his senses. He steps back and sheathes the rapier so that it becomes once more a fashionable walking stick.

'I beg your pardon, ma'am,' he says to Mrs Pyle. 'Tell me where the gentleman is, and I'll bother you no more.'

Mrs Pyle draws herself up with surprising dignity for a woman with an infant suckling noisily at one large naked breast. 'I assure you, sir, there are no *gentlemen* here.'

Brava, Mrs Pyle.

Shad nods. 'And you, ma'am, are . . . ?'

'I am Mrs Margaret Pyle.' She pauses. 'Sir.'

'Viscount Shadderly, at your service. I am deeply sorry for any distress I may have caused, ma'am.'

She withdraws the infant from her breast and pins her gown back into place. 'You should be, sir, attacking defenceless women and babies.'

'I am looking for the gentleman who accompanied this lady.'

'He isn't here,' I say again. 'Why would I come here with Beresford?'

'Hold your tongue, ma'am.'

'Sir, you are mistaken,' Mrs Pyle says.

Shad takes another look around the room and sees the doorway through which Ann disappeared seconds ago. In a moment his rapier is drawn, the walking stick clatters to the floor and he has kicked the door open.

Ann screams from inside the room, doubtless the one where Mrs Pyle's clients lie in.

'What the devil are you doing here, Lady Beresford?'

Ann saves the day. She cries, prettily and helplessly, and Shad flounders in embarrassment, offering a handkerchief while trying to hide the rapier behind his back.

'You are making a terrible mistake,' she cries. 'We came only to see my old servant Mrs Pyle.'

'I thought she was Charlotte's old servant.'

'She was our servant in the country when Charlotte first visited us, when we were both girls,' I explain.

'Indeed, my lord. And then I married and poor Pyle went for a soldier leaving me with an infant so now I look after others' children,' Mrs Pyle says, the second baby at her breast.

'I see. Admirable.' Shad looks dazed by the exhibit of maternal and infant activity around him. You can see him trying to work out the children's ages and the chronology of the whole business, and I fear mathematical impossibility will be our undoing. 'But I understood your confinement was more recent.'

'Taken for a little angel, my lord.' She pins her gown into place and sobs into her apron. For all I know her tears may be real, or as real as Ann's. She tucks the infant under one arm and takes Emma from me, giving me the opportunity to examine the damage to my skirts.

The toddler, meanwhile, has recovered its equilibrium and begins a perilous climb from chair to table, reaching towards the teapot.

To my surprise, Shad is there first, plucking the child away by the skirts and depositing it on the floor.

Ann, with tears shining on her lashes (how does she do it? She really is quite annoying sometimes) pours tea, and we all sit at the table, Shad included. The toddler has taken a liking to him and sits on his lap while banging a spoon on the table top.

Mrs Pyle unbends a little. 'I trust little Tom is not bothering his lordship.'

'Not at all, ma'am. I am quite fond of children.'

He does not add *baked* or *boiled*, so I believe he has recovered from his fit of madness. Why on earth should he think that Beresford is the object of my affections? Beresford, whom I barely know, and try to like only for Ann's sake?

Ann, sitting opposite me, nods towards the door that leads to the back garden of the house, indicating that she will visit the outhouse, but shakes her head violently when I begin to rise to accompany her. She gives a meaningful glance at Shad and Mrs Pyle (the two of them are deep in conversation about the age at which children begin to talk, Shad referring, of course, to his 'niece' and 'nephew'). I understand her. If Shad asks any leading questions, neither Ann nor I will be there to deflect the conversation.

After she has returned, I make a trip into the garden and the small shed, covered with rambling pink roses that do not quite mask the smell.

Shad rises as I come back into the cottage. 'We should return to London,' he announces. 'Thank you for your hospitality, Mrs Pyle, and my apologies, again, for my, ah, intrusion. Ladies, if you please.'

Ann gives Emma a longing gaze. I know she yearns to kiss her.

So I go and kiss the baby's soft cheek and Ann does the same. I then kiss the toddler's rather grubby, sticky face and he has a fit of shyness and buries his face in Shad's coat.

Shad pats the child on the head, opens the cottage door and ushers us outside. The carriage is waiting, with Shad's mare tethered behind.

He hands me and Ann into the carriage. Ann flutters around and I find myself insisting that she face forward; Shad sits next to me opposite her.

'How did you know where we were?' I ask.

He shrugs. 'I followed the carriage. I would have been here sooner, but Sheba cast a shoe as we entered the village and I met Matthew and James at the inn. They told me where you were.'

'And you thought . . .' But I can't talk of it with Ann opposite me. She has been giving me reproachful looks ever since the uproar of Shad's arrival died down. I know she suspects I told him where we were going; and, even worse, maybe she now suspects I nurse a *tendresse* for her husband. But where did Shad get the idea? It's not as though I have scattered strawberry-embroidered handkerchiefs around like Desdemona. I barely talk to Beresford unless I must. I remember that tonight we are to dine with Ann and Beresford and want to groan in frustration. I foresee an evening of verbal traps (Shad), wounded reproachful looks (Ann), and, worst of all, good-natured, oblivious jollity (Beresford).

Shad yawns and closes his eyes. His head slumps against my shoulder and I flinch, but he's fast asleep.

Ann stares out of the window. She doesn't want to talk to me and I feel resentful that she has not thanked me once for arranging this ill-begotten outing. My gown may be ruined, too (I chide, myself, slightly, for my worldliness, but I like this gown).

The carriage bumps and sways. Shad's head rolls from my shoulder, over my bosom, and on to my lap. But a few days ago, and if we were alone, I am sure that would have led to indecencies.

'You stink,' he mumbles.

'It was the baby.'

'Wasn't suggesting otherwise, ma'am.'

His head is hot and heavy on my lap. I slide the back of my hand against his forehead. 'Are you unwell, Shad?'

He pushes my hand away, scratches the back of his neck, disarranging his neckcloth, and falls asleep again.

Ann produces some embroidery from her reticule. I am full of admiration. Under the circumstances, even in a carriage as well sprung as this one, my sewing skills would be severely challenged. I should most likely sew the piece to my skirt.

'Are you well?' I whisper to her.

'Quite well.'

'I'm sorry about . . .' I nod downwards at the sleeping man on my lap who radiates heat like a coal fire. Despite my anger and sadness, I feel an odd tenderness towards him.

'Oh, he was quite heroic, wasn't he,' murmurs Ann with a touch of her gentle satire. 'Protecting his good name.'

I glance down. Shad sleeps on.

'Ann, I assure you, there has never been anything of that nature between me and Beresford. I don't know why Shad thinks it is so. Maybe it was because I was alone in your box at the play, and masked.'

'Oh dear.' She doesn't sound over-concerned and I am glad of it. 'Beresford thought it a great joke.'

'I think he is unwell.'

'Beresford?'

'Shad.'

'Oh, you mean he is insane? I think it all too likely.'

'No!' A little, maybe. 'I think he has a fever.'

Ann makes a face. 'I hope he is not contagious. I should hate to miss Lady Alving's soirée on Wednesday.' She looks at me. 'You have something on your face.'

'Where?'

'On your cheek. Allow me.' She shifts forward and rubs at it with her own dainty handkerchief. 'It must have been from that grubby little boy.'

'Whom I kissed for your sake—'

'Sssh!' She glances at Shad. He doesn't move.

'And I thought he was a rather nice baby. Emma will be like that in a few months, when she learns to walk.'

'No, she won't!' Her needle dips into the fabric. 'What will you wear tonight?'

'I doubt we'll attend if Shad is unwell.'

She nods and performs some complicated sort of embroidery stitch.

I lean my head against the window and long for this wretched journey to be over.

Shad

'Wake up.'

Damned impudence. Even if it's a French ship sighted this unfamiliarity is unforgivable. My bed shifts beneath me. Rough seas.

'Shad, wake up. We're home.'

Ah, now I remember. I'm in the carriage and Charlotte shakes my shoulder.

I sit upright, embarrassed that I fell asleep on her lap, although memories flood back of the rest of the embarrassing things I have achieved this day, and it is certainly not as bad as waving a rapier around in a room full of women and infants. I'm still not convinced that visit was as innocent as Charlotte and Ann would have me believe, but I feel confused by the whole business.

'Where's Lady Beresford?'

'We took her home,' she says. 'Sir, you're not well.'

'Mind your own business, ma'am.' Actually she's right, but I don't want her fussing over me.

My head aches abominably, the rest of me too. A glass of brandy will set me to rights, and I tell Roberts, who holds the front door open, to bring one to the study. I reel into the house like a drunkard and start the long, arduous ascent of the stairs.

'You should go to bed.' My wife is hot on my heels.

'Enough, ma'am.' I get into the study and slam the door in her face. Appallingly rude, but I've had enough with today's wild goose chase and female silliness.

I find the tinder box and get a candle alight, and then attempt to light the fire, for I'm chilled to the bone. The kindling flares briefly and goes out as Roberts enters the room.

'Oh, sir,' Roberts says. 'That is not the way, sir.' He

takes the candle from me and lights the fire, then lights the lamp that stands on the mantelpiece.

'A touch of fever, I think,' I say. 'Nothing to be concerned about. Where's that brandy?'

Roberts reaches for the glass on the desk, turns and looks at me, and drops it. Brandy splashes on to the carpet and the glass rolls away. He backs away from me.

'What the devil is wrong with you? Get me another glass.'

'My lord,' he says. 'My lord, you . . .'

And then I see my reflection in the glass over the mantel. For a moment I'm frozen in horror.

'Fetch me more brandy. Tell Lady Shadderly to return to her parents' house. Don't let the Bastards upstairs and do not admit any visitors.'

'A physician, my lord, I'll call a—'

'If you wish. It will make little difference.'

He hesitates, shifting from one foot to the other.

'Go, man. I must put my affairs in order.' I sit at the desk and papers rattle in my hands as I search for my will. The miniature of my mother rolls out on to the writing surface of the desk and I stare at it. I may meet her soon, but not, I hope, my father.

Here's the will. Yes, I've left Roberts fifty guineas. The other servants on the estate are provided for, as are the Bastards. I write short farewell notes to friends and to my sister, hoping that the letters will never be read.

And Charlotte. I try to remember the terms of the settlement and seem to remember that her money will return to her. I should write to her before the illness overtakes me fully. I grab a clean sheet of paper and wish I did not feel so damnably ill. Who the devil will succeed me? I can't remember; not Beresford, he's too distantly related, and there's dozens of family members, but the lawyers will work it out.

Unless my wife is with child; she will not know for some time and I may never know, but then children without fathers are something of a family tradition. My fingers are clumsy and will not obey me but I manage to sharpen a pen and stare at the dizzying whiteness of the paper. My first action is to create a large blot of ink on the paper.

And then I begin to write.

Charlotte

'Get me out of this gown immediately!' I snap at Withers.

She moves behind me to untie the laces. 'I have put out the cream gown with the gold netting for milady.'

'It doesn't matter. We shall not dine out tonight. His lordship is ill.'

I wash my face and let Withers drop the evening gown over my head. As she finishes tying the laces, someone knocks at the door.

Roberts stands there. He looks terrified. 'Beg

pardon, milady, his lordship wishes you to leave the house immediately.'

I sit on the bed rather more abruptly than I expected.

'He says you may return to Mr and Mrs Hayden's house, milady.'

He is casting me out! He must be convinced of my infidelity. 'Why?' I hardly have any voice at all.

'He has smallpox, milady.'

I hear a scuffling sound behind me and realise that Withers is running for the door. 'I'll not stay in this house, milady. I'm giving notice. Good evening, milady.'

She pushes past Roberts and I am grateful that I have not had to sack her, but it seems a small and insignificant victory now. I find my voice again. 'Smallpox?'

Roberts nods. 'Poxes on his forehead, ma'am, and a dreadful fever. He won't let me near him.'

I stand. 'We must get him to bed. I'll help you. You've sent for the physician? Good.' And then I remember something Marianne told me about her children. 'Roberts, you are quite sure?'

'What else could it be, milady? I'll send one of the maids to help you pack.'

'Very well, but first bring me pen and paper to the morning room. I must write to Mrs Shillington.'

He bows and runs out of the room.

Smallpox. I remember a woman in the village who survived it, blinded and with her fingers bent into claws by the scarring. She looked like a crone. She was five and twenty.

I hope to God I am right that it is not smallpox.

Shad

'Milord, you must go to bed.'

I've fallen asleep writing, or not a sleep exactly, but into a series of dreams populated by dead shipmates, my brother, any number of odd people and crazy situations. Roberts' voice intervenes occasionally, telling me I should get up, that I must go to bed.

I tell him to go away.

'If I've caught it, I've caught it, milord. 'Twill make no difference now.'

And Charlotte. Thank God we have not shared a bed these past nights and she may be spared.

'Has she gone? Her ladyship, that is.'

'Yes, milord.'

He doesn't sound quite certain. Then he comes and hoists me from my chair at the desk, his shoulder beneath mine. The room spins crazily and I am glad to lean on him for support.

'You'll go to bed now, milord.'

'The letter I was writing. Burn it. Anything else that may shame the family.' I'm not even sure what I've written but I have a vague memory of writing to Charlotte and knowing I might regret what I said, if I live.

'Yes, milord.'

The few steps from office to dressing room to bedchamber – those few steps I could not bring myself to take when I slept alone, and now I am both glad and sorry for it – take hours, or so it seems.

I fall flat on the bed. The sheets are cool, blessedly cool.

Roberts struggles to remove my clothing and drop a nightshirt over my head. I try to help but I make things more difficult.

The sheets are cold enough to make me shiver and then hot and tormenting like the fires of hell. Is that where I am bound?

I dream again. I dream that my ship is on fire, a nightmare of falling spars and the shrieks of wounded men and then I'm plunged into freezing waters and my teeth chatter.

'Milord, the physician is here.'

Roberts' wrist is gripped in my hand and I can see new poxes between my fingers.

A black-clad physician lurks in the doorway, a handkerchief over his face. 'I shall instruct your manservant to burn pastilles against the infection, milord.'

He sidles into the room, removing from his bag an implement the like of which I last saw used on a horse. 'I recommend also an enema and some bloodletting will do your lordship much good.'

I use a vulgarity from my naval days to encourage

him to leave the room and take his instruments and pills with him.

He draws himself up, quivering. 'If you reject science, my lord, there is little hope for you.'

I invite him again to leave and this time, to encourage his departure, I hurl the water carafe in his direction.

'Oh, sir,' says Roberts.

'You get out, too. Bring me some brandy. Then leave me here to die.'

For I have made up my mind. I shall die. I want to die, feeling worse by the moment.

Roberts trudges in again, bearing a bottle of brandy and a glass and another water carafe. He has tears in his eyes.

'You're a good fellow, Roberts. You're provided for in my will. Now leave me.' My teeth chatter as I speak and I am racked by chills.

No matter. I wait for the heat to build and set me afire, and fling off the bedclothes and the nightshirt, which is rubbing my skin. Inflamed bumps rise on my skin, all over me, and they itch like the devil.

The brandy helps a little.

The bedchamber door opens again. 'You don't have smallpox.'

I grab the bedclothes to cover myself. 'I ordered you to go to your mother's house, ma'am. Now leave me. I wish to die in peace.'

Charlotte takes a couple of swift strides to the bed. 'Shad – sir – it is not smallpox.'

'Yes it is. I'm dying. Go away.'

'Your sister says—'

Tears spring to my eyes. My poor sister. She is about to lose another brother. I turn my face into the pillow. 'Get out of my bedchamber.'

'Your sister says she and your brother, and you, were all inoculated. Do you not remember? A surgeon cut your arm and put some nasty stuff in it?'

'No, I don't remember. I'm tired. Please go away.'

She holds out the discarded nightshirt. 'But she also told me you never caught chickenpox.'

I swat the nightshirt away. 'Children get chickenpox. Please leave.'

'She said you were sent to play with the gamekeeper's children so you would catch it.'

That I do remember. We ran around and got horribly dirty – I was five or so, and the gamekeeper's daughter, who was also five and covered in livid poxes, kissed me and told me she would marry me. By the end of the day, though, she'd jilted me for my seven-year-old brother and later he boasted she'd shown him the poxes on her bum.

Shortly after that both my brother and sister became unwell.

I did not.

My niece, I remember, has recently suffered a similar indisposition. Nevertheless . . .

'I have smallpox,' I insist. 'I am dying.'

'You are not at all well,' she says. 'The illness will

make a grown man or woman very unwell, more so than it will a small child. Your sister said your niece was hardly out of sorts at all and I suspect you caught it from her. But I regret to inform you that you are probably not dying.'

'As you will.' I take a swig from the bottle of brandy, my teeth chattering against it. I don't have the energy to argue; I must save my strength for my imminent demise. 'Fetch Roberts.'

'What—'

'Now!'

She bounds across the room, fetches the chamber pot (mercifully empty), and holds it and my head while I vomit up the brandy.

This must be the most embarrassing moment of my life. I am glad I am too ill to appreciate it fully.

'You may go now,' I say, when I can speak again.

There is a pregnant pause and I wonder if she contemplates tipping the contents of the pot over my head.

Instead, tight-lipped, she offers me water to rinse my mouth, pushes me back on to the pillows, and wipes my face with a cool wet cloth. 'Your sister also sent this over.'

I view the large bottle with mistrust. After that dolt of a physician I don't know what to expect. 'And what do you intend to do with that?'

'Your sister says it will ease the itching.' She adds, putting to rest my worst fears after the physician's suggestions, 'I shall apply it to your skin.'

'You may leave it and go.'

'Hold your tongue, Shad, and take the sheet off.'

'Certainly not. Send for Roberts.'

She shakes the bottle in a very determined way. 'Roberts is having his dinner. It will not hurt, I assure you.'

That does it.

'Very well.' As I shove the sheet down to my waist, I realise she knew exactly how to break down my resistance. The Navy could have used a skilled tactician like Charlotte. I turn over, presenting my back to her.

She gives a small gasp. 'Oh, my dear. That is, oh dear. I am afraid you have broken one of the ones on your neck – you must not do so, for they'll scar. Surely they have not all erupted today?'

'I thought it flea bites.'

I yelp in surprise as she dabs the lotion, cool and slightly tingling, on to my neck and back. A lot of dabs.

She murmurs under her breath, counting. At thirty-three, she pushes the sheet down, revealing my arse and legs. At ninety-two she orders me to turn over and I grab the sheet to preserve my modesty.

She dabs me from head to toe, including inside my ears.

'Done!' She reaches for the cork. 'One hundred and seventy-four.'

'I regret it is one hundred and seventy-five. The bottle if you please, and avert your eyes.'

She hands me the bottle but my hand shakes so I almost drop it. Hers closes around mine, steadying it.

'Where is it?'

'Where do you think?' I clutch at the sheet.

'On your prick?'

'Who taught you that word?' I try to sound shocked.

'You did, sir.'

So I did. 'It's indecent. Allow me.'

She flushes. 'We are married.'

'Yes, but . . .' I am feeling too wretched to argue and relinquish control of the sheet and my anatomy to her. 'Oh, very well.'

I shut my eyes tight.

'I can't see . . .' she says.

I utter the words that later, I know (if I live), will make me writhe in shame, although at the time I scarcely care. 'Draw back my . . . you know, as I showed you when we . . .'

'Of course.' I am grateful that she is so matter-of-fact.

'Ow!'

'I'm sorry.'

And then the unthinkable happens. I can't believe it – I am at death's door, the stuff stings like the devil, yet her touch arouses me.

God help me, she giggles.

'I beg your pardon,' I say. Stiffly. I make things worse by blundering on, 'Sometimes it happens for no reason; it means nothing, well, that is to say, I mean you no disrespect, and I daresay it will go down on its own, it—'

'Sssh.' She touches my lip with the cloth, silencing me.

Charlotte

I've told him he isn't dying and he seems almost disappointed.

But I'm not so sure he isn't. Even though one part of him seems very much alive, he is running a high fever and I am afraid for him. In the few hours that have passed since we returned to the house he now seems very ill, and I suspect it was only rage and jealousy that kept him on his feet for the better part of the day. I am particularly alarmed when, as he falls into a restless sleep, he looks beyond me as though someone else has entered the room. His eyes bright with fever, he says one word.

Mama.

Don't dying men call for their mothers?

Before I can brood on this further, Roberts returns with a footman who, as I have instructed, brings barley water, and leaves with the chamber pot. Roberts and I stand together at the bedside while Shad mutters in his sleep.

'I told him it was chickenpox.'

Roberts nodded.

'He is most distressed. I think he would prefer smallpox.'

Roberts allows himself a smile. 'Downstairs they're all weeping and praying.'

'Pray allow everyone extra ale this evening.'

'Thank you, milady.' I have a suspicion he has anticipated my order.

We then begin a mistress-servant round of polite bickering over who will sit with Shad. Roberts has had his dinner; I have not. Roberts, who shows himself alarmingly protective of his master, agrees with some reluctance that I shall sit with Shad later that night. Footmen, he points out, are available.

Yes, but I am his wife, who vowed to honour him in sickness and in health.

Roberts insists with the greatest of politeness that it is his job and I allow him to take over until after I have dined.

As I leave the room, I turn to ask, 'Roberts, do you know if the children have had chickenpox?'

'Apparently so, milady, so Mrs Price says.'

'Good.'

It's still too early for me to dine and I'm not hungry. I then remember we are engaged to dine with Ann and Beresford, and call for a lamp to be brought into Shad's study so I may write them a note. Sitting at a small table in the room – the desk is scattered with papers – I compose another note to Marianne, thanking her for the lotion. I tell her that it made him a great deal more comfortable and chew my pen while trying to think of a way to warn her her brother is quite ill, without worrying her unnecessarily. She was remarkably calm about her own daughter's chickenpox, but then, as she said, the child was quite well in herself although a hideous sight.

I settle on writing that Shad is asleep although feverish and that I will send word in the morning. I dispatch a footman with the notes, lean back in the chair and regard the office, Shad's male sanctum where he conducts his private business.

Naturally I am more than eager to poke around and find out what I will. Besides, he will be grateful that someone tidied his papers. So, after closing the door – I do not want the servants to see what I am about – I approach the mess on his desk.

A couple of miniatures slide from the pile of papers as I touch them. One I recognise, from her portrait in the dining room, as Shad's mother. The other, according to a scrap of paper tucked beneath the glass back along with a coiled lock of hair, is of his brother Frederick, who died a couple of years ago while Shad was at sea. There does not seem to be a miniature of his father.

His letter opener is an elegant ivory knife, with an

engraving of a ship on the handle, and inscribed *HMS Arcturus*. That, I remember from my rather difficult conversation with Captain Carstairs, was the ship under Shad's command. I wonder who made it, and as I do so, I notice other small carvings of wood and ivory on the top of the desk, on the mantelpiece. Some are delicate, others have a vigorous unschooled quality. I pick up one of a bird, and turn it over. On the base there is an inscription so small I have to find a magnifying glass in one of the pigeon holes of the desk to read it: *Made this day, 7 June, 1807 by John Ketching, seaman*, HMS Arcturus.

I examine others, similarly inscribed, gifts to Captain Trelaise from sailors and officers of *HMS Arcturus*. All date from a few days in early June, almost two years ago, when Shad heard his brother was dead, and resigned his position in the Navy to take over his family's obligations. Several inscriptions note that the wood is from the ship itself, damaged during the capture of a French ship a week or so before.

I smile at a rather saucy depiction of a mermaid and wonder how many of those men still live. Was this outpouring of sentiment towards their departing captain genuine, or ordered by one of the officers? I hope they liked him. Shad's never volunteered any information about his life at sea. I've never asked. I will, I swear, when he gets well.

I examine the papers on his desk. He has written, folded and sealed letters, to his sister, Beresford,

Carstairs, and Roberts, and to some other people whose names I don't recognise. He has written on the front of each, underlined, <u>In the event of my death</u>. His writing is spiky and firm.

I stack the letters neatly. My hands shake. I am tempted to throw them on the fire.

He has not written to me.

The papers include a copy of his will, some bills, a letter dealing with estate business, a couple from gentlemen applying for the position of the children's tutor – oh God, who will be responsible for his children if he— I take a look at the will. To my relief, generous sums of money are settled on the children who are to remain in the care of Susan and Matthew Price.

There is no mention that I shall be involved in their upbringing in any way.

If he dies it will be as though our marriage never existed, never mattered. I lean my elbows on his desk among the piles of paper and put my face in my hands.

I don't know how long I sit there, but eventually I move and my foot touches something that makes a slight crackling sound. I bend and retrieve a crumpled ball of paper.

I smooth it flat. The writing here is agitated, a great blot of ink on the paper, and the lines run at odd angles. I'm not sure whether it is a first draft or whether he was delirious.

My dearest wife, my beloved,

It is with great sorrow that I have not told you before this how passionately I love you for I realise it is now so. I pray you may be with child so you may remember me. If it is a boy, name him for my father and brother Frederick as family tradition demands.

Charlotte, try to think well of me when I am gone. Kiss the children from me and

The letter ends.

He loves me? Oh God, I don't know whether to laugh or weep. He barely knows me, I barely know him, and there's only one place, or one activity we've undertaken, where we have been in accord. Furthermore he has accused me of being unfaithful – the man has a vivid imagination, for sure – and we have been married less than a week.

He loves me.

And he's dying. *Oh, Shad.*

No, he isn't. I'm so angry I pick up the nearest object, a wooden candlestick, and hurl it across the room. How dare he play with my affections so, claiming he is dying when he is fool enough to have a childish ailment he should have caught twenty-odd years ago! Not to mention the vulgarity of growing a horn – another indecent term he taught me – while lying on his so-called deathbed and while I was ministering to his needs as though I were a lowly servant. How dare he! I feel like storming into his bedchamber and brandishing the stupid letter in his spotted face. Instead I run to the fireplace, throw the letter into the coals, and watch it flare and disintegrate.

Afterwards I pick up the candlestick, which is broken in two, drop to my knees in front of the fire, and give way to tears.

'Milady?'

I didn't even realise Roberts had opened the study door.

'I want some glue,' I say, surely the most absurd statement of my life.

'Milady, his lordship asks for you.'

'Is he worse?' I wipe my eyes on my gown and rise to my feet.

'I don't believe so, milady.'

'I broke this, Roberts. It's a candlestick one of the men from the *Arcturus* made for him, and—'

'Don't you fret, milady.' He takes the broken candlestick from me with great kindness. 'I'll put it to rights. I have glue downstairs. You go and see his lordship, milady, if you please, and dinner will be served directly.'

I find Shad sitting up in bed, his eyes too bright, cheekbones sharp and flushed. He's examining one foot.

He looks up as I enter. 'I must know whether you're with child.'

'I beg your pardon?' I start to draw myself up in outraged modesty. 'I won't know for weeks yet, Shad. Is that why you wished to see me? Shouldn't you lie down?'

'Damnation, another one between my toes. Devil's bargain, Charlotte. I get to scratch the ones on my feet.' And he does, a look of bliss on his face that I've only seen – well, under equally intimate circumstances.

I pour him a glass of barley water to cover the blush that rises to my cheeks.

'Bring me some brandy.'

'You'll only puke it up and I may not be so ready with the chamber pot.' I push the glass into his hand. 'Drink, please.'

He makes a face, drinks, and then drops back on to the pillow. 'I saw Frederick.'

'Your brother?'

'Yes.' He closes his eyes.

'Oh?'

'He told me he'd got another bastard. Damned nuisance, my brother. Leaves me to pick up the pieces.' He mumbles something incoherent into the pillow. 'I loved him. I hated him for dying, the fool. Could have stayed in the Navy if he'd lived, wouldn't have had the title or the mess.' His eyes close.

As I move away from the bed he shoots out a hand and catches my wrist. 'Damn you, you won't go to him!'

'Shad, stop it!'

'What?' He blinks and stares at me. 'Kiss the Bastards for me. I don't want them to see me like this.'

'Shad, nobody wants to see you like this, believe me. You look dreadful.'

I can feel his pulse, a rapid and fluttering beat. I stare at his wrist where it emerges from the creamy cotton of his nightshirt, at the jut of the bone, the blue trace of vein, curling black hairs, and the poxes that erupt, ugly and livid, on his skin. I put my hand over his.

'Don't die,' I whisper. 'Please, don't die.'

Roberts comes back into the bedchamber a few minutes later. 'Your dinner is served, milady.'

I rise and Shad's hand slips from mine. 'Do you think we should send for the physician? He's still so hot.'

Roberts retrieves a cloth from a bowl of water, wrings it out, and lays it on Shad's forehead. 'Give him time, milady. The fever will break this night or the next, I expect.'

Shad jumps at the touch of the cold wet cloth and mutters a word that I believe may be common aboard ship.

'Oh, sir,' Roberts says. 'And in front of her ladyship, too.'

I don't have much appetite for dinner, but I drink a lot of wine, hoping it will stop me thinking too much about things. The words from Shad's letter bounce through my mind. He said he loved me. Maybe he said so because he was ill and distressed; yes, that must be it. He would doubtless be highly embarrassed if he knew I had read his declaration.

However, I feel it would be distressing to the servants if I drank myself insensible, so I return upstairs and enter the bedchamber. Shad lies quite motionless while Roberts dabs lotion on his ravaged back.

'There, milord, you're done. Her ladyship has come to see you.'

I tell Roberts to go to bed – we have decided that we should stand watch, like sailors, each for four hours at a time – and take my seat in the armchair by the bed. The room is dim and golden by the light of one lamp turned low. I lean forward and place my hand on Shad's forehead. He moves away with a grunt of annoyance.

'Where's Roberts?'

'I sent him to bed.'

He opens his eyes. 'Get him back.'

'No.' I offer him a glass of barley water. 'If you drink this all up, maybe Roberts will allow you some gruel.'

He erupts into fearsomely profane mutters, and then: 'You realise the inevitable consequences of forcing large amounts of liquid into me?'

'I shall provide the receptacle, sir, and avert my eyes.' His extreme modesty is proving tiresome.

Roberts, yawning and rubbing his eyes, returns at about one in the morning, and I retire to the guest bedchamber. To my embarrassment, one of the maidservants, her gown untidy from having to dress herself in the dark, and rubbing sleep from her eyes, waits to unlace my stays and help me to bed. I shall wear my front-lacing stays for the immediate future.

I don't think I shall sleep, but I do, waking with a start to see grey light seeping into the room. The house is very quiet, or as quiet as a London house can be. I look out of the window to see a servant, hands reddened, on her knees scrubbing the front steps that lead down to the servants' quarters. A horse and cart dawdle by in the street.

I wrap myself in a large shawl so as not to alarm Roberts' sensibilities and open the bedchamber door. I nearly jump out of my skin as a small figure, clothed in white, stumbles to her feet, rubbing her eyes.

It's Shad's daughter Amelia.

'What are you doing here?' I ask. 'Did you sleep outside all night?'

'Roberts would not let me see Uncle Shad. Ma'am, is he dying?'

'No! Of course not.'

She snuffles and wipes her face on her sleeve. 'I meant no harm.'

'Mrs Price may be worried about you.'

'Oh.' Then, tearfully, 'Please, milady, may I not see my uncle?'

'I'll ask him, but he is very unwell and looks dreadful. I don't want you to be frightened.'

The look on her face makes me wonder. She looks so adult, so surprised to be treated as a child, this girl whose mother left her to seek work in a factory and has not been heard of since. Perhaps after that nothing, or everything, will frighten a child, and I wonder whether it is her love for Shad that makes her so fearless; and his undoubted love for her.

I tell her to wait, and enter the bedchamber. Roberts is asleep in the chair.

Shad mutters, turns over, and looks at me with bright, feverish eyes. He frowns. 'Charlotte?' He runs a hand over his chin. 'I'm not shaved yet.'

'You can't shave. You must not break the poxes.'

Swearing ensues.

'Amelia wishes to see you.'

'No. No one except you and Roberts are to come in this room.'

I come and put my hand on his forehead. Still hot and the poxes look worse than ever. He shakes my hand off as usual.

'She slept outside all night, waiting to see you.'

'Very well, but only for a few minutes and the shutters must be closed. Wake Roberts so I can wash.'

I consider this request. Roberts sleeps with his head at a dreadful angle that will surely give him a sore neck, but on the other hand he sleeps like the dead – an unfortunate choice of words. I suspect Shad has not had a good night, and therefore Roberts has not either.

'I shall serve as your valet since Roberts is still asleep.'

A kettle sits at the side of the fireplace and I pour hot water into the bowl on the washstand, ignoring the fluent torrent of bad language that erupts from the bed. There is some further argument as to whether he should get out of bed, and I, who tire at his refusals of help, allow him the attempt.

'I admit defeat.' He sinks back on to the pillows. He looks alarmingly grey and hollow around the eyes.

'You know, I don't enjoy this much, either,' I say, wielding soap and towel. 'And doubtless your relatives will descend on the house today and I shall have to deal with them.'

'I am sure you will be the mistress of tact and sweetness.'

I ignore him.

Washed and his hair combed, and with a fresh nightshirt, Shad announces that he is ready to see Amelia, and Roberts, who has woken, yawning, opens the door.

She runs into his arms. 'Uncle Shad!'

'Come now, no crying. Your Aunt Shad will take you to the park today. Give your brother a kiss and tell him all's well. Are you practising your lessons still?'

'Yes, sir.' She wipes her eyes on the hem of her nightgown.

'Your uncle is tired,' I tell her. 'He needs to sleep again.'

She slips obediently from the bed. 'May we go to the park, Aunt Shad?'

'Of course.' A happy thought strikes me and I decide I shall pen a note to Ann, asking if she would care to take her brand new equipage for an outing, with two small passengers. I intend to ride the horse Shad bought for me. I hope fervently that he and I will ride together when he is well.

For he must get well. I cannot consider the alternative.

The outing to the park is a great success, with Ann proving herself an excellent whip, and my new mare proves to have a soft mouth and excellent paces, as Shad predicted. She is fresh from her sojourn in the stables, and eager to gallop, which, since it's early in the day we can do (although I have been awake for many hours, it is early only by the standards of polite society). I give her her head to work out most of the fidgets, while Ann keeps her team to a sedate trot.

When my mount is quieter, I take John up on the pommel of the saddle, to his great delight.

Ann and I do not have the opportunity to talk of intimate matters, but she is cheerful and full of smiles, sympathetic and sensible about Shad's illness. She tells me excitedly of the ball she is planning and how Shad must be well for it, and we discuss gowns and decorations. We kiss each other affectionately and with some difficulty, me from horseback and she on her high perch, before I hand my mare, who I have decided is to be called Cassandra, over to a groom.

Amelia and John run to tell Mrs Price of their great adventure and I enter the house. Outside the bedchamber I talk with Roberts, who has shaved and changed his shirt, but who looks weary and concerned.

'When the fever breaks, he'll do well, milady.'

'I hope so.'

I go through the study into the dressing room, not wanting to disturb Shad, and call for hot water. This dressing room is used mostly by Shad and his clothes are stored here. I open the linen press and run my fingertips over the crisp cotton of his shirts, the soft weave of his stockings, and lay my cheek against the supple smooth leather of his breeches; if I cannot touch him, I can touch what will lie next to his skin.

Then I shut the linen press doors, telling myself not to be so foolish, and what would I do if a servant were to walk in?

I have heard the front doorbell ring several times and, dressed and washed, and thankful that all I have to do to my hair is run a comb through it, I descend the stairs to greet my visitors in the drawing room.

My mother, red-eyed, surges forward to embrace me. 'My child, my child, *Widowed Before Her Time*!'

'He's not dead yet, ma'am,' I respond, aware of how

surly I sound, and how tired I feel. Furthermore, I see the distress on the faces of Carstairs and Marianne and Beresford, and about a dozen Trelaise family members whose names I can't recall.

I address the whole room. 'Shad runs a high fever still but I believe he is in no danger. And he's very bad-tempered, which I believe a good sign. I regret he refuses to receive anyone, but he is so hideous a sight you would not want to see him at the moment.'

After my announcement they smile and seem much relieved, as I am also. I order fresh tea and offer Madeira from the sideboard and attempt to remember who everyone is. To my surprise, it is Beresford who, with a surprising degree of tact, reminds me of people's names.

'Ann sends her best love, ma'am, and regrets she has another appointment, so she cannot call herself. You'll remember Cousin Maria, ma'am, my second cousin once removed to be precise; and this is Cousin Telford, a good fellow who can talk only of horses, is not that right, sir? I believe Shad bought a mare from him recently.'

'Oh, indeed, sir.' I shake his hand with great enthusiasm. 'She – Cassandra, I have named her – is perfectly splendid. My papa has a great interest in horseflesh too.'

'Now, Lady Shad, I've a perfectly good pair of greys if Mr Hayden or Shad is interested.'

'No, they aren't.' Beresford takes my arm. 'Mrs

Garrand and her daughters you already know, ma'am, and this is Captain Burge from my mother's side of the family. Do not play cards with this fellow, ma'am . . .'

And so I am absorbed into the bosom of the Trelaise family, who receive me with surprising warmth (apart from Mrs Garrand, who comports herself with icy formality) and are soon enough addressing me as Charlotte. We chat of the usual things – servant problems and town gossip – and I find myself agreeing to a visit to Vauxhall Pleasure Gardens that very evening with the family, for as everyone assures me, my health will be jeopardised if I do not take some fresh air.

'But Shad—' I say.

'Nonsense!' Beresford is all warmth and good humour and I understand, a little, why Ann loves him. 'You must come, my dear Charlotte. I insist upon it. Why, Ann will not give me a moment's peace if you do not.'

Shad

Charlotte tells me I'm not dying so often I think I probably am. She also insists that the hideous scabs that now adorn my person are a sign of returning health. Moreover, she has told my family I am getting better, and they have spent half the morning depleting the household's stock of wine and tea.

What does she know? She's only a woman, and not a particularly accomplished or well-educated one at that. She told me she liked to read, but I've never seen her with anything other than a fashion paper in her hand, like the one that has fallen to the floor while she sleeps. I suspect she has helped herself quite liberally to the Madeira while playing hostess.

'Don't scratch.' Her eyes are still closed but apparently she's not asleep.

Furthermore, my condition encourages her to bark

orders as though I'm her servant, while acting as my valet. And now, devil take it, she's pouring out yet another glass of that tasteless barley water. I long for a pot of ale. Soon she'll force gruel upon me again.

I wish she'd undress and get into bed with me. No! It's indecent. My own wife!

But if I am to die there are things I must tell her. 'Charlotte?'

'Chamber pot?'

'No. It's the Bastards.'

'You are not dying, sir. You do not need to summon family members for a deathbed scene.'

'I should have told you about them before.'

She frowns. 'You should have, sir, but they're nice children.'

'Amelia is my half-sister, one of my father's by-blows. John is my nephew, my brother's child.'

There is a long silence. I'm not sure she believes me.

I continue, 'I tried to tell you this after our wedding.'

'Oh, yes. You were interrupted by the arrival of your mistress. Or are you to tell me she was someone else's mistress?'

'As a matter of fact, yes.' Since I have been sworn to secrecy on the matter by Beresford I say no more on the subject. 'When I returned to England after Frederick died and I inherited the title, I learned of the Bastards' existence and sought them out. Amelia had been put into service by the parish when her mother left and was worked half to death and starving. And I found John half starved. How could I not take them in?'

She draws in one quick, painful breath. 'It was very good of you. Thank you for telling me, but I think you a fool for not telling me before.' She gives the bottle of lotion a vigorous shake. 'Pray remove your nightshirt.'

'Shameless seductress,' I murmur, purely to provoke her, pulling the nightshirt off. 'Charlotte, I am telling you the truth about Mrs Perkins.'

'Most amusing, sir.'

I yelp as a large blob of lotion lands cold on my back. I'm damned if I'll argue with her.

She works her way down my back and legs with an air of annoyance – I'm not sure how she conveys this by touch alone, but Charlotte can do it. Regrettably her touch also has the usual effect on me.

'You may turn over.'

'I'd best not, ma'am.'

'If you please.'

I do so.

'Oh.' She hesitates, bottle and cloth held aloft. 'I trust this does not happen when Roberts attends to you. He would be extremely embarrassed, I am sure.'

'No, ma'am, it does not, and a little less avid interest on your part would be becoming.'

'I am not avidly interested, sir. How could I sustain such a level of interest in so frequent a phenomenon?'

'Thank you, ma'am – ow!' Damn her, she drops a large blob of the cold lotion exactly where I feel it the most intensely. 'I think you'd best rub it in, Charlotte.'

'Don't be indecent. You may attend to it yourself.'

'And now, pray, ma'am, who is being indecent?'

Her lips twitch. I shall say this for Charlotte, as ill-tempered and sharp-tongued as she is, she does not bear a grudge for long. It is altogether remarkable, considering her trying family, that she possesses such generosity and good temper.

I try not to think that her generosity may extend beyond the marriage. It is time to mark my possession. I drop my hand to her skirts and tug.

'What are you about?' She does not sound particularly welcoming or aroused.

'I wish to claim my marital rights, ma'am.'

'In your condition, sir? I don't believe so.' Her laugh is mostly a contemptuous snort.

My hand has reached her garter. 'I'm inclined to agree, ma'am. Maybe you should take the uppermost role.'

'Roberts would be most distressed that you exert yourself at all.' I am pleased to hear now a certain breathlessness in her voice.

'Well, *I* shan't tell him. Pray lock the door.'

'Certainly not.' She pushes the cork into the bottle – somehow I find that extraordinarily arousing – and shoves my hand from her skirts.

'Then kiss me, at least.'

She lays the bottle and cloth aside, her gestures slow and deliberate.

I shiver and not with fever.

Her hands come to my face and she brushes her lips with mine. And again.

Our tongues touch and slide. I haul her on to the bed with me.

'I wish you were better,' she murmurs, hooking her leg over mine.

'You can make me so.'

The door opens.

'Beg your pardon, milord, milady.' Roberts, his face flaming scarlet, closes the door.

Charlotte buries her face in my neck, exploding into giggles. 'Poor Roberts. Oh, goodness, you are all bristles, Shad, and so hot.'

I rub my face against her hair. She smells of rosewater. I pull her against me more closely and close my eyes. *My wife, my Charlotte. My love*.

When I open my eyes next I am alone and it's evening. The lamps are lit and the room glows and pulsates; my fever has risen again.

The dressing room door opens, and Charlotte, dressed in a gown that shifts and shimmers between gold and grey in the lamplight, enters. She dips her head to avoid her ostrich feather headdress brushing against the doorway.

'Beg your pardon, ma'am. I fell asleep.'

'I know.' She seems to be waiting for me to say something else. 'Your family invited me to attend a party at Vauxhall tonight. I didn't want to go, but . . . how are you?'

I shrug. 'I think my fever has risen.'

She takes a towel from the washstand, dips it into water, and places it on my forehead. 'Roberts will sit with you until I return home. He'll bring you some gruel.'

'Better than Vauxhall ham and punch.'

She laughs, but there's a reserve about her.

'Who else is going tonight?'

'Ann and Beresford, Carstairs, Telford and his wife and daughter. Oh, Shad, I forgot to tell you I rode Cassandra – the mare you bought me – this morning. She is lovely. I'm sorry we couldn't have ridden together. And the children had an excellent time. Ann took them in her phaeton. They seem much happier for it.'

'Good.' I can't help but notice the change of subject. 'Take one of the footmen with you.'

She frowns. 'I don't think that's necessary, sir. Beresford and Ann will take me in their carriage and I shall be perfectly safe.'

'As you wish.' The thought strikes me that I should

get out of bed and follow her to see what she and Beresford get up to, but when I try, the room spins horribly and she grabs my arm to steady me.

'What's wrong, Shad?'

'Thought of something,' I mumble, shamed by the concern in her voice. 'Send Roberts.'

My attempt at delirium satisfies her – good God, what have I said these last couple of days? – and I settle back into bed.

Charlotte

As he fell asleep he said the words: *My wife, my Charlotte. My love.*

I don't know what to think except he cannot be in his right mind. He did seem to be speaking the truth about the Bastards, but there is still the matter of the dreadful Mrs Perkins, on which he either would or could not elaborate. And then he'd fallen asleep against me, his feverish head burning against my neck, his body hot (and undressed) against mine, my arms round him. He had not stirred when I disentangled myself; how I shall look Roberts in the eye, I do not know.

I dress myself in my newest and most alluring gown, and decide that if he mentions the episode, I shall discard the ostrich feather headdress (and more) and turn wanton with him (as his health allows). If not . . . well, I shall keep everything on and go to Vauxhall for I have promised Beresford and the rest that I shall attend.

I feel guilty when I see how ill he looks but I hardly think he will be of much use in performing any acts of wantonness, or even of talking coherently. I pray God the fever breaks soon.

I know Roberts will take excellent care of him, and I shall return home early (by *ton* standards) so that I may sit with him for the rest of the night. I must talk to someone about my fears and concerns, and who else but Ann, the person who knows me best in the world?

Charlotte

I always enjoy Vauxhall. I cannot help it – it is a vulgar place and I come from vulgarity. I love the hint of danger and disrepute that hangs over the place, the ease with which dukes and drabs mingle, the shoddy prettiness of the lantern-hung trees. Many attend masked; your dancing partner may be one of the highest in the land or, by day, an obsequious assistant from behind the counter at the draper's. Vauxhall casts its tawdry glamour, bestowing a magical charm over all who pay the admission and step inside the enchanted environs. Inside its walls you can find whatever you desire – dancing, entertainment, intrigue, spectacle – enough for a whole night.

Even the notoriously expensive refreshments, the paper-thin ham and weak punch, taste better than they should. The musicians always seem to play and sing in tune, and if they do not, well, what is the harm? We attend determined to be entertained and captivated, and so we are.

As soon as we are settled at a table Beresford orders punch, and, with a wink, produces a small flask, the contents of which improve matters greatly. To my dismay I do not sit with Ann as I had hoped. I am with my mama and papa and George, who has invited himself along. My father has found a kindred spirit in Cousin Telford, and the two of them immediately start trying to sell each other horses. My mother fans herself and sighs gustily but is cheerful in her way, particularly after a few glasses of punch.

The tables are set in painted boxes forming a theatre, with the dancing area where the pit would be and musicians on the stage at the end. Already couples leave the tables to form sets as the musicians tune. Above our heads, a tightrope promises other entertainment to come.

'I'd ask you to dance, Lottie, but you'd look a fright dancing with your own brother,' George says, helping himself to punch.

'Most obliging of you, brother, but I shan't care.' I tug him to his feet and drag him out to join the other dancers despite his protests. The music begins as we take our places.

I'm still wondering about Shad's mistress, or whoever's mistress she might be – why, even Ann doubted he had time to have a mistress in town. So I decide to ask George, who always manages to give the impression that he is a man of the world. Besides, Beresford, who with Ann forms the next couple, may know.

'George, you mentioned the other day—' He treads on my foot and turns me the wrong way. 'Do have a care. You told me that Shad looked for a mistress.'

'Did I? Oh yes, sniffing after actresses. Don't worry, sister, everyone does that.'

'They do?'

'Of course.'

I grab his sleeve to prevent further disruption to the dance. 'To your right, George. What do you know of Mrs Perkins?'

'Who?'

'Mrs Perkins. I can't remember her Christian name. She's a courtesan.'

'Oh, Jenny Perkins.'

We break hands and stand aside to let Beresford and Ann chassée between us, turn, and thus progress up the set.

'Yes, Jenny Perkins – have a care, Beresford, you're meant to turn round me, so.' I shove him into position as Ann giggles. What is wrong with these men, who surely have had as many dancing lessons as we, that they turn into such fools when they stand up?

My brother stands still for some reason, possibly to think hard, for he has trouble doing two things at once unless they are of a crude nature (scratching and belching, for instance). His immobility is problematic, since we are supposed to be linking hands in a circle now with Ann and Beresford. Someone else bumps into him, we all apologise, and sort ourselves out.

Beresford takes my hand. 'Lady Shad, I must talk with you. No more,' he mutters. 'Not now. After the dance.'

'But—'

My brother takes my other hand and swings me away. 'Ssh!'

'What? Why?'

'So how does Shad?' my brother continues with hearty male tact. 'Devilish bad-tempered, so Beresford said.'

'He is quite ill but the family insisted I come out tonight. Shad thought I should, too.' To my annoyance I sound defensive.

'That's right, enjoy yourself before you're in whelp and as great as a house.' My ever-delicate brother treads on my foot once more. 'Beg your pardon, Lottie. We have a bet as to who'll get with child first, you or Lady Ann.'

'Who does?'

'Oh, everyone. All the fellows at the club. It's great sport, I tell you. My money's on you although you married after Ann. You have the bigger arse. Built for it, I'd say.'

'Don't be obscene.'

'Besides, there's the evidence that Shad has—'

I interrupt him. Having learned the truth about John and Amelia, I don't want to hear vulgarities regarding their parentage; it is a subject that makes me strangely protective, of Shad as well as the children. 'Oh, George, look at that tightrope dancer. She's wearing tights!'

Sure enough, George turns to stare and is quite distracted, looking over his shoulder when he is turned away, and his dancing becomes even worse.

Now and again I catch Beresford's gaze on me, and he too performs abysmally, stepping on Ann's feet, blundering into strangers, and offering effusive apologies that somehow make it worse. He also, like my brother, is extremely interested in the tightrope dancer, who might as well be naked for all the coverage her costume affords.

'She's fat!' Ann sounds outraged.

'The men don't seem to mind.' The dancer slides into the splits on the rope with a coy smile. 'Besides, could you do that?'

'Dear me, no. She definitely has the advantage,' Ann murmurs.

The dance comes to an end, we curtsy, and the gentlemen bow and turn their full attention to the fat woman on the tightrope.

All of them, that is, except for Beresford, who makes his way to my side. 'A word, Lady Shad.'

'Certainly.' I expect to sit next to him at our table, but he draws me aside.

'We'll take a stroll,' he says and leads me away down one of the gravel walks.

'Is something wrong?' I'm afraid that he may ask my advice on the problems of his marriage bed.

'Yes, there is. What the devil do you mean by talking about Mrs Perkins before my wife?'

'But—' Then I remember what Shad said, or rather implied. She was someone else's mistress. 'Sir, she is your mistress?'

'Sssh!' He looks around guiltily as though Ann spies on us. 'She was, ma'am, but no longer. However, Ann is so delicate a creature – I'm sure you understand.'

'Ann is a delicate creature? What about me, sir? That woman came to our house the morning after our wedding to be paid off!'

He stops and scratches his head. It's on the tip of my tongue, after dealing with Shad, to tell him not to scratch, but I restrain myself. 'You mean,' he says in bewilderment, 'you thought she was Shad's mistress?'

'What else would I think, sir? Why did she apply to Shad for the money she was owed?'

He shrugs with a boyish grin that I imagine has got him out of many a scrape unscathed. But not this one. 'Well, you see, ma'am, I asked Shad if he'd tidy up a few odds and ends for me when Ann and I went out of town. He must have forgotten. Besides, he could have told you. Can't think why he didn't.'

I'm inclined to agree with him – it would have saved a great deal of trouble. 'I hardly think you can blame Shad for this. Possibly he was silent from loyalty to you.'

Beresford is having trouble maintaining the boyish grin and careless attitude. 'Well, I daresay he thought you might blab to Ann, for you're as thick as thieves. Now I think of it, I did remember asking him to be discreet about it, or some such.'

'Ann and I are friends, sir, but that does not mean I would share information with her that would injure her. Neither do we ask each other to – to do each other's dirty work.' No, but Ann will hint and look helpless and I will jump in and rescue her.

'I've done a few favours for Shad,' he says.

'Indeed.' I don't want to hear about what these favours might be. 'How very loyal of you, my lord. I believe you assist him in the search for a mistress.'

'You are mistaken, ma'am.' This is said with such lofty disdain I am sure he is lying.

'And I suppose Ann would not want to hear of that, either.'

He turns and lays a hand on my arm. I am aware that we have progressed beyond the well-lit public area. Hushed voices, furtive movements beyond the pathway, and the rustle of bushes speak of illicit intrigues. 'I'm sure you don't mean to threaten me, ma'am. Let us think of it as a misunderstanding between friends, eh?'

I look at his hand on my arm. 'Very well, but Ann is my friend. I will not injure her, and I hope you shall not either.'

'Of course, Lady Shadderly. But you're in no position to condemn a fellow for former indiscretions. I know your little secret.'

'What little secret?' For one horrible moment I wonder if he knows of the journey I made with Ann to see her daughter and somehow he thinks it is I who am the mother of an illegitimate child.

'That you harbour a *tendresse* for me.'

'Oh!' I gasp, horrified. 'For you! What are you thinking, sir? I have never given you the slightest encouragement!'

He smirks. 'I'm aware that fashionable females deny such attraction. Your secret is safe with me, I assure you.'

'I've had enough. You, sir, are an idiot and I am sorry Ann married you.'

He laughs in a foolish, good-natured way. 'Deny it all you wish, Lady Shad, but you came quite willingly to this spot alone with me.'

'Shad would kill you if he knew.'

'But he won't know, will he?'

Beresford must be drunk, for he sat next to the punchbowl and I noticed he helped himself liberally. But this is Beresford, friendly, slightly stupid, well-meaning Beresford, Shad's friend and Ann's husband, who is no threat to me.

However, I shall not take any chances. I kick him in the shin as hard as I can and he releases me. 'Now, Lady Shad, there's no need—'

I turn, and collide with a couple emerging from the greenery. The woman shrieks and raises her fan to protect herself, smacking me in the mouth. We make mutual apologies and I turn away to meet a familiar and unwelcome personage, Mr Harry Dunbury, the gossip hack. Well, I suppose it his business to turn up where he is not wanted.

He bows. 'A very good evening to you, Lady Shadderly. Lord Beresford, your servant, sir. How is Lord Shadderly, ma'am? I hear he is unwell, and I am most sorry.'

'His poxes improve by the day,' I say. 'He should be well soon.'

There's a loud crack and flash from overhead. Fireworks. I take advantage of the distraction to pick up my skirts and run, dodging others who saunter slowly down the path, and meet the rest of our party. I am greatly relieved. They tell me they are going to find a better spot than our box to watch the fireworks.

Ann takes my arm. 'Where have you been?'

'I met someone I knew – my dressmaker,' I improvise wildly. 'And we talked and I—'

Ann frowns. 'What happened to your face?' She produces one of her dainty handkerchiefs, and dabs at my lip. 'You've bled a little.'

'Someone bumped into me. An accident.' I'm babbling like a fool and out of breath. 'Please call on me tomorrow. I must talk with you. Or I could call on you and help you with your preparations for the ball. But now I think I should go home.'

'Oh, Charlotte, I'm sorry. I'll ask Beresford to call the carriage.'

'No! That is, I do not wish to break up the party. George can escort me.'

'If I must, I shall,' says my gallant brother. 'Are you ready to leave?'

'Go away. I'm talking to Ann.'

'Of course, Lady Shadderly.' My brother performs an elaborate bow. 'Where is Beresford, anyway?'

'Here, my dear fellow.' Beresford is followed by a waiter, bearing a tray with glasses and bottles of champagne. 'I sought out some more refreshments for us.'

I make my farewells to everyone, my mother waxing dramatic as usual, and George accompanies me to the entrance. 'What's the matter, Lottie?'

'I don't know what you mean.'

He waves to get the attention of a hackney carriage driver. 'You disappear, so does Beresford. Fortunately Ann didn't notice. Don't come between them.'

'Between whom?'

He hands me into the carriage and ducks his head as he follows me inside. 'Shad and Beresford, of course. Provoke Shad and he'll have to call Beresford, his best friend, out. He'll never forgive you.'

'Oh, don't be ridiculous. What do you think I was doing?'

'Be careful, Lottie.' He puts his booted feet on the

seat next to me and whistles tunelessly through his teeth.

'I'm sorry you had to leave early.'

'Doesn't matter. I'd rather go to the club and see the fellows. Vauxhall's a bit of a bore, isn't it?'

I make a noncommittal reply as the hackney bumps its way back home.

My brother breaks the silence that has fallen. 'Do you think all is well with Ma?'

'With Mama?'

'She got Ann and you married off one after the other. I think she's lonely and Pa's no help. All he's good for is buying horseflesh and selling it at a loss.'

'She seems much the same to me.'

'Call on her, Lottie. Take her shopping or whatever women do together. Otherwise she sits at home and broods with the cordial bottle.'

'Very well.' To tell the truth, I'm not over-concerned about my mother. Was not her aim in life to have me make a brilliant match? 'But, George, you're living at home. Why don't you take her shopping?'

He offers a fearful grimace in reply. It's a pity he cannot take my mother to Jackson's or any other of his disreputable haunts. I can imagine her making sonorous pronouncements as the cream of the male members of the *ton* beat each other black and blue. Besides, I'm anxious to get home, where Shad is.

Shad's house is my home. It has not felt like it until this moment. My husband waits for me at home. I feel as though I roll a delicious sweetmeat around my mouth, anticipating the moment when I shall bite into it.

The carriage draws up at our house and I fairly leap out of it. Manners demand that I should invite my brother inside, but we are used to mutual incivility.

I rush inside the house – I wonder if our footman thinks I need the water closet – and up the stairs. I unfasten my cloak and let it fall, the satin drifting on to the wooden floor like a great dark blue feather.

As I open the door to the bedchamber, Shad stirs beneath the covers. Roberts, who is sitting at the bedside, stands and bows.

'You're home early, milady.'

I stand inside the doorway, beyond the light, so he cannot see my bruised lip. 'I am. You may go downstairs, Roberts. I'll see his lordship settled for the night.'

'Very well, milady.' He murmurs to me, 'His fever still runs high, but I think he feels better in himself. Very bad-tempered, still.'

Shad pushes himself up on to one elbow as Roberts leaves the room. 'What do you want, Charlotte?'

'I've been to Vauxhall.'

'I know. Why did you come home so early?'

'Because I wanted to be where you are. This is my home and I love you.'

There, I've said it. It comes as a great surprise, a huge release as though something has confined me until this moment. I don't even care if he does not say he loves me in return, or if he says nothing at all.

He stares at me, his eyes bright with fever. His face is covered with poxes in various states, and the beginnings of a copious black beard. He does not look handsome at the moment. He looks merely ill. Ill but alive, still.

'Very good. Turn.'

I turn.

He pulls at the tapes that fasten my gown at the back and it falls to my ankles in a rush of silk.

Apparently he's more alive than I thought.

'So,' he says. 'Keep the ostrich feathers on. The stockings and garters, too. Everything else may go.'

I open my mouth to say his demands are indecent but he speaks first. 'And I love you, too. I'm not sure why, but devil take it, I'm stuck with you, Charlotte.'

Oh, thank God.

And then commonsense rears its ugly head as he tumbles me on to the bed and continues to make his intentions clear. 'I don't believe this is a good idea for a man in your condition.'

'Nonsense. I believe any physician would advise me to balance the humours.'

'Like this?'

He looks up from where – well, where he is, although I have discovered his bristles to be no bad thing under the circumstances, and says, 'Absolutely. Would you like me to stop?'

'I believe a physician would recommend a blood-letting.'

He says something exceedingly vulgar about a leech and an ostrich feather snaps.

'I need a maid,' I say with excessive stupidity.

'Exactly at this moment? What would you like her to do?'

'Withers left when we thought you had smallpox.'

'The Almighty works in mysterious ways. Get on top of me, girl.'

'Why?'

'Because . . .' He brings his appalling bristly face to mine. His lips are chapped from the fever and his body is hot, so hot, and rough from the infamous one hundred and seventy-five poxes. His mouth is hot too but not unpleasantly so.

'Because I must conserve my strength; don't look so shocked, Charlotte, the Church of England recommends this position, except during Lent of course. It's somewhere in the Prayer Book, I believe.'

'Oh, certainly.'

The position has a particularly jolly air about it – I am inevitably reminded of riding astride my brothers' ponies in childhood, in the beginning at least, and then I'm not reminded of anything at all, for the moment and Shad drive everything else from my mind.

And as I come to myself I realise his chest beneath my cheek – hard, bony, rough – is also cool and wet.

Nature, it appears, has effected a cure. 'Your fever has broken!'

He is in the extraordinarily flattened, limp state he assumes after performing our Marital Relations, even though this time I was the one who made the greater exertions. 'Mmm.' He raises one hand to scratch at his beard. 'Don't say it.'

'What?'

'You're about to tell me to stop scratching.'

I remove myself from his person. The bed is a mess of tangled, smelly sheets. 'Maybe we should ask Roberts to have the sheets changed.'

'No, we'll make them smellier in a little while.' He yawns.

'Shad, when did you fall in love with me? Or become stuck with me, as you so elegantly put it?'

'Let's see.' He considers. 'When you were drunk and fell down those steps at my sister's party, perhaps. I don't know, Charlotte. When you almost said you loved me but told me instead you loved your horse. You crept up on me like moss. In a good way, that is.' He closes his eyes and mumbles something about half an hour, then turns and falls asleep against me, his face against my neck.

'I love you,' I whisper into his ear.

He's fast asleep and doesn't reply. It doesn't matter.

I remove the ruins of my headdress, pick out a garter from beneath me – heaven only knows where the other is – and put my arm round him, pulling the smelly bedclothes over us both. So this is love, this need to shelter and find shelter; to be with the one person of whom you will never tire and whose infinite quirks and thoughts and actions become a part of yours.

Shad

It's a miracle. I am whole, if spotted.

Roberts, with extreme embarrassment (it must have been he who drew the bedcurtains on our scene of depravity during the night) urges me out of the bed to change the sheets, much the worse for wear, thanks to my excessive sweating and Charlotte's efforts last night.

She, it appears, rose some hours ago to send notes to relatives that I am well, or becoming so, which means another influx of visitors when all I want to do is be alone with her. I want to talk with her, to learn about her. We shall leave London as soon as possible for a real honeymoon. What a fool I was to think she considered adultery with Beresford or that she loves anyone but me.

Washed, decently clad in a clean nightshirt, and tucked between sheets that carry the faintest scent of a hot iron, I am served breakfast and joined by John and Amelia who fling themselves on me with great enthusiasm.

I regard the boiled egg and toast that comprise my breakfast with somewhat less enthusiasm.

'Aunt Shad says you are to eat it all,' Amelia says.

'It is a country egg from our ducks,' John informs me. 'Sir, you have scabs coming off your beard.'

'Thank you, John. Where is your Aunt Shad?'

'She is talking to the housekeeper.'

'Ah.' Doubtless she plans to allow the family to spend the entire day eating and drinking. 'Who would like the top of the egg?'

'I would, sir!' they both chorus and share the delicacy. I cannot understand why the top of a boiled egg is considered so desirable, but remember my brother and me clamouring for the same from our father in one of his rare good moods.

Amelia cuts my toast into strips and dips one into the egg yolk. 'Uncle, it is most important that you eat and get well.'

I'm intrigued by my children's attempts to look after me and assure them that I am capable of feeding myself. I am glad that they do not recoil from my appearance in horror; John, in fact, seems quite fascinated by my condition and offers to help me remove scabs. I turn down his kindly offer and they tell me of events below stairs and a new litter of kittens that has arrived in the stables.

After they leave I fall asleep, much to my surprise.

I am awakened by something of a commotion in the dressing room, footsteps going to and fro, the slosh of water, and the sounds of voices.

Charlotte enters the bedchamber. She sports a long linen apron and a glint in her eye. 'You are to have a bath, sir.'

'Am I, indeed?' I consider this new, officious person I have married. 'And you are to supervise my bathing?'

'Yes, sir. You stink.' She turns her head to glance at the activities in the dressing room and bellows, 'Mop that up immediately!'

I see resistance is futile. She insists on helping me from the bed and I reject her arm and then wish I had taken it by the time I reach the doorway to the dressing room. I grasp the wood of the doorway as though I have to discover sea legs on land.

'I told you so.' She takes my arm and this time I allow it.

'You are the most annoying and provoking woman and I have no idea why I love you,' I retort. 'I can bathe alone, Charlotte.'

'Nonsense.' She tugs at the hem of my nightshirt.

'I can do that – you know, ma'am, giggling under the circumstances, and in such a lascivious way, is most unbecoming. What of your wifely modesty?'

'What of yours? Your husbandly modesty, that is. Have you no shame, sir? You are supposed to be *ill*.'

'I am. I have been. It's a sign of returning health.' I

climb into the water as fast as I can. 'Besides, removing my clothing is improper behaviour on your part.'

She rolls her eyes. 'Next you will say your condition will subside on its own.'

'You could help.'

Her response is to pour a jugful of hot water over my head and then wash my head with great vigour, using some herbal concoction that her family swears by, so she says. Since the Haydens are not famous for the beauty of their hair, I suspect the stuff is a legacy from their livery stables days and formerly used on the stock.

I can't believe I thought this woman plain. Even with dark shadows beneath her eyes and wearing a plain gown and plainer apron she is desirable to me. I gaze at the length of her neck, the elegant jut of her collarbone, the fascinating wisps of hair at the nape of her neck, her slender fingers. And her scent, a blend of womanly sweat (for she scrubs me down like an efficient groom), rosewater, smoke from the fire and wax (from sealing her letters, I suppose).

Her mouth interests me greatly, the turn and shape of her lip.

'Did I do that to you?' I touch the flaw on her lip, a slight puffiness. 'I'm sorry.'

She shakes her head. 'No. A branch at Vauxhall sprang back into my face. It is nothing.'

A doubt creeps into my mind. I dispel it. If she were to lie, would she not blame it on me?

'Tell me about yourself.' A strange thing for a husband to ask a wife.

'Well.' She sits back on her heels, wiping her hands dry on the apron. 'There is little to tell. I'm ordinary enough. Whatever my family has told you is probably untrue, particularly the bit about coming over with William the Conqueror. My grandfather on Papa's side had a livery stable and married an heiress whose fortune was made in the china business. We have some money but no breeding. I have an eye for a horse and can mend a broken cup and paint a plain one. I had an education you would probably find laughable at an establishment to make young ladies more genteel. And Ann is my best friend.'

'Am I not your best friend?'

'No. You're my husband. Now you must tell me about yourself. Lift your foot out so I may wash it.'

I do as I am bid. 'I— my God, Charlotte, don't tickle me.'

'You're ticklish?' She looks up with a calculating grin.

'I have been a fiendish tickler in my time. I shall have revenge if you persist. So, my life story. I went into the Navy when I was fourteen, and left after ten years with the rank of Captain, when my brother died and I inherited the title and lands.'

'Your ship was the *Arcturus*, I know. Roberts showed me the carvings your crew made when you left. And?'

'There's little else.' I withdraw my foot.

She rummages around in the cloudy water and pulls out my other foot with a great surge of soapy water. 'Tell me about your mother and father and brother.'

I'm silent. I find the touch of her fingers on my toes extraordinarily arousing in a drowsy, sleepy sort of way. My eyes close. 'My father loved us in his way, I think. He was not a kind man. He wore my mother down with his infidelities and bullying. She died when I was ten. I was at school. They took me from my classroom – we were parsing Virgil – and told me she was dead. I could not weep for the other boys would have thought me unmanly. My father died when I was abroad, some five years ago, and my brother's death, as you know, came about suddenly two years ago, and so I inherited the title. They left me with many responsibilities, including John and Amelia.'

She strokes my foot, silent.

I continue, 'I want to take you to the estate in Suffolk. I hope you'll like it. The skies are huge, like the roof of a cathedral. The house is old but it's in good repair now and you'll meet my tenants.'

'You know, Shad, you really don't come up to snuff for a wicked rake. I find you distressingly dutiful and responsible. I'm almost disappointed John and Amelia are not your children.'

I open my eyes. 'I've been most careful not to produce unwanted children.'

'Indeed. With whom?'

'Oh, no one for some time. Come here.' It's time to distract her and by the time I have finished distracting her she is almost as wet as I and her lips are thoroughly red and swollen.

'You are wicked,' she pronounces. 'Now you must get dry and go to bed.'

'With you?'

'Certainly not. You should rest. Ann is coming to drink tea with me.'

She swabs me off as though I am a horse, employing a brisk swatting technique with the towel on my arousal, and leads me back to bed.

Thoroughly exhausted, I fall asleep again.

Charlotte

Ann arrives accompanied by a young woman I do not know. She's as well dressed as Ann or I, but her deferential manner and modestly lowered eyes suggest she's a servant. 'This is Betty Tillyard, cousin to my maid, who is in need of a position. You mentioned you had sacked your maid.'

I open my mouth to correct Ann; the dreadful Withers had run from the house without my assistance, but Ann shakes her head. I see her point; this Betty Tillyard may not want to join a household where servants leave after a few days.

I ask her who she worked for and read the letters of

reference she produces from her reticule. Betty Tillyard is a paragon of all the virtues: industrious, respectful, quiet, and skilled with cleaning and mending clothes, and dressing hair. In contrast to Withers she has a sweet, ready smile. 'I left my last position because Lord Harrington's dog made me sneeze all day, and Lady Harrington said either the dog or I must go, milady, and his lordship would not hear of the dog being sent away.'

I express myself satisfied and offer her the position. I then turn her over to Roberts to negotiate a salary and arrange for her box to be brought from her lodgings, and thank Ann.

'Oh, I think she'll do well enough,' Ann says in response to my effusive thanks. 'What are those awful stains on your gown? If she can remove those she'll be worth double her salary.'

I glance down. 'Oh, that's the stuff we put on Shad's poxes.'

'Couldn't Roberts have done that?'

'Some of the time he did.'

'That's dreadful,' Ann says. 'You look tired, Charlotte. Were you at his bedside all last night after you returned home?'

'Yes.' So I was, when I wasn't in his bed. 'But he is much recovered today. I am so glad to see you, although we may not have much time together. I fear the entire Trelaise family will descend upon the house soon.'

We drink tea and she tells me in great detail of the preparations for her ball, and then she asks why it was I wanted to see her. I can barely remember, except that in my agitation I wanted comfort; thinking of it since, I am not likely to tell her that her husband had a mistress (she may already know) or that he insulted me.

'No particular reason. I miss you, Ann. I like to have you to myself, now and again.' I find myself blushing. 'Shad and I are in love.'

'Indeed?'

'Yes, and Ann, the Bastards are not his. Of course they are not, for he has been at sea all this while. They are his illegitimate nephew and half-sister.'

'You didn't know that?'

'You mean it was common knowledge? I feel like such a fool.'

'Certainly among the family.' She gazes at me quite calmly as though I am an idiot, which I suppose I am. 'I am very glad Shad is better.'

'His fever broke last night.' A blush creeps over my face as I remember the exact circumstances. 'Ann, what do you intend to do about Emma?'

'Sssh!' She looks around wildly as though her husband's spies hide behind the curtains or up the chimney. 'I cannot tell Beresford. He would—'

'Of course you do not want to tell him. But consider what you will do when she is grown. Surely you would want her to have the advantages of education and the opportunity to make a sensible match? Shad is hiring a tutor for the Bastards – I really must stop calling them that, it's unpleasant – and maybe—'

'No! Charlotte, I know you mean well, but—'

I plough on relentlessly. 'She will not be a baby forever. When she is weaned, shall you leave her with Mrs Pyle?'

She shakes her head.

I continue, 'Why do I not ask Shad if he knows of a family on his estate who could raise Emma? I would not betray your confidence, I promise. She would receive an education and you would be able to see her. Please, Ann, think about it.'

'If you are my friend, you will talk of it no more.' The inevitable tears brim at her eyes and the uncharitable thought crosses my mind that Ann can produce them at will.

'Very well. But since I am your friend I want only the best for you and your daughter.'

'I know.' She sniffs. 'I am glad Shad is getting well, although I suppose this means you will have to resume your wifely duties.'

As I try to think of a suitable reply, the drawing-room door opens to admit Beresford, who bounds into the room like a large friendly dog, followed more decorously by Carstairs and Marianne Shillington. I am glad others are there and I do not have to receive Beresford alone. He is affable enough but does not meet my eyes and I hope Ann does not notice.

I send all three of them upstairs to visit Shad, and turn to Ann. 'I am glad we have had this time to talk alone. I miss your company now we are both married.'

'I, too.' She stares away from me as she says this, and I am saddened that Ann, whom I used to know and love, does not trust me as much as I had hoped. Part of me hoped that now we were both married, we would once again be close; but was our intimacy merely an illusion? She kept her greatest secret from me when I thought we were the best friends in the world.

She stands and ties her bonnet in place. 'I must go.'

'You shan't wait for Beresford? Or stay, please do. I'll have the house full of family for the rest of the day, and I should like to have you there so we can laugh about them together.'

'Thank you, but I must return home. I have so much to do with the ball and I am sure something will have been mishandled while I am away.'

After Ann has left, I meet Marianne on her way downstairs. 'My dear, it is becoming a male club upstairs. They have just sent Roberts for ale, so I thought it politic to leave. I am glad to see Shad recovered, although I suggest you rescue him before long.'

I invite her to drink tea with me, but she has to return home to see to domestic duties. 'You plan to attend the Beresfords' ball the day after tomorrow? You should if Shad is recovered enough to shave – I cannot decide whether he looks more like a wolf or a bear.'

I peer round the bedchamber door. All three men are sprawled on the bed with glasses and a jug of ale, talking with great animation of politics. They ignore me. Downstairs the front doorbell jangles. I change into a clean gown, or at this point a cleaner one, and descend to meet the next round of visitors.

And so it continues, all day long, I entertaining the majority of guests in the drawing room while the carousing continues upstairs. At about four of the afternoon, Shad has the sense to discharge Beresford, and Carstairs from the bedchamber so he may rest. I declare myself not at home for the remainder of the day and join my exhausted husband.

To tell the truth, he is not as enervated as I might have expected.

So, bliss. All is well. We are in love. Nothing shall destroy our happiness.

'A shave is a wondrous thing,' Shad says. He stands in the dressing room in that peculiar stance of a shaving man, feet spread, head tilted, and making curious grimaces in the mirror. He shakes foam from the razor and applies it to his neck.

Tilly, my new maid, giggles. She giggles at most things, particularly anything Shad says, and I suspect she's a little in love with him. 'Carmine for your lips, milady?'

'Milady does not need carmine,' Shad replies. 'I'll kiss her lips to redden them. Will that suffice, Tilly?'

'Sir!' I feign shock, although delighted by the idea.

Tilly giggles. 'Which stockings for milady?'

'The ones with scarlet clocking? Or the ones with gold thread? I don't know, Tilly. You choose.' In truth, I'm busy watching Shad. There's nothing so lovely as watching someone who's unaware of your observance perform a simple everyday act, particularly when that person is your husband, and you know what lies beneath the pristine cotton shirt, the silk breeches. His cuffs are unbuttoned and rolled to reveal his forearms – I note a new pink scar or two from his chickenpox – and I think with pride that I am the only woman who sees him so.

He bends to splash water on his face, the baggy seat of his breeches tightening as he bends (and of course they are fashionably tight in front in a most delightful and revealing way).

He reaches for a towel and buries his face in it; then, as though feeling my gaze, looks up and smiles. He watches with appreciation as I roll a stocking up.

'I'm not sure I'm well enough to attend the Beresfords' ball,' he says in a thoughtful way. He uncorks a bottle and tips a little of the lotion, witch hazel and lemon, into his palms, and anoints his freshly shaven face.

'Nonsense.' We both know he'll be the one to roll my stockings off later. 'I want to go. It will be the event of the season. But if you feel weak, we can leave early and I'll order you gruel when we return home.'

'You're too kind, ma'am.' He pauses in the act of tying his neckcloth. 'Where's my waistcoat?'

'On the bed. It's nice to see your face again, Shad.'

He runs a hand over his chin. 'I looked like a ruffian.'

'You looked worse as a spotted ruffian.'

He nods and saunters over to the bed. 'You look very pretty, Lottie, but is there a gown to go over that?'

'Also on the bed – please have a care, Tilly spent a long time ironing it.'

He stretches out on the bed and reaches for the newspaper.

Tilly snatches the gown from the bed before he pushes it aside with his foot, and drops it over my head. I spend a little time fighting my way through the folds; the gown has three layers, silk and gauze and net, festooned with twists of fine gold wire. I am afraid something will break if I push my way through too fast.

When I emerge Shad has changed his attitude on the bed completely, from a man at rest to a sort of dangerous alertness. If he were a dog he'd be twitching with his ears cocked. Tilly feels it too – she glances at him, then at me, then moves behind me to tie the laces of my gown.

'Send her out,' Shad says, his voice tight.

Tilly curtsies and runs from the room, pausing only to snatch my discarded afternoon gown and stockings.

'What's wrong?'

He looks at me and then at the newspaper in his hand. 'You are discovered, ma'am.'

'What do you mean?'

He stands and holds out the newspaper. He points to a paragraph.

> The secluded walks of Vauxhall Gardens recently saw an assignation between the Earl of B— and the crop-haired Lady S—, whose precipitous

> marriage to Viscount S— raised many a well-bred eyebrow. Blushing from an adulterous embrace, Lady S— was good enough to inform your humble servant that his lordship takes the cure for the p–x; doubtless many ladies of the night and of the *ton*, protesting innocence in the matter, wish his lordship a speedy recovery.

'I said chickenpox! I swear it! At least, I think I did . . .' I trail off to a miserable conclusion, shocked by the contempt on Shad's face. 'It's not true.'

'So you were not alone with Beresford in one of Vauxhall's secluded walks?'

'He asked me to accompany him. I could not very well refuse.'

'I see.' He tosses the newspaper aside. 'You have lied to me all this time.'

'Shad, I love you, not Beresford, and I have never lied to you!'

'Indeed.' He steps aside as I reach out a hand to him and shrugs into his coat. 'Your jewels, ma'am. We shall leave soon.'

My hands tremble as I reach for the heavy, old-fashioned family heirlooms. I fumble with the catch of the necklace and make several attempts to thread the wires of the earrings through my ears. Meanwhile Shad stands and regards me with cold indifference, as though I am a stranger.

'And your lip? He did that?'

I've told him I have never lied to him. It's not quite true, for I lied my head off regarding the visit to Emma. So I tell him the truth in a blundering, stupid sort of way. 'No. That is, it would not have happened if . . . I bumped into someone.'

He's quite still but I sense a surge of violence in his being that he keeps under control only by the greatest effort.

'Do you take me for a fool, ma'am?' He takes one step towards me.

I shake my head, no. 'I was alone with Beresford because . . . because I found out Mrs Perkins was his mistress and he was afraid Ann would overhear and . . .' I stumble to a halt as I see the contempt on his face. He doesn't believe me.

He watches as I fumble my feet into gold slippers and slip the silk loop of my fan over my wrist and place the gold headband with silk flowers on my hair. With the greatest politeness he places my cloak on to my shoulders.

Outside the bedchamber Roberts awaits with his master's cloak, and we make our way downstairs and outside into the damp smokiness of a London evening, and into our carriage.

Shad does not say a word but stares out of the window. I stare at him with a sick helplessness. I know what is to come, and there is nothing I can do to prevent it. My brother warned me, but already then it was too late.

I pray for the traffic to be so bad we must return home; or maybe Beresford has caught chickenpox, or we break an axle, or . . . but it is no use. In what seems a remarkably short time we arrive at the Beresfords' house. Carriages stand outside disgorging their fashionable occupants, and as I watch Marianne and her husband ascend the steps to the door. She releases her train now she is out of the muck of the street and turns her head to say something to her husband.

Our coachman waits for a carriage in front of us to draw away and we jolt forward a few yards and come to a halt. As though I could extend time, I take great notice of the small actions that comprise our arrival. Our footman, who rode with the coachman, comes to open our door and lower the steps. Shad stands – his face is close to mine for an instant and I breathe in the scent of lemon and witch hazel before, with a rustle of silk, he brushes past me and out of the carriage.

He holds his hand out to me. 'Please, let me explain,' I whisper, far, far too late.

Maybe he doesn't hear me. He shows no reaction at all.

I place my hand in his, hold up my skirts to protect them from the dirt of the pavement, and descend.

So. We take the stone steps, pass between the tall pillars of the portico, and enter the house through the open front door. Our footman takes our cloaks and disappears into the depths of the house with them. A crowd of people mills around in the hall, on their way to the ballroom – a vast cavern of a place, according to Ann, and musty and dusty; she has had a devil of a time (not that she would ever use such a term) making the place clean. She's told me how Beresford's steward (for his house is large and grand enough to justify this position) has hired extra footmen and china and glass and all the rest of it. But she is convinced it will look splendid, and most important, she has a new gown she wishes me to see; how I wish this was an evening where I could concentrate only on these trivialities.

Shad tugs me forward as I linger. I debate whether I should express an interest in visiting the ladies' withdrawing room, but discard the idea. Shad may think I'm afraid of what is to come. Even here, as guests prepare for their grand entry, are there some sidelong glances and whispers, or do I imagine it?

Marianne and Mr Shillington are ahead of us, and they pause as Shad and I approach. Marianne looks at me, or rather through me, as though I do not exist, but bows her head in her brother's direction with a slight smile.

My footsteps falter and once again Shad urges me on. The crowd slows down. Ahead of us a footman announces guests, red-faced with the effort of bellowing to be heard above the conversations that take place all around. Ann and Beresford greet their guests just inside the ballroom, a glowing vault filled with flowers in pots and wreaths and hundreds of wax candles. I can smell perfume and sweat and the scent of crushed flowers mixed with those of spilled wine and baking and roasting, and we move along borne on a tide of fashionable people.

Shad waves the footman away and for a moment I think everything will be well. Ann beams at me and Beresford is his usual jolly self; they have not read the paper. But other people have; I hear a snigger, a muttered aside, an exhortation to watch what will happen now, for there will be some good sport.

Beresford's expression turns from good humour to perplexity as he sees the cool, set look on Shad's face.

'Why, Shad, we won't stand on formality, my dear fellow!' Beresford tries to clap him on the shoulder. I can imagine Shad's face as he hears this and I have to give Beresford credit for attempting to soothe his savage demeanour; or perhaps Beresford is merely being stupid.

At any rate, so fast I am barely aware Shad has moved, Beresford staggers back and would have fallen if a footman had not caught him, and I realise Shad has hit him.

Ann stares at him, and then at me, in horror. She starts to come to my side, but Beresford, now recovered, puts out a restraining arm.

'What the devil's the matter, Shad?'

'You have insulted my wife and my name. Send your friends to me, sir.' He turns on his heel to face me. 'Home, ma'am.'

Shad's gaze shifts over my shoulder and he darts past me. 'You despicable cur!'

The crowd breaks and jostles as Shad swings his arm back and hits Mr Harry Dunbury, who lands sprawling on the floor.

'Send me your friend, if you have any, you filthy scribbler.'

My face burns as I see the greedy stares and eyes bright with malice. Marianne has moved to Ann's side, talking rapidly, and Ann gives me such a look of horror and betrayal I want to burst into tears, but I'm damned if I'll do so here. Shad will not see me cry. The last I see, before Shad pulls me away, is Ann and Marianne retreating together, and Beresford looking simply bewildered and shocked, and yes, a little guilty. As indeed he should.

I stumble as we leave and my gown rips a little at the hem. Somehow it is the last straw. I wrench my arm from Shad's grip.

'You are a fool,' I hiss.

'But not an adulterous fool, ma'am. Hold your tongue. Do you wish to afford the *ton* even more entertainment?'

We're outside the house now, standing on the portico. Beresford's footmen linger, hoping for vails. Shad glares at them and they retreat, then apparently he realises that to find our footman and our carriage, he will need their assistance. The footmen all seem tremendously busy and occupied, refusing to notice him.

I'm most relieved to see our footman, Jeremiah, wander out of the house. He must have heard what has happened, for he sets off in search of the carriage. It takes some time; I suspect the coachman and postilion had settled in for several hours of merrymaking for they return reeking of beer and with their buttons done up wrongly.

More icy politeness as Shad hands me into the carriage and a silent ride home (is it my home still? I don't know), where he retreats into his study.

I wonder who will be chosen as seconds and whether they can bring about a reconciliation so it will not come to a duel, but deep down I know the injury to Shad's name is such that no apology could be accepted. Beresford, publicly insulted, will probably not back down. In a day or two the matter will be resolved and the outcome does not bear thinking of. Whoever survives will have to flee the country.

It is quite possible I shall never see Shad or Ann again (or Beresford, but that prospect is quite agreeable).

I go to bed but can't sleep. After tossing and turning, damaging the pillows, and making an attempt to read (I throw the book down in disgust after a few pages) I get out of bed and walk quietly through the dressing room. The door to Shad's study stands open and a candle burns inside.

Shad sits at his desk, a velvet-lined case open in front of him. As I watch he removes one of the duelling pistols and cocks it, sighting down the barrel. The wood glows blood-coloured in the candlelight. It's a beautiful object, this delicately crafted instrument of death.

I wish I hadn't seen it, or the hard, set expression on my husband's face.

I return to bed and finally weep, not sure whether it's for Shad, or Ann, or myself.

Shad

So I'm setting my affairs in order again and I'm devilish tired of it, and simply devilish tired; a result, I suppose, of my illness. I long to sleep, even on that dreadful sofa; Roberts has brought bedclothes and a pillow for me with the mysterious tact of a good servant. First, a letter to Carstairs, asking him to act as my second in both affairs of honour. Then the more difficult letters to my sister and the children – I wish I had not destroyed the previous set.

No letter to Charlotte. I wonder if I wrote to her the last time I thought I was about to die.

And now what? Our seconds will go through the formality of seeking apologies, which they'll certainly not receive, nor any encouragement to prolong negotiations. We shall probably meet not this morning but the next; everyone will know of it, but since duelling is illegal, it will not be spoken of. Appearances must be maintained, even if you have lost the woman you loved and expect to kill, or be killed by, your best friend. The worst of it is that it will tear the family asunder.

Last time I remember thinking with great pain and distress that I might never know if Charlotte had conceived. I still don't know, and I shall never know whose child it is.

I inspect my pistols; pretty things, delicate and deadly, made to kill. I'm fairly sure that's what Beresford will choose. I have no idea of Dunbury's choice of weapon and the ludicrousness of the situation strikes me for the first time. I may be unable to fulfil the second obligation, although there is a better chance that Carstairs and Dunbury's second may negotiate apologies, the insult being less.

But Beresford, dear, stupid, good-hearted Beresford – there's no going back there.

My candle burns down, gutters, and flares out in a puddle of wax. Outside the sky shows grey.

I walk quietly in stockinged feet for a last glimpse of the woman who has betrayed me and, God help me, I still love. She lies in bed, making her familiar whiffling sounds, the bedclothes wrapped around her. A book lies open, face down, on the bed beside her; the spine is probably ruined. I want more than anything else, more than anything I have ever wanted in my life, to touch her one last time.

Instead I walk away.

Later that morning Carstairs comes to call and confirms that pistols are Beresford's weapon of choice and the meeting place is still under discussion. He offers silent sympathy and assures me he will act as the children's guardian should I not survive the duel.

My children, my poor children who are already fatherless but who have had some sort of happiness over the last two years, will now have their lives destroyed. I remember when I found Amelia, hungry and her hair matted with lice, worked half to death as a parish servant; little John, covered in filth in a hovel, looking up at me with my brother's eyes; Carstairs, gripping my hand as his leg was sawed off; Charlotte in that hideous drawing room like a surly, captured animal and I fool enough to want to give her something more.

My damned necessity to rescue others has become a curse and now it impinges upon my honour, for I cannot abandon my children.

So the day continues. Charlotte apparently keeps to her bedchamber and I have no wish to see her. By afternoon I am restless and agitated. I seek the company of the children who are delighted to receive their uncle, and I take them for a drive in the phaeton.

John bounces on the seat next to me. 'May I take the reins, sir?'

I allow him to hold the reins, my hands over his, and then give Amelia a turn. 'I wish Lady Shad could have come with us,' she says.

'Oh, Lady Shad is busy. She has to meet with the housekeeper and so on.'

'I like her so much, Uncle.'

'Yes, she is very good at marbles,' John says. It is his turn again with the reins and his face is creased with concentration.

'We'll turn right now, so tug gently on the offside rein – very good.' I slow the horses as we take the corner. This is a further complication, the fondness my children have for Charlotte, who, if she is not pregnant, may choose to return to her family.

'Oh, look, sir, there's Aunt Shad.'

Indeed it is. She approaches us on her mare and is accompanied by a groom. All very decorous. We both rein in as the distance between us closes.

'Ma'am.' I raise my hat to her.

She nods. She looks terrible, dark shadows beneath her eyes, but she manages a smile for the children. 'I hope you've had a pleasant drive.'

'We wished you could have come with us.' Amelia gives me a beseeching look.

It would be so easy to turn the vehicle and accompany Charlotte, but so difficult a thing for me to do. I can scarcely find any words, any polite, meaningless phrases to fill the silence between us.

'You handle the mare well,' I finally say. 'I regret we never rode together as we intended.'

She bows her head in acknowledgment. 'I too. I'll wish you good day, sir.'

A small flick of her whip and the mare moves off at a smart trot. I watch her ride past us, and command the team to walk on.

If there was any way to avoid being killed the next morning I would do it for their sake; and I will. I will swallow my pride and apologise to Beresford; if society laughs at me for being a craven cuckold, so be it.

The children squeal with delight as I whip the horses to a canter. I am anxious to get home and write the letter that will protect my children and ruin my honour.

Charlotte

'Milady, wake up!'

I could have sworn I did not sleep a wink, but apparently it is not so, for Tilly, clad in a nightcap, shawl, and nightgown, shakes me awake. She holds a candle in the other hand.

'What the devil's the matter?'

'Wake up, Charlotte!' Another figure pushes past her, this one swathed in a dark cloak.

'Ann! What are you doing here? What's the time?'

'A little after three in the morning.' She unfastens her cloak and drops it on to the bed. 'We know where they are to meet. We must stop them, Charlotte.'

My bed has never been more inviting. 'Why? It's too late. Let them do what they will. I don't care any more.'

'Liar,' she says with great cheer. 'Out of bed. You must get dressed.'

'Where's Shad?'

'Left already, milady.' Now Roberts has joined us. 'I'll summon a hackney for you, milady, and Jeremiah will accompany you.'

Sure enough, Jeremiah, grinning broadly, with his waistcoat half buttoned and a nightcap on his head, lounges in the doorway.

'Oh, do go away, all of you. No, Tilly, you stay.' I flop back against the pillows and regard Ann with amazement. She's all smiles, as fresh as a daisy, and beautifully dressed in a new morning gown and pelisse.

As though reading my mind, she says, 'Why don't you wear your new bonnet, Charlotte?'

'Oh, I'm sure that will be a great help,' I grumble. 'Besides, I think Withers may have taken it.'

'No, she didn't milady,' Tilly chirps. She has lit more candles and produces the bonnet with a flourish.

'At least I shall have the satisfaction of being well dressed while our husbands kill each other.'

My sarcasm is wasted on Ann. 'They will not kill each other if we are there.' She looks away, tight-lipped. 'Now do hurry up, Charlotte. I am exceedingly angry with Beresford. Shad wrote a letter of apology but Beresford would not accept it. And I fear it is my doing.'

'How could it be your fault?'

'You may leave us,' Ann says to Tilly, who obligingly retreats to the dressing room, all the better to listen at the door. She leans towards me, her voice lowered. 'I regret that last night was one of the nights when he . . . well, you know to what I refer. And I refused him because of this – this business. So I fear he was in an uncertain temper.'

'I'm sure it wasn't your fault.' I'm so touched by her loyalty that I want to weep. 'And I assure you that nothing untoward happened at Vauxhall between me and Beresford.'

'Of course it did not!' she cries as though the idea never entered her mind. 'That is why this whole business is absurd and it is our duty to prevent bloodshed.'

Suppressing the grumbles that come naturally to me and of which I am ashamed, for Ann means well, I climb out of bed. I splash water on my face and dress as quickly as I can, regretting that fashion papers so infrequently display what the well-dressed lady should wear to interrupt a duel.

Ann fusses around me, attempting to comb my hair, and places the bonnet on my head with small noises of satisfaction, as though she is preparing me for a jaunt in the country (and so she is, but not in the usual manner of things). When we go downstairs we are in time to see Tilly break away from Jeremiah, who is pink in the face and grinning hugely. She frowns at him, but with a flirtatious twinkle in her eye, and straightens her cap.

'She could do better than a footman,' Ann says.

'I don't know it's any of our business,' I reply.

'Of course it is! They are your charges.' She looks quite astonished and I think again of how easily Ann has assumed the position of countess.

Feeling like a killjoy, I order Tilly to sit inside with us and send Jeremiah outside to sit with the driver, thus depriving Ann and me of any chance of a real conversation.

'And how do you think we should stop this duel? What are the weapons?'

'Pistols, I believe. We must use our feminine wiles.'

'I trust you won't add to your duty in the bed-chamber.' I see Tilly look up with interest. 'Tilly, don't you have something to mend?'

'Beg pardon, milady, I quite forgot I'd brought it with me.' Sure enough, she pulls out a stocking and a needle and thread and sets to work.

We must be insane. We are about to face two men who want to kill each other over me – something I might have thought exciting if it were to occur, say, in a novel – armed with our feminine charms and a needle. And – Ann pokes around in a basket that Jeremiah loaded inside the carriage – we are to have a picnic.

'We must keep up our strength,' she says, and hands me a buttered roll. 'I told Jeremiah when I arrived that he should pack us some breakfast. How I wish we had some tea! But here is a bottle – oh, it is champagne. Several bottles, in fact. How very thoughtful.'

She releases the cork in a messy, amateurish sort of way while I attempt to chew and swallow a roll that has the texture of glue. The champagne goes down much more easily and although I find the situation of three giggly, drunken women come to placate two men intent on killing each other on Hampstead Heath even more ridiculous it does not worry me quite so much. Perhaps after sunrise we can make merry and enjoy a donkey ride or sketch the view. How delightful!

'Charlotte, please stop frowning,' Ann says.

'I'm sorry. I know you mean well.'

'I am sure Beresford will be entirely gentlemanly about the matter.'

'How are you sure? I'm not convinced Shad will be.'

'But Shad offered an apology.'

'Which Beresford refused, so—'

'Oh, you are such a cross thing!'

Three bottles of champagne later we arrive near the place where the duel is to be held; Ann swears she knows the exact spot, as told by Beresford's manservant to a footman, who then told her maid, with Jeremiah charged to give directions to the hackney driver. I think it will be a miracle if we even make it to Hampstead Heath, but apparently we are there. The hackney carriage stops and we all get out, Tilly carrying the basket.

A complicated shuffle into bushes, the natural

result of the champagne, now takes place. We are guarded by Tilly, who is guarded by Jeremiah, but the main threat to our privacy seems to come from the hackney carriage driver perched aloft.

Ann, having emerged from the bushes, asks the driver prettily if he will wait until we have found the gentlemen, and seems surprised that he expects to be paid for his time. We find out how much he has charged so far, an exorbitant sum in my opinion, and dismiss him. He turns the carriage and drives off.

'Now what?' I feel, and sound, less than gracious.

'Now we shall find them,' Ann says with a pretty smile. 'Jeremiah, you are not to bother Tilly.'

'I wouldn't dream of it, milady.'

And we three, or rather I, followed by Tilly and Jeremiah (who I suspect are indeed bothering each other as much as they can while carrying a basket between them), set off behind Ann. It's getting a little lighter now and she stops suddenly. I bump into her and champagne sloshes from my glass on to the back of her pelisse.

'Listen!' She holds up one hand, sheathed in a beautiful pale yellow kidskin glove.

Sure enough, men's voices come to us quite clearly, and we can see that horses took this path recently, a fact I have discovered by stepping in the evidence.

'Over here!' Ann whispers. 'Tilly, can you clean your mistress's shoes?'

'Not now,' I say, becoming more surly by the minute. I grab the last bottle of champagne from the basket and open it, using my skirt to silence the pop of the cork. 'Does anyone want any of this? Good.' I toss my glass into the basket and take a swig from the bottle.

'Charlotte!' Ann grasps my arm and leads me aside. 'You cannot arrive drunk at the duel.'

'Why not?'

'Because we must convince them of our moral superiority.' She adjusts my bonnet. 'And you must smile.'

'Smiles be damned. I have had enough of this idiocy.' I shake her off and walk through furze bushes, my shoes darkening with the dew, in the direction of the male voices.

Behind me Ann squeaks of robbers and *oh, do be careful, Charlotte*. I have a strong suspicion that Tilly and Jeremiah have bothered themselves right off the path for I hear her calling for them in a loud whisper. The ground slopes down into a wooded hollow where a little mist lingers. The voices have ceased now; I break into a run, after another fortifying draught from the bottle, and find myself bursting into a little clearing. I am sure Ann would think it a perfect spot for a picnic, were I not faced with Shad, in his shirtsleeves, pointing a pistol straight at me.

There's a flash and a loud bang and he's obscured by a cloud of smoke as something streaks across my upper arm. Surely it's too early in the day for a bee. But this bee spins me round and knocks me flat on to the ground in a mess of spilled champagne.

'Damn it, it's all over me.' I thought I'd drunk most of the bottle. Why then is it so very wet and—

'Damn you, you're drunk!' Shad roars as he kneels over me and rips at my pelisse.

It hurts like the devil.

He's shouting now to bring a knife, a scalpel, quick, while I thrash to get him off me, but my sleeve, I see now, is darkened not with champagne, but with blood. Shad's blood? No, mine.

'You shot me!'

'You bloody stupid woman, getting in the way.' Someone has given him a blade. I see it flash silver in the newly risen sun.

I scream as the blade rips up the sleeve of my pelisse and the cool morning air hits my skin. 'What are you doing? That's new! You've ruined it!'

'If you get cloth in the wound you'll die.'

I look at my exposed arm. Blood runs scarlet against my skin and I feel cold. A lot of blood, mine, runs into my ruined sleeve and pools on the grass.

'Look at me, Charlotte.' It's Shad, his eyes steady on mine, hands clasped on my injured arm. Blood runs over his fingers. 'We must let it bleed, to clean it. The ball scraped along your arm and it's left a furrow, but it's not so bad. Breathe. Don't swoon on me like some silly miss.'

'I want a drink.'

Shad picks up the champagne bottle. 'Empty. You've had enough.'

'No I haven't. And even if I am drunk, at least I haven't shot anyone recently.'

I become aware of others, now, Ann sobbing and Beresford's soothing tones, and someone, who I gather is a physician, telling Shad that leeches are ready for immediate use.

Shad tells him to desist, using a term I can only assume is nautical.

'My dear Lady Shad!' It's Beresford, leaning over me as Ann, with tears running down her face, clings to his arm. 'I'm so dreadfully sorry.'

'Did you shoot me?' I thought it was Shad, so why does Beresford apologise?

'Why, no, ma'am!'

'Then stop apologising and leave me alone. You idiot,' I add, feeling a lot better for it.

'Hold steady, Charlotte.'

'Why?' I let out a loud shriek as Shad pours something over my arm that stings enough to bring tears to my eyes.

'Brandy, to clean the wound,' he explains.

'I want to drink some.'

'Certainly not.' He sits back on his heels – he's knelt beside me all this while – and wipes his forehead with the back of one hand. He looks older, tired, and his hand shakes.

'Milord, milady, what shall I do?' Tilly, looking terrified, approaches us. She has twigs in her hair, doubtless Jeremiah's doing.

'Finally, a woman of sense.' Shad tugs at his neckcloth. 'Your kerchief is clean? Good. Fold it and lay it over the wound and I'll bandage it.' He unwinds his neckcloth and uses it to bandage my arm which now no longer stings but throbs like a bad headache.

'You shot me!' I repeat.

'I know. I'm sorry. I was trying to shoot Beresford.'

'And, damn it, I deloped!' says Beresford, as though firing a shot into the air qualifies him for a medal.

'More fool you,' says Shad. He stands and holds his hand out. 'My apologies, sir.'

'Damn you!' Beresford says and flings his arms round Shad. 'You're my best friend.'

The two of them stagger slightly as they thump each other on the back and Shad treads on my bonnet.

'Beg your pardon, ma'am.' He stands on one foot to remove the mangled straw mess from the other. 'Pretty hideous, if I may say so.'

Ann scowls. 'It certainly is now, Lord Shad. The bonnet was a gift from me to Charlotte.'

'It was, ma'am? This? For Charlotte?' He shakes his head. 'Most, ah, generous.'

Shad

I am convinced I have married, and now nearly killed, the silliest woman in England.

What is worse, I love her to distraction.

I suppose the servants of both households conspired to tell her and Ann where Beresford and I were to meet. Certainly the last thing I expected to see, my finger on the trigger, was my wife headed straight for me with a bottle of champagne in her hand, weaving slightly as she ran, and with a scowl on her face beneath a bonnet of hideous floral fussiness. I'd hardened myself to being killed by Beresford, although I know he is a dreadful shot; I had made up my mind that my shot would miss him, but come close enough to give him a fright.

And instead I shoot Charlotte.

As she dropped to the ground I thought I would die myself of a broken heart, convinced that she was dead at my hand. A barrage of cursing from the lady convinced me she lived, although bleeding copiously. The ball left a bloody furrow in her arm, messy and shallow, and I believe she will heal well, but I cannot stop shaking.

To hide my weakness I find myself bellowing orders – for a blade to cut off her sleeve, to bring brandy and my coat, to arrange who shall ride in whose carriage.

'Stop shouting, Shad,' Charlotte says. 'You are so very bad-tempered.'

'Hold your tongue. Can you sit?' I ease her up, holding her arm close to her side.

'Brandy?'

At this second request, I am so glad she is alive I will not deny her, even though I do not think it advisable.

'Very well.' I hold the bottle to her lips and allow her a sip. She grabs the bottle and takes a large gulp.

'I think I shall puke,' says my lovely bride after a moment's reflection.

'No you shan't.' I wrap my coat round her. 'Breathe through your nose.'

'She is most unwell,' Ann pronounces. 'I shall ride with you and Tilly must come with us too.'

'Thank you, no, Lady Beresford. I'll look after her and you may take Tilly with you, if you please.' I don't think Ann is used to gentlemen finding themselves immune to her charm. She frowns, albeit in a pretty and feminine way, but turns away with an eloquent, affronted swish of her skirts.

Beresford smiles when I refuse her presence, but scowls at the mention of his other passenger. He has been casting amorous glances at his wife all this while – I suspect she continues to refuse his advances – and takes her hand in his. She flinches and moves away from him, and I don't know which of them I feel sorrier for.

But Beresford and his cold bride are not my concern.

'More brandy.'

'Not advisable, ma'am. Can you stand? If I lift you from the ground I'll do myself an injury.'

She stands and flops like a boneless creature against my chest. 'Ow, that hurts.' She giggles and – regrettably there is no elegant way to express this – belches.

Carstairs, who stands nearby with my pistols, hat, and other possessions, blushes.

I hoist Charlotte into my arms and carry her – she is a dead weight and solidly built for such a slender woman – to the carriage. She swears at me as I squeeze her through the doorway, and I can hardly blame her as her injured arm is jostled in the process.

I put my arms round her, medically necessary as I do not wish her to be jolted by the movement of the carriage, or to fall over on to the injured arm, for she is as drunk as a sailor.

'You shall go to bed as soon as we get home,' I tell her.

'Do you think of nothing else, sir?'

'You shall go to bed *alone*.'

'I'll need help undressing.'

'Tilly can help. Behave yourself.' For one hand creeps towards my breeches.

'Oho,' she says happily. 'You are not as indifferent as you protest.'

'Charlotte, you are drunk and do not know what you do.'

'Oh yes I do. Did you yourself not say I was quick to learn?'

'Yes, but you're hurt. This is not the time. Ma'am, please remove your hand. It is indecent.'

'Balderdash.'

It is like dealing with an amorous octopus. She has somehow trapped me in the corner of the carriage, using one of those strong, long legs to pin me down. I am afraid to put her aside for fear I'll hurt her.

The problem is resolved by her sudden slump against me, followed by a gentle snore. She is fast asleep. I remove her hand from my breeches and fasten as many of my buttons as I can reach. A fine thing it would be to arrive at the house and have my breeches fall round my ankles as I step out of the carriage with my dead drunk wife in my arms.

Shad

'This is a great bore. First you are ill, with something you should have caught years ago, and then you shoot me so now I am the one abed.' My wife scowls horribly at me. She has been confined to our bed since we returned home from the duel yesterday and we are both heartily sick of it. She's as strong as a horse, this descendant of livery stable keepers, but I won't let her get up. Neither will she let me forget that I was the one who fired the shot, but I cannot say I blame her.

'Stop complaining and drink this soup.' I dip a spoon into a bowl of beef broth that the physician (not the guardian of the leeches at the duel, but a fellow who seems to know his profession) deems fit for an invalid. 'It's a good thing I love you, else I'd have sent you to your mother's house to recover. I may yet.'

As I thought, at this she swallows the offered

spoonful. 'Ah, but you wouldn't, because you wouldn't be able to crawl into bed with me every hour.'

'Once, ma'am, yesterday evening, at your request, as I remember.'

'It was most ungentlemanly of you to accept.'

I ignore this. I know she's picking a fight from boredom and pain.

She continues, 'And then you spend the night on the sofa in your study. If indeed, you were there – I should not be surprised if you had gone to the theatre to pick up a whore.'

'Roberts may vouch for my whereabouts if you care to question the servants.'

'Who are doubtless all in your pay!'

'More soup?' I enquire after a short pause.

She shakes her head, eyes downcast.

'Does your arm pain you?'

Another shake of the head.

I place the soup bowl on the bedside table. 'Charlotte, look at me.'

'No.' Her voice is muffled, and I see then that she is weeping and trying to hide it from me.

'Ah, sweetheart.' I draw her to me and let her weep and snuffle all over my waistcoat, absurdly touched that she trusts me enough to do so. 'I am sorry, truly I am sorry. For everything, for doubting you . . .'

'For shooting me. Don't forget that.'

'Yes, that too. I believe I shall not be permitted to forget that for some time.'

'At least a decade. And for shouting at me after you'd shot me.'

'I wasn't shouting at you, my love. Well, I must confess I did, a little, because I was so frightened of what had happened.'

She nods and blows her nose on a handkerchief I offer her. 'I am dreadfully hurt that you thought I was unfaithful.'

'I thought you were in love with Beresford.'

'What have I ever done to make you think that?' She looks at me with absolute astonishment.

'Well, to be honest, it was an idea Beresford first put in my head.' And I relate all the other episodes: her reaction to the letter sent when they were on honeymoon, her eagerness for their return, the visit to Camden Town, and then finally, the episode at Vauxhall Gardens that left her with a bruised lip and a mention in the newspaper.

She leans back against the pillow and sighs heavily. 'It was Ann.'

'Ann?'

'She is my friend. My best friend. She knows me better than anyone in the world. When she fell in love I was lonely. I felt I had lost her and part of myself, too.'

I am silent. I have friends; I have lost friends, too, an inevitable consequence of the times in which we live and my former profession. But I have never felt incomplete without anyone – or rather, until now, I have never entertained the possibility that I could feel this way. For I realise fully now what Charlotte means to me; my other half, my love, the one to whom I can turn and who knows my secret self. It has taken her confession of love for another to make me see how deeply I love my wife, an extraordinary business to be sure.

'I see. And does Ann feel the same way about her friendship with you?'

She looks at me. 'I don't think so. It doesn't matter.'

In an odd sort of way I understand. I have observed often that regard is unequal; as far as one can tell from the outside, there is one who is loved, and the other who loves. Beresford, for instance, loves Ann; so does Charlotte; but I am not sure whom Ann loves.

'Do you mind?'

'No. No, of course not. My concern only is that Ann may not return your regard and may injure you.'

'Well.' She shrugs and winces. 'I shall have to learn to shrug one-shouldered, I believe. It is a risk I have to take. Love is a risky business, I think.'

She reaches for the soup and finishes it, with me steadying the bowl on her knee.

But since she's in a confessional mood, there's something I must ask her. 'If it is not a betrayal of your friendship, may I ask what the real purpose of the Camden Town visit was?'

'I can tell you nothing more on the matter.'

As I suspected, Charlotte guards Ann's confidence and I must resign myself to never knowing the truth of the matter. I am not pleased, and to hide my feelings I rise and light more candles.

'You're angry,' she says.

'A little, yes. I love you, Charlotte, and I am your husband. You made vows to honour and obey me.' I see her reflection in the mirror on her dressing table. She's prodding gingerly at her injured arm. 'Don't do that, Charlotte; you'll make it bleed again. I trust it will not come to the test, that you must choose between old and new loyalties.'

'I hope so too.' She yawns. 'Where's my fashion paper? I hate this. I hate being looked after. Even by you.'

I find her fashion paper, which has fallen to the floor, and hand it to her. 'You'll be well soon. I'd never have shot you if I'd known how bad-tempered you would become. It's a good thing I have a thick skin.'

She pauses from turning pages. 'You may be thick-skinned, but inside you're as soft a fool as I ever met. Sometimes I think I'm another one of the sorry misfits of your collection.'

'Stop trying to fight with me, ma'am.' I pause, much entertained. 'My collection?'

'Yes, your doltish friend Beresford who can't talk sensibly and Carstairs who barely talks at all, and the children, and Jeremiah – you do realise he has grown an inch more in the last month? Oh, Shad, what do you think of this bonnet? Do you think I should get something made up like this?'

I view the representation of a woman with a tiny head and tiny feet in a hat that suggests a bird laid a fruit basket. 'No, it's far too much like that monstrosity Ann gave you.'

She lays the paper down. 'You don't like her very much, do you, Shad?'

She's not trying to provoke me now, but I answer very carefully. 'For your sake, and Beresford's, I try to, but she strikes me as someone who uses others to her own advantage, and I cannot admire that.'

'I see.' She lays the fashion magazine aside and yawns. 'I'm so tired.'

She settles herself in the bed and closes her eyes. I watch her sleep for a time. I love her so much, even when she's behaving like a fretful child. There's little endearing about her foul temper; my children would bear an indisposition with more grace than Charlotte does. I love her beyond reason.

Charlotte

I wake later that afternoon to the sight of Ann accompanied by her maid. The maid staggers beneath a great sheaf of flowers, a pile of books, and a quantity of fruit, and is followed by footmen bearing vases and tea things.

'I had to give Shad quite a talking-to to let me in,' Ann says. 'He told me you were asleep.'

'I was, but it doesn't matter.'

She bends to kiss me and then flits around dividing the flowers among the vases and placing them here and there. 'Does your arm pain you very much?'

'No, but I'm bored. Shad won't let me get up. I'm so pleased to see you.'

She batters my pillows into submission; it is rather annoying, but I let her do it.

'Well!' The room arranged to her liking, she settles herself on the bed and proceeds to peel and quarter a peach. 'Beresford sent for these from the country for you.'

'How very kind.' As a peace offering it is quite acceptable.

'I am afraid you will scar.'

'So Shad says.'

'And with the current fashion in sleeves, it is most unfortunate.'

'Oh, maybe I'll start a new fashion. I'm not too concerned. Besides, I think we intend to live mostly in the country.'

'How dreadfully unfashionable,' Ann says. She lifts the lid of the teapot and gives the contents a vigorous stir. 'Where is your maid?'

'Entertaining yours, I expect. Why?'

'I need to ask your advice.' She hands me a teacup. 'I shall not give you a saucer since you have only the one arm.'

My heart sinks as she explores the dressing room and, I suspect, looks through the keyhole into Shad's study to make sure he is not lurking, ear pressed to the door. I am afraid that once again I shall be pressed into some sort of dubious plan.

'Well?' I say with little grace when she returns.

Ann leans forward and dabs peach juice from my chin. 'Promise me you will not tell Shad.'

'Well, I . . .' I know I should not make this promise, but she looks so innocent and happy I want to oblige her. 'Very well.'

'It is to do with a letter I have received.'

'Indeed?'

She blushes, something else I suspect she can do at will, like the decorative weeping. It has the beauty of a sunrise, quite unlike the usual red blotchy effect of other women. 'From little Emma's papa.'

'I thought he had washed his hands of you both.'

She fishes in her reticule for a letter. 'Oh, no. Quite the contrary. He has had a change of heart. He loves me still, Charlotte.'

'So does your husband.'

She dismisses Beresford with a dainty wave of her hand. 'I shall read to you what he says.'

If there is one thing I loathe it is having letters read aloud to me, and Ann knows this.

'So. Here is the passage.

' "My darling girl, I have thought much of you of late and of" . . . there is something crossed out here . . . "the baby and I hope he is as pretty as you." '

'*He?*'

'I last wrote to him when she was born and that was almost a year ago,' Ann says.

'It's no excuse!'

'Do you wish me to continue or not?'

Not really. 'Of course. My apologies.'

'No, I am the one who should apologise. I forgot you are not well after your husband shot you.' She looks at me with such sweetness that I try to convince myself there is not a hidden barb in her words.

'Ann, I have no quarrel with you. Pray proceed.'

'Oh dear, his spelling is quite atrocious. I am afraid it becomes somewhat private here for the next few lines. "In short, lovely Ann, I have decided I cannot live without you and we must be together. Pray leave that dolt of a husband. When I arrive in London next Monday I shall send for you and we shall once more enjoy the bliss of our . . . onion.' I think he must mean *union*, don't you agree? Although his hand is not very clear and I may misread it.'

'I should think so, unless he intends to practise the cultivation of vegetables. What is his profession, anyway? Will you not tell me who he is?'

She shakes her head and returns the letter to her reticule. 'You will know soon enough. Is it not wonderful, Charlotte?'

'Wonderful?'

'He loves me, Charlotte. After so much unhappiness and our long separation, he loves me.'

I take a handful of grapes from the bowl of fruit.

'Yes, but . . . Ann, what about Beresford? Surely you do not mean to leave him?'

'What else can I do?' She blinks at me as though I suggest she fly round the room.

'You will lose all respectability and I hope this gentleman has money, for Beresford will keep yours. You will have no friends, no one to protect you, no family, only this gentleman who has ignored you and your child for almost a year.'

'But I will have you as a friend, shall I not? I shall have everything: my little Emma, someone who truly loves me, and—'

'Shad will side with Beresford and the family. You know that. Our friendship will suffer, as you also know. If he forbids me to see you, I shall—' I hate to say this, and I look around for a place to deposit my grape pips while I search for words – 'I must abide by his wishes. I do not wish to deceive him any more, not even for your sake.'

Ann offers me her saucer for the pips. 'I see. I thought you would be happy for me. I thought you might understand.'

I take her hand in mine. Unfortunately, since I am for all purposes one-handed, the last of my grapes compress between our fingers. 'How can I advise you to do something so foolhardy? He may love you, but that does not mean you should give up everything for his sake. What if he leaves you again?'

She grips my hand so hard pulverised grapes

squeeze from between our fingers. 'He loves me! Don't you see, this is the only way I can be baby Emma's mama.'

I disengage my hand, search for a handkerchief, and wipe us both clean. 'I beg your pardon, he says nothing of that, unless it is elsewhere in the letter.'

'He doesn't need to say it! It is what he wants, too. Why, he mentions Emma in his very first sentence.'

'Yes, as the child whose name and gender he cannot recall.'

'Sometimes you are quite cruel, Charlotte.' I am afraid she will cry, but she stands and pulls her gloves on with an air of righteous anger. 'I thought you would act as my friend in this matter. I have given it much thought and I am disappointed in you. I have no recourse but to leave Beresford and be with the ones who truly love me – Emma and her papa.'

'I truly love you, too, and that is why I must advise you, please, to think before you do anything hasty.'

She turns and regards her reflection in the mirror as she ties her bonnet strings. 'I trust you will oblige me in considering our conversation confidential. I hope you recover soon. I have other calls to make. Good afternoon.'

And she's gone with no kiss or smile or even a hint of friendliness, the door of the bedchamber closing quietly behind her.

I don't like this at all. We've quarrelled before, certainly, but not like this. I do hope she'll be sensible.

I tell myself she may sulk for a little, but then she'll relent and we'll be as good friends as ever. As soon as Shad stops fussing over me like a mother hen I'll call on her; for next Monday, when her lover arrives in London, is only four days away.

Charlotte

'Beg your pardon, milady, her ladyship is not at home.' Beresford's butler closes the door in my face and I'm left fuming on the doorstep.

The note I sent Ann after her visit yesterday has not been answered. Neither has the one I sent today. I promised her – before finding out what she intended, it is true – that I would not tell Shad, but I am at a loss. If I do not speak up to someone, I become an accessory to her proposed plan. If I do tell Shad (and I am not a fool, I know I should) he will careen around in typical male fashion, doubtless instigating at least one duel, and possibly with Beresford again, who will not believe his sweet Ann to be capable of such perfidy.

I am left with only my feminine wiles to assist me, a situation Ann no doubt would approve of, even though I suspect I am wearing the wrong sort of hat for the occasion. So I decide I should talk to another woman. Since Marianne, Shad's sister, is out of the question, that narrows the field considerably.

My mother. I should visit my mother. Did not George say I should? And I know Shad turned her away yesterday, thinking quite correctly that her dolorous pronouncements, however well meant, would not improve my state of health.

'Milord said I should send you home as soon as your calls were made,' Jeremiah says, lurking on the steps of Beresford's house.

'I haven't even started making calls,' I tell him, annoyed that his loyalties have switched entirely to Shad. 'We'll go to Mr and Mrs Hayden's house. You'd like to visit your friends downstairs again, wouldn't you?'

'Indeed, yes, milady, most kind.' He shambles ahead of me to open the carriage door and I climb inside, resigning myself to a visit with my mother. I hope George and my father will be there too, to add a little good-natured cheer.

Luck does not smile upon me. I find my mother alone, prone on a couch, handkerchief clutched in one hand and the cordial glass in the other.

'*My Poor Wounded Child!* I have *Such a Headache*.'

'I'm sorry to hear it, ma'am.' I send the footman for tea. 'My arm is much better today.'

'That *Monster*,' she murmurs.

'It was an accident, ma'am.' As far as my family is concerned, this is the only version of the truth they shall hear. I do not embroider upon it; I know that the more elaborate the deceit, the more tangled I shall become, incompetent liar that I am.

'Poor dear Henry no longer *Approaches Hymen's Bower*.' I notice now a creased and stained letter next to the small table that holds the cordial bottle.

'Oh dear. What a shame.'

'*The Young Woman in Question Severed the Amorous Connection*.' An entire sentence of emphasis; not a good sign.

'I'm most grieved to hear of it, ma'am.' Thank God the girl had some sense. 'Is Henry much upset?'

'I fear so. How *My Soul Laments* that I cannot be with *My Darling Boy* in *His Grief and Distress*.'

'Oh, I expect he'll recover soon enough.'

'You do not understand. Like his mama, Henry is possessed of a *Delicate Sensibility*.'

I did not call on my mother expecting an excess of sympathy – I suspect I missed my chance yesterday, thanks to Shad's vigilance – but her harping on about Henry proves tiresome.

She rouses herself enough to wave with a tragic air in the direction of the tea caddy and I make tea and pour. The effort takes its toll; with an air of exhaustion she sinks back recumbent.

'Where are George and Papa?' I ask.

'They are engaged in *Equine Pursuits*.'

'Why do you not ask them to take you for a drive? I'm sure the fresh air would do you good, ma'am. It might take your mind off things.'

She shudders. At her bidding I take the letter, marking Henry's usual execrable spelling and lack of coherent expression. Other than announcing the end of the engagement, a vague promise of a visit to London soon, and a significant comment that military life proves more expensive than he anticipated, he has little to say. Lacking a mother's feelings, I cannot detect much agony between the lines.

'He doesn't sound too out of sorts, and don't you think it good that he puts such a brave face on things?'

She groans at my attempt at cheerfulness.

I discreetly move her cordial glass to one side and replace it with a cup and saucer. 'I am sorry you are so unhappy, ma'am.'

She's always unhappy to one extent or another and I don't know what I can do for someone who's determined to suffer. But she is my mother, and I must ask her advice. So I launch into the sorry story of Ann and her baby – I mention that her marriage to Beresford has 'some difficulties', admiring my own discretion – and the sudden appearance of her former lover and his demand that they should run off together.

'So, ma'am, what do you think I should do? She will not talk to me. And she will be ruined. I cannot believe such a scoundrel should have a change of heart as she claims. I cannot talk to my husband of it. Mama, please advise me.'

A sound emerges from my mother's lips. A faint snore. Has she slept throughout?

'Ma'am! Rouse yourself!' I clatter the china to gain her attention.

She does not stir. I shake her, my hand on her shoulder. 'Ma'am!' I bellow in her ear.

She mumbles something, smacks her lips, and sleeps on. She's dead drunk. I should have known. I tuck her shawl round her and wedge a pillow beneath her head. I wonder if she will even remember I was here.

My mother has failed me, and there is only one other I can think of who may help.

'You again,' says Lady Renbourn. 'Has he run off with an actress? I heard he dallied overmuch with some slut at the theatre and fairly dragged her out of Beresford's box.'

'No, ma'am. That was me.' I push a cat from a chair and sit.

'You'll take some claret. We don't have tea in this house.'

One of the languid young men steps forward to pour.

'And what's all this about him shooting you? Have you taken a lover already? No, I didn't think so. Now, I heard Lady Frinchingham had her lover hidden behind a screen in the bridal chamber for her enjoyment after Frinchingham had consummated the marriage, and then they sent for oysters and champagne and started all over again, but this time—'

'And don't forget the boy from the fishmonger's who delivered the oysters, ma'am,' purrs Francis, or Tom, or possibly even Johnny, for I really cannot distinguish them.

'Manners!' screeches Lady Renbourn, smacking him with her fan. 'Don't interrupt when I'm in the middle of a story. Well, miss, what do you want?'

'Your advice, ma'am, on a serious matter, but . . .' I wonder how I can ask if her pack of pretty young men could remove themselves.

To my surprise Lady Renbourn anticipates me. 'They may be the most shallow creatures on earth, but they're discreet and loyal,' she says. 'And if I tell them to keep a secret, they'll do so. You'd have more trouble if I sent them from the room and they listened at the keyhole, for then it would give them carte blanche to gossip all over London.'

It seems an odd sort of arrangement, but I have no choice but to trust Lady Renbourn's judgement, and so the young men stay as I relate, once again, Ann's story.

'So that milk and water miss has claws,' Aunt Renbourn comments. 'Aye, I thought she was too good to be true, and that booby Beresford turns a blind eye to her faults.'

'She is my friend!'

'Sit down, girl. Have some more claret. To be sure, this is a pretty pickle. But what if this young man truly loves her and she him?'

I shake my head. 'She will be lost to all others who

love her, ma'am, and he may prove false. He has done so before.'

'You're too good for her, I think, but you won't heed the advice of an old woman and she won't heed yours. You did quite right in not telling Shad, for it would only cause more trouble between him and Beresford, and I'd rather see those two friends than not. Besides, we'll have a great deal more entertainment this way. No, don't pull faces at me, miss. I must think.' She picks at a cat on her lap, idly pinching a flea or two between her fingernails. It makes me itch just to watch her. The young men rearrange themselves into new picturesque poses.

Lady Renbourn speaks like a Sybil making a pronouncement. 'So, Lady Ann has a maid, I presume? You, too? And they're cousins? Ah, that's easy. You shall get your maid to find out the meeting place and then we'll go and intercept the adulterous couple and—'

'We?'

'It will afford me great entertainment and the boys do not get nearly enough exercise. In the fresh air, that is.'

I open my mouth to argue. My plan, such as it was, was to bring pressure to bear upon Ann so that she would not meet her lover at their rendezvous. So far I have been unsuccessful and someone may have to intervene at the last moment.

But the thought of Lady Renbourn and her assorted exquisites making Ann see the folly of her actions makes me snort with laughter, although didn't Shad tell me Lady Renbourn usually made young women cry? She may be able to frighten some good sense into Ann.

'And you don't know the name of the young fellow, I suppose? Not that it makes any difference, but I've heard no scandal in the offing concerning Lady Beresford.' She cackles. 'We'll have your Ann locked back into her marital cage before you know it.'

'But what about her child?'

'God's teeth, girl, she'll be in whelp to Beresford soon enough and that will be quite enough to occupy her.'

'She loves her daughter, ma'am. I don't think she would agree.'

'Then she's an even greater fool than I thought.' She bangs her stick on the floor, shaking her claret glass from the small piecrust table in front of her. It rolls on to the floor to be batted around by one of the cats. 'We'll play cards now. A shilling a point, I think.' She leans towards me and whispers, 'These boys owe me fortunes. They know their place.'

I thank her profusely but turn down her invitation to cards. My arm is becoming sore and I want to see Shad.

Shad

Something is worrying my girl and I don't like it at all. Neither do I like the fact that she refuses to even confess that something is concerning her, but dismisses her anxiety as pain from her wounded arm. The arm is healing well, with no hint of fever, and indeed Charlotte shows great dexterity and appetite distracting me in the bedchamber (how I love her).

Something is going on. I notice that Tilly sports new lace on her caps and wears one of Charlotte's hideous gowns from before my sister took her in hand; it looks better on her than I suspect it ever did on my wife. Ann, the pretty spider who spins her webs of deception, must be involved, for Charlotte has been unsettled ever since her visit. I am fairly sure now that one of the children in that cottage in Camden Town was Ann's, a theory for which I have no proof whatsoever.

I notice also that Jeremiah and Tilly exchange languishing glances and smiles, and one is apt to come upon them in odd corners of the house, respectively giggling or grinning, fresh from an embrace. Roberts confirms this disgraceful behaviour is taking place and I send for Jeremiah.

He shuffles into my study; he gives an impression of being about to fall apart, as though the stuff of his new livery holds his limbs in place, and only mere chance and fustian prevent him from exploding in all directions.

Roberts, meanwhile, stands behind me, arms folded, and doesn't utter a word, like a threatening thundercloud.

I assume my sternest expression as though Jeremiah is a midshipman who has been derelict in his duty and he, looking exceedingly nervous, trips over his own feet. I fear he will land on my desk, but with great effort he manages to keep upright. I look at him steadily for a good minute.

He shifts from foot to foot and licks his lips.

'You know why I have sent for you, Jeremiah.'

'No, sir, I do not, I'm sorry, sir. For whatever it is I've done.' Poor lad, I fear he is about to blurt out an inventory of offences. I'm not too sure I wish to hear them – I don't want him to admit to ill-doing that would justify his dismissal. After all, a well-run household depends upon a delicate balance of what is known and what is acknowledged by the folk upstairs (and by those downstairs, for that matter).

'Well, Jeremiah, Mr Roberts and I are most pleased with your work.'

That takes him by surprise. He gapes at me.

'But,' I continue and pause for a good ten seconds. 'There is something that concerns me.'

He looks quite unsettled now, unsure of whether I want him to confess or plead ignorance.

'I fear it concerns Miss Tillyard.'

To his credit, he says nothing.

'Well, man, what do you have to say for yourself?'

'Sir,' he says, 'my intentions towards Miss Tillyard are strictly honourable.'

'Are they indeed?'

'Oh yes, milord, but we can't afford to marry yet – tell the truth, milord, I haven't asked her, but I'm sure she'll say yes – and I know we must wait, and, oh, milord, she's the prettiest thing I ever saw and so sweet-tempered and good . . .'

By this time a huge, foolish smile lights up his face and despite myself I'm touched. However, there is work to be done here. 'Admirable, but I can still sack you if your attentions to Miss Tillyard interfere with your work or with hers.'

'So you can, milord, but I am sure neither will happen.' He's not being cheeky; he has some pluck, this gangling lad. But he bites his lip, uncertain of what is to happen next.

I let him wait again while I pretend to read through a paper on my desk. I look up. 'I have a specific task I require of you, Jeremiah.'

'Yes, milord.'

'Any note Lady Shadderly sends out or receives is to come to me first, and if Miss Tillyard is good enough to share any secrets regarding her ladyship's activities, you'll tell me.'

'Beg your pardon, milord, but I can't deceive Miss Tillyard. Nor Lady Shadderly, milord, for she has always been good to me.'

'I'm sure you'll find a way to satisfy your

conscience. Otherwise . . .' I end with a shrug. I don't like to make an implied threat to a man I believe is basically honest, but Jeremiah must understand the seriousness of the situation; and I have decided this is the only way.

To sweeten the bait, I add, 'I should be prepared to make you a handsome reward if you are successful, for if you're to marry you'll need some capital.'

This time it is he who creates a long pause. 'Thank you, milord. I'll do my best.'

I don't have too long to wait. On Monday morning, after painstakingly unsealing and reading several tedious notes to and from Charlotte's dressmaker and milliner, Jeremiah brings me a note from Charlotte addressed to Lady Renbourn, of all people. I remember my aunt's taste for mischief and open it to find that a rendezvous is planned for eight o'clock this evening at the White Horse in Piccadilly. I know this inn; most do, for it is a coaching inn. What the devil is Ann up to now?

When Charlotte mentions to me in a casual sort of way that she plans to keep her mother company this afternoon and may well dine with her too, for the lady has been lonely of late, I praise her for her filial obedience. I recommend Jeremiah accompanies her and she agrees quite happily. Bless her, the children could (and do) tell more convincing lies. I stroll along to the schoolroom where they practise their penmanship, and listen to them recite some Shakespeare.

Unfortunately the play is *Othello*, not the best choice for my state of mind. Although I am cheered by the children's sweetness, my mood changes when I am alone again. Deep in my mind my old suspicions of Charlotte still fester. What if Ann is Charlotte's accomplice to adultery, and not the other way round?

I retire to my office and draw the blade from my swordstick. This time, whoever my rival may be, I shall kill him then and there; to the devil with the gentlemanly formalities of a duel.

I consider, briefly, writing another set of letters in case of my death, but frankly I have done it so frequently of late the prospect bores me. I spend some time going over the most recent letter from my bailiff and writing a reply, while the hands of the clock move too slowly for my liking. After a while I repair to my club, where I dine unfashionably early, and chat with a few Navy fellows there.

When I return to the house I am surprised to find a visitor who has been waiting for me a number of hours in the drawing room. Mrs Hayden's wobbly curtsy and the empty Madeira decanter tell me how she has spent her time. As I suspected, Charlotte did not visit her mother today; even though I knew it, Mrs Hayden's presence in my house serves to depress my spirits further.

'Sir,' she exclaims – this is not a woman given to conversation in the normal sense – 'I must *Rescue My Beloved Child from Folly and Iniquity*!'

'Which one, ma'am?' I cast a longing glance at the decanter; so does she.

She moans and sinks on to the sofa. 'My Charlotte.'

I relent and send for more wine, and listen to Mrs Hayden ramble on. Apparently when Charlotte paid her mother a visit a few days ago she told her of a dilemma concerning a former lover who wanted a reunion with her.

'A moment, ma'am.' I interrupt the sighing, declamations and handwringing. 'Are you absolutely certain Charlotte spoke of herself?'

'Sir! *A Mother Knows!* Naturally, not wanting to *Distress the Maternal Bosom*, my poor child pretended she spoke of *Another Who Contemplated Ruin*.'

I suspect Mrs Hayden is quite capable of distressing her own maternal bosom – she spills wine down it in her vehemence – and her account confirms my suspicions that Ann is at the bottom of this idiocy. Mrs Hayden slithers from the couch and falls to her knees. *'Pray Forgive the Errant Fruit of My Womb!'*

'Ma'am, I assure you I shall do nothing rash.' I hoist her to her feet. 'I am aware of the situation, although I assure you that you are mistaken; Charlotte is innocent. She does indeed protect another, as she told you, but I intend to prevent anyone performing any foolish actions.' I hope I believe this; saying it aloud to Mrs Hayden helps me convince myself.

'It is very good of you to say so.' She blinks and says in a fairly normal way, 'You know, I really do not see how Charlotte could have had a baby. I am sure I would have noticed. You are right, sir, it must be someone else. I do hope it is so.'

Now I'm faced with a dilemma. Mrs Hayden gazes at me, all plaintive trust, if somewhat glassy-eyed from the wine, and I must leave for the inn very soon. The lady may indeed have grasped the wrong end of every stick offered her, but she did come to me for help, for her daughter's sake. To keep the contents of my wine cellar safe, I invite her to accompany me to the assignation, to prove to us both that her daughter is in no danger.

She agrees quite readily, so I send for the phaeton, in the interests of speed, and we set off for the inn. Although I have assured Mrs Hayden of her daughter's innocence, I find myself doubting my own judgement regarding Charlotte's actions. Why should she inform Aunt Renbourn of her destination if she were planning an adulterous liaison? unless she has press-ganged my elderly relative into being a conspirator. Why did she not confide in me? Does she act as Ann's accomplice, or is she determined to stop her committing any foolishness?

I try to maintain my composure as we speed through the London streets, but with every yard it becomes more difficult.

Charlotte

I'm as nervous as a cat, an odd phrase, for Lady Renbourn's cats (or rather Aunt Renbourn's, for she has invited me to address her so) are the most slothful of creatures, with only the occasional savage maiming of people or rodents to relieve the monotony of their lives. For one, I am afraid that Ann has deliberately misled us by giving her maid the wrong information, knowing that I shall try to stop her; and second, I fear somehow Shad has found out what I am about, and will arrive with a great deal of shouting and bloodshed, angry that I have deceived him. The third dreadful possibility is that Shad may believe I have adulterous designs on – someone, I'm not sure who he has settled on to cuckold him this time; not Beresford, for they appear to be the best of friends again. Occasionally over the last few days he has tried to trap me into an indiscretion, I swear it, and I have had to distract him in the only sure way a wife can.

He has not complained, other than asking me to order more beef for dinner so he may keep up his strength.

Were it not for Ann's folly these past few days would be the best of times for me. Shad and I ride together in the park and he compliments me on my ability as a rider; we attend fashionable events where we retreat into corners to kiss and leave early; we've even been to Vauxhall where we explored the dark walks and did shocking, delicious things to each other. He tells me stories of life aboard ship, and confesses he has never before told anyone how frightened he was before each engagement with the enemy. I am full of admiration that he should have the courage to proceed and do his duty. And I advise him to buy a new team for the carriage, for they are not well matched, and he promises to take my advice, so long as he does not have to buy horses from my father.

So all is well, very well, except for Ann's imminent ruin hanging over me like a great shadow.

I pace up and down the parlour with adjoining bedchamber we have engaged at the inn, and return to the window again and again to look into the yard. Mail coaches arrive and depart, the passengers come and go; there are arguments over luggage and fares, and it is all fairly entertaining. But where is Ann?

'Calm yourself, Charlotte,' says Aunt Renbourn. 'Order some tea if you must, but stop that infernal pacing.'

'Lady Shad,' simpers one of the young men, 'I should so like to draw your footman's portrait.'

'Ask him, not me, sir.'

Then I see a familiar figure in the yard. It's Mrs Pyle's helper, the skinny, silent little girl, and she holds a bundle in her arms. So Ann has instructed Emma to be brought here. She really intends to leave Beresford!

No sign of Ann yet, though. I leave the room and run down the stairs and out into the yard. What a stroke of luck! I am quite prepared to use the innocent babe as a bargaining tool. The little girl sees me and smiles.

'Ma'am,' she says, 'I've brought the baby.'

'Very good, please come inside. Would you like me to carry her? She's quite heavy. Surely you did not walk all this way?'

'No, ma'am, I came in a cart; a man in the village was driving into London with some chickens to sell.' She hands the sleeping child over to me and slips a cloth bag from her arm. 'Mrs Pyle sends her regards to Mrs Longwood and says she will be at her service any time. Emma is now weaned and Mrs Pyle thinks she will begin to walk at any moment. Her clothes are in this bag.'

I offer the little girl, whose name I discover is Jenny, some refreshment, but she is too shy to come into the inn. I content myself with giving her a shilling so she may buy something at a cookshop, and she leaves, a small, determined figure picking her way through the throng of people and horses in the yard.

I lose sight of her as a mail coach draws into the yard, horn blaring, and when it halts the passengers step down and rush into the inn, to take refreshment in the few minutes allowed. Grooms run forward to change the horses, and servants remove luggage from the roof and the basket.

And then I see her. She's veiled and wearing a dark cloak, but I'd know her anywhere – the way she carries herself, the flowery femininity of her bonnet, the golden curl of hair escaping and curling round her neck. Of course she didn't arrive on the mail coach, but has slipped in from the street. She surveys the yard, obviously expecting her lover to be there, and I wait to see if she catches sight of him.

Emma stirs in my arms and yawns. She opens her eyes and looks at me with a smile. 'Mama?'

But my face is unfamiliar. The smile fades. Her face creases up, her mouth opens, and she howls.

Ann starts towards us. I can't hear her above the noise of the yard, or Emma's howling, but I see her mouth form my name.

I turn and enter the inn.

'Charlotte, wait for me!'

I pick up my skirts and run up the stairs with Emma bawling in my ear and Ann close behind me.

'Shut the door!' I shout as I burst into the room, Ann on my heels. As soon as we are inside I hand Emma over to her mother.

'There, there,' she says with little effect. 'Charlotte, what have you done to her? Why won't she stop crying?'

'She's crying for Mrs Pyle.' I'm ashamed of my cruelty even as the words burst from my lips.

'Give the brat to me,' says Lady Renbourn. She bounces Emma on her knee. 'Stop that noise immediately, child!'

To everyone's surprise, Emma gulps and stares at Lady Renbourn, startled into silence. The room is astonishingly quiet.

Ann turns to me. She's furious. I've never seen her so angry. 'What is Lady Renbourn doing here and who are these gentlemen? You promised you would tell no one—'

'I promised not to tell Shad. I cannot let you do this.'

'You have betrayed me. You are not my friend!'

'Lady Shad acts in your best interests, girl. And where are your manners?' Lady Renbourn has given Emma a teaspoon to play with and seems quite content to have a baby rather than a cat on her lap.

'Lady Renbourn.' Ann curtsies. 'Thank you for your assistance. I shall take the child and leave now.'

'I believe not, ma'am.' Aunt Renbourn smiles in a genial yet determined way.

'This is absurd!' Ann runs to the door but one of the lovely young men stands in her way and leans against it. 'Let me out, sir!'

'No, ma'am, I am not permitted.'

She draws herself up. 'I am the Countess of Beresford and I order you to let me leave!'

'No, miss, you're staying here,' Lady Renbourn says.

'How dare you!' Ann catches sight of the doorway that leads into the bedchamber, but discovers there is no way out when she gets there. She runs back and bursts into tears.

'Charlotte, please, please let me go!'

'No. We can't let you do this.' I step away. I cannot bear to see Ann in tears.

'I hate you,' she hisses and runs to the window. Even with her veil shading her face, I see her expression change to one of joy as a light carriage drives into the yard. I can't identify the passenger, clad in a caped greatcoat and whose face is hidden by his hat – besides, it's after eight now and almost dusk. He jumps down smartly from the carriage and stretches. He must be driving post, for a groom leads out a pair of fresh horses as his current ones are unharnessed.

Ann screams as I grasp her wrist to stop her opening the window. She breaks away from me and heads towards Francis (I think) at the door, hands poised to scratch. Halfway there she falls flat on her face and her bonnet falls off and rolls away.

'Oh no you don't, miss,' says Aunt Renbourn, withdrawing her walking stick.

I grab the bonnet and pull the cloak from Ann's shoulders.

'Ann, if you do not stop I shall tie you to the bedpost in the other room. I'm sorry, but you are not to be trusted.'

'You wouldn't dare!'

But Jeremiah has removed his neckcloth and holds it out to me.

I ignore Ann's pitiful weeping, her threats, and her insults. Later, I know, I shall remember what she said, and feel hurt that she could say such things, but I make good my threat and tie her to the bedpost.

'What if I need the chamber pot?' she whimpers.

'Here, beside the bed.' I open the cabinet door.

'I'm thirsty.'

'We'll order tea when I come back. Ann, sit down and rest. Would you like Emma brought in so you can play with her?'

'You are a vulgar, unfaithful girl,' she says tearfully. 'You were never my friend.'

I go back into the main room and look out of the window. There's no sign of the passenger, and the driver is drinking from a tankard and chatting with the grooms. The fresh team is harnessed.

'I'm going down to talk to him. I want to find out who he is.'

'Whatever for?' Aunt Renbourn says. 'Let him cool his heels and then he'll go away.'

'What if he doesn't? We'll be stuck in here. I'll tell him Ann no longer wishes to see him and her husband the Earl is inside the inn and will come out to kill him at a moment's notice. I'll see if the inn has some milk or pap for the baby, too. Please untie Ann once the carriage has left.'

I put on Ann's hat with the veil. Now, I daresay it is exceedingly foolish of me to even approach Ann's lover but I'm afraid he might be someone we know, and in that case I do not want him to guess my identity. Furthermore, if Ann has told him she will wear a hat with a veil, he will not attempt to conceal himself from me.

By the time I'm downstairs and in the yard, the horses have turned towards the archway leading out, and it is obvious he is ready to leave. I walk up to the carriage but can't see anyone. As though taking the air, I stroll round to the far side.

The door flies open and a pair of strong arms haul me in.

'Drive on!' the gentleman shouts.

The carriage moves off with a great jolt and I am flung to the floor. The gentleman seems overeager to help me and I give him a good kick on the shin to dissuade him. Meanwhile the carriage rocks and lurches – we seem to be going very fast – and I lose my balance and fall again.

'So, my beauty, we are together at last!'

I smack his hand away from my waist. And then I look him in the face. Oh, no. It can't possibly be . . .

At this point the hat falls off.

'You!' we both exclaim.

He blinks at me in horror. 'What the devil have you done to your hair? What have you done with Ann? What in heaven's name are you up to?'

'I should ask the same of you. You! I don't believe it.'

He lurches to the window and pulls it up, shouting at the driver to turn the carriage, by God, turn it now, back to the inn.

Shad

'Hold tight, ma'am!'

Mrs Hayden whimpers as we take yet another corner too fast. There's more traffic on the streets than I had anticipated. A church clock strikes eight and I know we are already a good half-mile away from the inn. I swerve to the side as a mail coach, probably having left the inn minutes before, speeds down the street towards us and passes with a blare of its horn.

'We're perfectly safe,' I assure my mother-in-law.

She seems to be praying while clutching my sleeve in a death grip.

I whip the team into a gallop and see another carriage approach us, rather too fast, and taking the crown of the road. As we close, the driver swerves his team to the left to avoid us, but with a large vehicle he has less control than I have of my smaller, lighter phaeton. I stay as close to my side of the road as I dare; people on foot leap out of the way of both vehicles, employing colourful language. In our wake I hear a crash of splintering wood and shouts. I don't know what's happened, whether the carriage has run off the road or hit another one, but I don't care.

I pull into the courtyard of the inn, my horses' necks and flanks darkened with sweat and their shoes striking sparks from the cobbles. A groom runs out to take their heads and I leap out and run for the inn, leaving Mrs Hayden to fend for herself.

The innkeeper tells me there is no Lady Renbourn or Lady Shadderly present, but upon further questioning he reveals that a hideous old lady, three nancy-boys, a fellow in livery and some other ladies have rooms above. And a baby, he adds.

I hear the baby as I go up the stairs, shrieking its head off. I knock at the door from where the sound originates, and since no one answers – it is hardly surprising, the baby's cries are so loud – I open the door and enter. What I find is quite unexpected.

A young man, totally undressed, stands quite still in one corner, holding a boot aloft in one hand. Seated in front of him, an exquisite young man with a sketchpad and pencil is hard at work, another one peering over his shoulder. I recognise them as my aunt's hangers-on. Aunt Renbourn is seated at a table, enjoying some wine and a game of cards with the third of her collection of effete young men.

The men stand and bow, except for the naked one who is told to stand still.

'Where's Charlotte?'

I don't wait for a reply but continue straight into the other room where Ann sits on the bed with the baby. Both of them are crying, Ann quietly, the baby not at all quietly.

Ann looks up as I enter. She doesn't seem particularly surprised to see me. 'Oh, sir, I cannot stop her crying! What shall I do?'

'Where's Charlotte?'

'I don't know.'

'The child is probably either hungry or wet, ma'am. I regret I can't help you. I must find my wife.'

I go back into the parlour. 'Where's Jeremiah, my footman?'

'Milord?' The naked young man lowers the boot and blushes.

'Jeremiah? Good God, man, I didn't recognise you without your livery. For heaven's sake, put your clothes back on. What are you thinking?'

'He has remarkably classical proportions, sir,' says one of the young men, licking his lips. I can never remember their names.

I look at his sketch, in which the boot has been transformed into a classical spear. 'You've drawn his feet too small. They're not at all classical. I regret I'll need his assistance. Jeremiah, where is Lady Shad?'

'She's talking to Ann's lover. I told her it was a ridiculous idea,' says my aunt.

'Beg pardon, ma'am, I believe she went to find

something for the baby to eat,' Jeremiah says.

'Why the devil didn't you go with her?'

'The gentlemen had asked me to stay,' Jeremiah said. 'She did not ask me, milord.'

Once he's decently clad, I send Jeremiah downstairs in search of Charlotte.

'Where is Ann's lover?' I ask the room at large.

'Oh, his carriage left, and good riddance I say.' My aunt scoops up her winnings.

The door opens to admit Mrs Hayden.

'Ma'am, have you seen Charlotte downstairs?'

She ignores me and walks into the bedchamber, where I hear the baby's cries diminish into the occasional sob and then into a happy burbling.

After a few minutes Mrs Hayden emerges from the bedchamber carrying the baby, who is wearing fresh clothes, and beaming. Ann follows behind, and I can see she is doing her best to retain her composure.

'Charlotte has ruined my life,' she says to me. She turns away to sit at a chair by the window.

Aunt Renbourn meanwhile dandles the baby on her lap and Mrs Hayden joins them at the table where she pours herself a glass of wine.

I am feeling more and more uneasy. When Jeremiah returns with a cup of pap and a spoon to feed the baby, I find myself in a room full of cooing, infant-obsessed fools, none of whom seem to care particularly where Charlotte is. The artistic young man sketches the baby, Ann sits alone and cries, and the others gather round the table encouraging little Emma to eat and exclaiming at her prettiness and sweet smiles.

It's a pity they were not so kindly inclined towards the child when she was unhappy and screaming.

'So you did not see Lady Shad downstairs?' I ask Jeremiah.

'No, milord. Oh, look at her little toeses! Does she like to have them tickled, then? Oh yes, she does!'

'She got into the carriage,' Ann says, quite quietly.

'What?' I turn on her. 'You knew this all along but said nothing?'

She shrugs. 'No one asked me. I saw her from the bedchamber window.'

'Ma'am, she is your friend but you allowed her to be abducted by a perfect stranger and kept silent?'

She smiles. 'Oh, I think she knows the gentleman rather well.'

For a moment I am dizzy with rage and jealousy. Have I been a cuckolded fool all along? Surely Charlotte has not betrayed me. I cannot believe it of her. And then common sense takes over, and I find I am more shocked by Ann's betrayal than anything else, and terrified for Charlotte.

I lean towards her. 'You would see Charlotte ruined to protect your own precious skin? What are you thinking, to allow her to drive off in a carriage with an unprincipled adventurer? What do you think will happen when he discovers he has the wrong woman? You are a vicious little fool, Ann.'

'You don't understand!' Her eyes fill with tears but they have no effect on me.

'I most certainly do, ma'am. Charlotte deserves better friends than you and Beresford deserves a better wife.'

Someone breathes wine fumes over me. Mrs Hayden, slightly unsteady on her feet, touches my arm. 'I told them to cool the team down, sir, but to keep them in harness. Just in case.'

Never have I been more grateful that my wife is the granddaughter of the proprietor of a livery stables. I thank Mrs Hayden and dash down the stairs and out into the yard, where I question the grooms about the carriage that has just left. They're not sure which direction the gentleman and lady in the carriage took, but the road north seems the most likely. In the space of a few minutes I'm turning out of the inn yard and on to the road. I groan. Ahead of me is the most appalling mess, a carriage rocked on to one side with a smashed wheel, people milling around arguing and waving their arms, and something – blood? – spilled on the cobblestones.

I rein the team in. I can't get through this mess. And then I remember the carriage that I nearly collided with – can it be the same one? According to the comments of bystanders, after our near miss the carriage made a sudden turn and collided with a wagon carrying casks of wine. Some of the casks have fallen on to the road and broken although no one was injured.

In fact the scene has something of a holiday atmosphere, as people try to salvage spilled wine, scooping it up with plates or ladles; one broken cask has been righted, and people converge on it with saucepans and other household receptacles.

Then I see Charlotte, and naturally she has a china teacup in her hand, doubtless full of purloined wine. She's standing by a horse that cocks one foreleg on its hoof, a casualty of the accident, and talking earnestly to a man who carries a whip, one of the drivers. She bends to grasp the horse's hock, and I see her fingers move over the joint. She straightens and pats the horse's neck.

My first thought is, thank God she is alive and well.

My second, blind jealousy and rage, as a fellow in a caped greatcoat appears and puts his arm round her shoulders.

With a roar of rage I spring forward, knocking him away from her, and push him down on to the cobblestones. I pull my knife from my boot and place the blade against his neck.

My wife giggles. 'Shad, allow me to introduce my brother, Lieutenant Henry Hayden.'

Charlotte

I've never seen Shad so angry or look so dangerous, and regrettably it gives me something of a delicious thrill; his hair is disordered and he holds a knife of a most lethal appearance, with a blade honed into an uneven curve, suggesting it has been used often and with deadly purpose. It's a far cry from his gentlemanly swordstick or elegant duelling pistols, and I believe he pulled it from his boot in true buccaneer fashion.

Nevertheless I do not think it advisable for Shad to protect my honour by killing Henry, even if my brother has behaved abominably.

'This is your brother?' Shad says. The knife moves, a little, away from Henry's neck.

'Yes. Please don't kill him. Mama would be most upset.'

Very slowly Shad withdraws the knife and stands.

My brother does too, brushing wine and filth from

the skirts of his greatcoat. He holds his hand out to Shad. 'A pleasure to meet you, sir, and congratulations on your nuptials.'

Shad hesitates and takes Henry's hand. 'Your servant sir. What the devil are you doing abducting your sister?'

'Beg pardon, I thought she was Ann, but as soon as she was in the carriage I realised my mistake. Gave me quite a turn.'

'You are an idiot, and a dissolute one.' Shad turns to me. 'What were you thinking, to put yourself in such danger?'

'I—'

'No matter. I don't believe I even want to hear whatever ridiculous excuse you have.'

'Then why ask me?'

He ignores me and turns to my brother. 'The Countess of Beresford will not be going anywhere with you, Hayden, but she yearns for your child whom she cannot acknowledge. You are responsible for an extraordinary mess.'

'Good God, sir, I thought that was all taken care of. You mean she brought the child with her?'

'Yes. You've broken her heart, Henry.' At my words he looks a little shamefaced. 'You were about to tell me before the accident – you really should not have instructed the driver to turn round right at that moment – about your liaison with her.'

'We'll return to the inn,' Shad says. 'I can't let the

horses stand. Where are you going, Charlotte?'

'To return the teacup.' I find the woman who lent it to me, now well on her way to getting roaring drunk, who embraces me with great affection.

When I rejoin the two men they are examining Shad's knife and are deep in conversation.

''Pon my word, that's a fine blade, and seen some service, I'll be bound,' says my brother.

Shad nods. 'I used it when boarding enemy ships. There's not room for a sword at such close quarters. I find it's best to—'

I shall never understand men. 'May we concentrate on the matter at hand, gentlemen?'

'Very well.' As we start walking back to the inn, leading Shad's horses, my brother relates how he met Ann while visiting friends in the country and realised the family connection. 'And I remembered when she visited us when we were all children, and she said it was almost like discovering a grown-up brother of her own. She was quite bored as housekeeper, you know, and lonely. Of course we became very close, and one thing led to another.' He concluded. 'I couldn't marry her, though I wish I had, for I needed money. I was never more sick when I heard she was her cousin's heir.'

'But you could have married her, before she met Beresford.'

Henry laughs at my indignation. 'I was in some difficulties, don't you remember, Charlotte? Besides,

Ann wouldn't have anything to do with me, and married Beresford.'

'You were engaged to several ladies, as I remember. You are an idiot, Henry.' We turn into the courtyard of the inn. 'She probably knew you were after her money.'

'Well,' he says, shame-faced, 'I was, but I do love her. At least I think I do. When she told me she was with child I said I didn't think it – the baby, ah—'

'Emma.'

'Emma was my child.' He addresses this mostly to Shad, making an attempt to gain male support. 'It's the sort of thing one does say, you know, under the circumstances. Otherwise, well, it gets damned uncomfortable for a fellow.'

'How could you! You appalling scoundrel!' I slap my brother's face, much to the entertainment of the grooms and passengers who mill around in the courtyard – another mail coach has arrived, so we have a full and appreciative audience.

'Indeed. Almost as being uncomfortable as a ruined woman,' says Shad, who has not yet grasped my brother's immunity to irony. 'And if I'd hit you, Hayden, which I'm strongly tempted to do, you'd have more than a red mark on your face. Mrs Hayden is here,' he adds as he turns over the horses to a groom.

'Oh, lord,' mutters Henry, rubbing his reddened cheek. 'How is Ma, Lottie?'

I shrug. 'Pretty much the same. Papa is no help to her. Let me go first and tell her you're here.'

When we arrive at the rooms upstairs I'm somewhat surprised to see that Ann has captured the attention of the three beautiful young men: one sketches, one admires; the third scribbles and crosses out words on a scrap of paper, occasionally running a hand through his perfect curls, and I suspect he writes a poem about her. Emma crawls round the room under the watchful eye of Aunt Renbourn, who directs her with her stick rather as a shepherd does a lamb.

My mother sits at the table, with a bottle for company. She looks up as I enter the room.

'*My Dearest Child,*' she intones. '*Returned Unsullied to the Maternal Bosom.*'

I take her hand. 'Mama, I'm very pleased to see you, but why are you here?'

She raises her gaze to mine and I see my face in hers, our eyes the same colour, but the lines and faded beauty speak of lost hope and the disappointments of years. 'I came with Shad to rescue you, Charlotte, for I knew you were in trouble.'

'Thank you.' So she did hear something of what I told her.

'Because that is what a mother does.'

I'm humbled and can think of nothing to say.

She reaches for her bottle. I lay my other hand briefly on her wrist. 'I wish you would not, Mama.'

She smiles with a hint of sadness. 'I too, my dear.'

I take my hand away and watch her fill her glass. Then she pushes it aside and stands to greet her firstborn son, who follows me into the room. Her face fills with happiness at his appearance, with some of the gaiety and vitality she must have had when younger.

'How d'ye do, Ma,' says Henry, grinning.

'*My Darling Boy*, returned to the *Grieving Maternal Bosom*! But, my dearest boy, why did you not send word?'

The grin on Henry's face fades. He's looking past our mother at Ann and Emma, who has crawled across the room to her and pulled herself to a standing position, fists knotted in her mother's skirts.

We're all silent. We (everyone except Emma, who is busy exploring this new world and the people in it) know it's too late for Ann and Henry; theirs is a finished chapter. Tears well in Ann's eyes and she cries in a helpless, red-eyed, nose-running sort of way. Henry spreads his hands out, in a gesture that could be a plea for help, or forgiveness, and mutters something about what a pretty child Emily is. 'Emma!' I hiss at him.

Shad is the first to move, producing a handkerchief for Ann, then taking Henry by the shoulder and escorting him away. I suspect he's taking him down to the taproom.

Ann stands and transfers Emma's hands to the chair. Then, handkerchief at her face, she runs into the bedchamber. Emma, left clinging to the chair and alarmed by the high flow of emotions, staggers a few steps and then drops to the familiarity of all fours to scramble across the room to my mother, who takes her on to her lap.

Ann has missed her daughter's first steps.

The beautiful young men blow their noses and Jeremiah, wiping his eyes on his sleeve, mutters something about fetching more coals and leaves the room. I discover that the woman who lent me a teacup and embraced me so heartily stole my handkerchief.

I give Ann some time to compose herself before going into the bedchamber. She sits on the bed, twisting Shad's handkerchief in her hands. She raises her face, revealing red, swollen eyes. Her hair is coming down in untidy, twisting fronds. She looks plain and unhappy.

'I want to go home,' she says.

As I wonder what she means, she says, 'Home to Beresford.'

Shad

'I think I am going mad.'

Henry, sitting opposite me in the taproom, slumped and dejected, shares his mother's fondness for grandiose statements. He turns his empty ale glass in his hands. 'What the devil do I do now, Shad?'

'I'd suggest you spend an appropriate amount of time with your family before you return to your regiment.' *And learn some good sense*, I want to add, but he has learned a hard lesson already today.

I gesture to the woman behind the bar to refill our glasses. The air is smoky and full of the scent of ale and roasted meat, and men hold boisterous conversations about their adventures on the road and in the city.

'I'm not even sure I'm in love with her now,' he says as though surprised by the discovery. 'I thought I was when I was in the north, but now I've seen her again, there's no, oh, you know, divine spark or whatever those old poets call it. She's quite an ordinary sort of pretty girl, really. Besides, I don't know if I could afford to keep a woman who dresses like that.'

'Chances are you'd be dead. Beresford's a crack shot.' A slight exaggeration, but Henry is not to know.

He sighs heavily.

'What about the child?' I ask.

'I should offer to pay for its support,' he says, brightening. 'Not this quarter, for I'm a little short, but next quarter I'll send money. To whom should I send it?'

'She's looked after by a Mrs Pyle in Camden Town.'

Someone reaches over my shoulder for my mug of ale and returns it to the table, empty. 'Mmm. Quite nice. I'm afraid Mrs Pyle has been paid off.'

'Charlotte! What are you doing here in the taproom?' We both stand, which gives Charlotte the opportunity to take my chair, leaving me to find another.

'Drinking your ale.' She takes another mouthful, oblivious of the stares she attracts from other customers, predominantly male. The only other women in the taproom eye her up as competition for the business transactions of the evening. 'Emma is weaned now and as I said, Mrs Pyle has been paid off. We need to find a family for Emma to live with, and I have an idea.'

'I beg your pardon.' Henry pushes his chair back, muttering something about fresh air, and leaves us.

'It's most improper for you to be here,' I tell her, which she ignores.

She stares at her retreating brother. 'Is he unwell?'

'He's drunk ale. Rather a lot of ale. So he needs to go outside.'

'Oh.'

'What is Ann doing now?'

'She's upset. She wants to go home to Beresford.' She takes her brother's glass and sips.

'And leave the problem of her child to us?'

'Why not? We can help.'

'We're under no obligation, Charlotte.' But it's a token protest only; we both know it.

'I was thinking that if Mr and Mrs Price took her she could be raised with John and Amelia. My mother would be able to see her – she is her first grandchild – and so would Ann when she visits us.'

'And Henry, I suppose. He offered to pay for her keep.'

'Of course, but I doubt he will.'

'So we deceive Beresford. That's what you suggest.'

The woman behind the bar approaches with a jug of

ale. 'The other ladies in here, sir, wish your companion to leave. They fear she will spoil their trade for the evening.'

'She's no lady; she's my wife.' I hand the woman a sovereign and she fills our glasses.

Charlotte scowls at me, something I have come to find quite adorable. 'Most witty. And, yes, we do deceive Beresford, unless Ann decides to tell him the truth. Do you think the Prices will agree to take her?'

'To oblige me, and if they receive money, yes. Mrs Price likes children.'

'We can sell my horse if—'

'Good heavens, no, Charlotte. You love that mare.'

'I do. I love you, too.'

'I love you, and because I love you I must tell you that . . .'

She looks at me over the rim of her ale glass, eyes shining, and not just with the drink. 'I know what you will say. You will say that Ann is unworthy and that she has deceived me and lied to me. I know, Shad. But she is my friend, or at least was my friend. And I have deceived you and lied to you for her sake and I am heartily sorry to have caused you pain.'

'You said yourself love is a risky business.'

She nods, and we sit quietly, hands clasped.

Henry returns. 'You know, Shad, you shouldn't have Charlotte here. The whores don't like it. They're taking bets on what her rates are and whether they should adjust their prices accordingly.'

'By raising them, I trust. Don't worry. We've rendered unto Caesar,' I respond with dubious logic. Henry looks confused. I tell him of the arrangement Charlotte and I have made and suggest he take his mother and the baby home for the night, accompanied by Jeremiah.

We go back upstairs and find Lady Renbourn preparing for her departure, which means much bullying on her part as the young men are instructed to collect various shawls, vinaigrettes, and packs of playing cards as well as their own drawing and writing instruments.

Jeremiah sits dozing in a chair with Emma asleep on his lap, Mrs Hayden contemplates her wine glass and Ann sits next to her, drinking tea. She's more composed, but her eyes are red and swollen. There is a hesitancy about her now she no longer hides behind the gilded mask of the beautiful young Countess. We tell her that a home has been found for her child and she thanks us and offers money, which I refuse even though Charlotte nudges me.

I don't want to take the phaeton through the streets at night, so we send Jeremiah out for hackney carriages, and to my relief Lady Renbourn offers to take Ann home. I badly want Charlotte to myself after the trying events of the night.

So at last I am alone with Charlotte who falls asleep on my shoulder as the hackney carriage takes us back home. She wakes and stretches when we stop at the house. 'I'm devilish tired. Do you want any supper?'

I shake my head. 'Let's go to bed.'

We dismiss Roberts and Tillyard for the night and climb the stairs. It's not late by *ton* standards, but I'm mightily tired and Charlotte yawns frequently.

'Do you think I drink too much?' she asks after one yawn so huge I fear she will extinguish the candle in her hand. She unthreads her earrings, her only jewellery tonight, and tosses them on to the chest of drawers.

'Not compared to your mother.' I unbutton my coat and untie my neckcloth. I reach for the bootjack and ease off my boots. They're muddy and have beer on them, too – Roberts will give me one of his reproachful looks when he retrieves them.

'Poor Mama.' She dips her toothbrush into the tooth powder. 'I saw myself in her tonight, Shad. I could end up like that, but I will not, for I have you.'

'On the contrary, you will not because you are yourself.' I pull the laces of her gown undone and watch it slither to her feet. Her stays are next, a slightly more protracted and fiddly process.

Yawning, she scratches her ribs and bends to splash water on her face. As I nudge her out of the way to clean my teeth she grumbles and retreats to the bed. In the reflection of the mirror I see her peel off her stockings and drop them to the floor.

I have the rest of my clothes off in a moment and crawl between the sheets, waiting while she dons her nightgown and pats scented lotion on to her face. She squints at her injured arm and smears ointment on it, wrinkling her nose at the smell.

'Are you asleep?' she says as she gets into bed.

'No. Not yet. I love you.' I turn to wrap her in my arms and her head settles on my shoulder with a small sigh. Her short hair tickles my skin. She smells of smoke and beer from the taproom, rosewater from her face lotion, herbs and tallow from the ointment; above all, of herself, the scent that both soothes and arouses me.

'I love you, too,' she mumbles.

She is the one who knows me, and whom I can tell anything and everything. There is only one exception – I shall never tell her of Ann's malicious poisoned words tonight suggesting that Charlotte was false. As for Charlotte, I suspect she will carry the secret of what happened with Beresford at Vauxhall to the grave. We value each other too highly to put unnecessary stress on the delicate strands that bind husband to wife, friend to friend.

I listen to the night sounds of London, the cries of the nightwatchmen, the rumble of traffic in the street, the chime of church bells near and far. Charlotte turns from me to wrap the bedclothes round herself, murmurs something and starts the small snuffling sounds I would not dare call a snore. And I sleep too.

little
black
dress